Why was there a spring in his step and a song in his heart at the thought of spending another evening in the company of his buddy's allegedly ditzy sister?

Scott could have told himself he was doing so only to satisfy his own sense of responsibility as a lawman and protector of the innocent. However, he wasn't into self-delusion. Miss Joy was turning out to be a whole lot of potent sex appeal packed into one tiny package, and when it came to sex, he was as susceptible as the next man. Maybe more so, considering how long it had been since he'd had any.

Scott groaned suddenly, realizing it was a little like chasing a perp through a swamp and coming around a clump of palmettos and finding the guy he'd been chasing was behind him instead of in front.

In short, he'd been had.

Dear Reader,

Once again, Silhouette Intimate Moments has a month's worth of fabulous reading for you. Start by picking up *Wanted,* the second in Ruth Langan's suspenseful DEVIL'S COVE miniseries. This small town is full of secrets, and this top-selling author knows how to keep readers turning the pages.

We have more terrific miniseries. Kathleen Creighton continues STARRS OF THE WEST with *An Order of Protection,* featuring a protective hero every reader will want to have on her side. In *Joint Forces,* Catherine Mann continues WINGMEN WARRIORS with Tag's long-awaited story. Seems Tag and his wife are also awaiti something: the unexpected arrival of another child Carla Cassidy takes us back to CHEROKEE C in *Manhunt.* There's a serial killer on the l the heroine's visions can help catch him— be in time to save the hero? *Against the W* SPECIAL OPS title from Lyn Stone, a welco to the line when she's not also writing for Harl Historicals. Finally, you knew her as Anne Avery, Harlequin Historicals, but now she's Anne Woodar in *Dead Aim* she proves she knows just what contem readers want.

Enjoy them all—and come back next month, when Silhouette Intimate Moments brings you even more of the best and most exciting romance reading around.

Yours,

Leslie J. Wainger
Executive Editor

Please address questions and book requests to:
Silhouette Reader Service
U.S.: 3010 Walden Ave., P.O. Box 1325, Buffalo, NY 14269
Canadian: P.O. Box 609, Fort Erie, Ont. L2A 5X3

Chapter 1

"I'd like to report a missing person."

Sergeant Stemple of the NYPD sighed inwardly and it was with some reluctance that he lifted his gaze from the reports he'd been slogging through. It had been a long day and his shift was about to end; another report added to the pile in front of him he did *not* need.

When he saw who was standing beside his desk, though, the first thing he did was suck in his stomach. He didn't intend to, it just happened. Automatically, as if somebody'd punched him there. Second thing was, the direction of his gaze had to be adjusted downward; the woman was shorter than her voice had made her sound.

"Yes, ma'am? Can I help you?"

The woman hesitated, then placed the manila envelope she was clutching as if it were the last remaining copy of the Declaration of Independence on his desk. "It's my room-mate. I think something terrible has happened to her." Her voice had taken on a breathless quality that made Sergeant Stemple feel as if his own breath was in short supply.

"Why don't you have a seat?" he said, putting on his gruff act to make up for the debilitating effect she had on him.

It was a not very well-kept secret in the precinct that Stemple had a heart like a marshmallow, but aside from that, he couldn't figure out what it was about this lady that was making it hard to remember he was a married man. Taken feature for feature she wasn't that gorgeous, not really. Okay, sure, she had nice, shiny brown hair that looked like it would be soft to touch, belling out from under the purple beret she was wearing. And when was the last time he'd seen a woman wearing a beret? True, her brown eyes had a way of angling upward through her thick dark lashes as she looked at him with a sleepy-eyed gaze, as if she'd just gotten out of bed.

He coughed and reached for a pen, pulling a pad of paper toward him. "What makes you think 'something terrible' has happened to your roommate? And…this would be a woman, right?"

"Well, of course." The woman seemed faintly surprised by the question, and Stemple looked down at his hands and felt unaccountably ashamed.

He muttered, "Ya never know, nowadays."

She lowered herself gracefully into the chair beside the desk, and when she crossed her legs, he saw that they were clad in jeans and high-heeled boots. That surprised Stemple because her light-gray jacket was feminine and curvy and nipped in at the waist, and was the kind that usually went with a matching skirt and that hardly anybody ever wore nowadays, either, come to think of it. And the rose-pink blouse with the deep V-neckline she was wearing underneath the jacket didn't exactly go with blue jeans, either. The lady definitely had her own unique style. Looked good on her, though.

"I haven't heard from her. And she always keeps in touch. *Always.*" There was that breathlessness again.

Stemple ran his hand over what was left of his salt-and-pepper hair, which, at his wife's suggestion, he'd just had cut toothbrush-short. He sat back in his chair, mentally refocusing on the job at hand. "Okay. So, when was the last time you saw your...uh... Sorry, this roomie got a name?"

"Oh— Yes, it's Yancy— Yancy LaVigne. Well, actually, her real name is Mary Yancy. LaVigne is more like her professional name, but it's the one she goes by, so I guess..." She floundered to a halt—probably, Stemple figured, because she was watching him pick up the manila envelope and pull out the photographs that were inside. Photographs of the roommate, he assumed; she'd come prepared, he'd give her that.

"Whoa," he said, rearing back. His eyes flicked to the woman in the chair and back to the photo again. Impossible not to notice that the woman in the photo *was* drop-dead gorgeous. "Nice lookin' girl," he said, mentally putting his eyeballs back in their sockets. "What is she, some kinda fashion model?"

"No, a fashion *reporter*. She works for *La Mode* magazine. You might have seen her on TV, too—sometimes she's on those morning news shows, and, you know, Regis and—"

"Yeah, my wife, she watches that stuff." Stemple put down the photograph reluctantly and picked up the pen again. "So, when was the last time you saw, uh... Ms. LaVigne?"

"Three weeks ago. She—"

He fixed the lady before him with a narrow-eyed stare, no longer noticing so much the cute beret and bedroom eyes. He was, first and finally, a cop. And, if he did say so himself, a pretty damn good one. "And you're just now getting around to reporting her missing? Why is that?"

"You asked how long since I've *seen* her. She went on vacation—to Florida."

Looking flustered, the lady placed one small hand on the desktop not far from Stemple's big meaty one. She leaned forward, and his gaze dropped—all by itself, he'd *swear*—to the deep V of her rose-pink blouse.

"It was supposed to be for two weeks. And she was supposed to *call* me." Her voice quivered, and she tightened her lips and quelled it like a misbehaving child.

"I know what you're thinking," she said, which Stemple devoutly hoped she did not. "But it's just that Yancy's very young." She smiled suddenly, which made Stemple feel a little like an adolescent himself. "She doesn't always make the best choices, so I guess I try and look out for her. She was supposed to call me every couple of days to let me know she was okay. I gave her one of those phone cards so she wouldn't have to use her cell. Roaming charges can be awful. And she did call the first week. Then, all of a sudden, she stopped. I thought she was just having a good time and forgot, but...she didn't come home. I went to the airport to meet her flight, and she wasn't on it."

It was a moment or two before Stemple became aware of the silence and realized she was waiting for him to say something. He shook himself, coughed, picked up the photograph again and frowned at it.

"Yeah—okay. Uh, you say she's young? How young, exactly? She's not underage, is she? Because if she is—"

"Oh, no. No, Yancy's thirty—just turned. In April. She's an Aries—an infant soul. I'm Pisces, we're very old souls. Which is why I..." She stopped once more. Her cheeks had turned a softer version of the color of her blouse. "Oh, sorry."

Stemple gave another inward sigh. He supposed it was just as well the lady was something of a dingbat; on top of everything else, brains would have been just too much. He shifted in his chair and started again.

"Okay, Miss—"

"Starr. Joy Lynn Starr. And it's Ms."

Perfect. "*Ms.* Starr. That's not a 'professional' name, too, is it?" He had unsettling visions of smoky rooms and the lady slithering naked around a pole. Which would explain a lot.

Possibly because she'd been reading his mind, Ms. Starr said in a chillier tone than the one she'd been using up to now, "Starr is my maiden name. I'm divorced."

"Okay...Ms. Starr," said Stemple, rubbing at his temples.

He was once more reminded that his day was drawing to a close and the pile on his desk wasn't getting any smaller. "Have you tried contacting the authorities down there in Florida?"

"Of course I did. Right after I called the resort and found out Yancy had checked out three days early. They told me—"

"Hold on. You say she checked out of her hotel. *She* did— herself, personally?"

"Yes, the desk clerk remembers—"

Stemple's pen hit his desk blotter with a gentle snapping sound. "Ma'am, it seems to me, wherever your friend might have gone, looks like she went there voluntarily and of her own free will." He realized he was frowning and drew a hand over his face to erase it. "You're not her mother, and even if you were, she's a grown woman, she's got that right. Now, maybe you feel like she shoulda called you and filled you in on her plans, but maybe she didn't feel the same way about that. I'm sorry, but I have to tell you, unless you can give me some kind of concrete evidence or a damn good reason why I should think otherwise, that's what I'm gonna have to go with here. It's just not the police department's job to go chasing after law-abiding adults, you understand what I'm sayin'?"

"Yes," Ms. Joy Starr said in a low voice.

Her hands, he noticed, were resting on her purse, and he thought they would have clenched if she'd let them.

"Sorry to have bothered you."

"Ma'am, it's no bother." Once again feeling vaguely ashamed, Stemple rose hastily as she did and scooped the photographs back into the manila envelope. "I wish I could help you. I do," he said as he handed it to her, and discovered he meant it. "Look— I know you're worried about your friend, but here's what I think. Young, good-lookin' woman like that, goes off to Florida to some fancy hotel to have herself a good time...checks out a couple days early—assuming she ain't lying in some hospital or the morgue—"

"She isn't. I checked." Her voice was flat, her lips tight.

There it was again, that effect she had on him. He couldn't seem to let her go away feeling bad about things. In the kind of tone he'd use to convince one of his kids the trip to the dentist wasn't gonna hurt him, he said, "Okay, so, what that says to me is, she maybe met somebody made her a better offer. You know? Made some new friends, maybe met a guy—anyways, chances are she's off somewhere having herself a good ol' time." Stemple reached into his jacket pocket. "Look here—you take my card, give it a few more days, see what happens, okay? You don't hear from her, you let me know."

"Thank you," she said softly. She turned and walked away.

Hey, you're a married man, Stemple sternly admonished himself. And his self answered, *Yeah, but I can look, can't I?*

And he did so, until the door of the squad room had closed behind the lady in the purple beret.

Joy Lynn Starr paused on the sidewalk outside the police station to dig a small fold-up umbrella out of her pocketbook. She wasn't surprised to discover it was raining again; it had been the longest, wettest spring anybody could remember in New York City. She'd been a New Yorker long enough to know that at that time of day and in that kind of weather there was no point in trying to catch a cab—which was okay because she needed the walk anyway, to help her calm down. Her hands trembled as she unfurled the ridiculously inadequate umbrella. There were knots in her stomach and her legs as she set out to walk the dozen or so blocks to her apartment, and she felt decidedly wobbly.

I know I'm right, she told herself. *I know it.* Just because nobody believes me, doesn't mean I'm wrong.

I shouldn't have mentioned the old-soul-new-soul thing, though.

She sighed mentally and closed her eyes. She should have

known better. Among her own closest family members there were cops and lawyers, teachers and nurses, pilots and truck drivers, and not one single believer in astrology, karma or past lives.

But at least, she thought with a shudder, I didn't tell him about the *other*. What could she have said about it, anyway? Even she didn't know what to call it. A *feeling?* But it was so much more. Like a dream, only she hadn't been asleep when it happened. Oh, yes, she was *very* glad she hadn't mentioned that.

Rain lashed spitefully under the umbrella, gluing long strands of her hair across her face and sneaking inside the collar of the nineteen-forties-style jacket she'd bought last winter on eBay, and it occurred to her that back home in Georgia right now the weather would be settling into its typical summer pattern, which was, of course, hot. And humid. Like a sauna. She hadn't missed that particular aspect of her Southern heritage, not before this year, anyway. But right now she was wondering what the Gulf Coast of Florida might be like in late May, early June. She'd never been there, but she was sure it would be hot. Probably not as sultry as Georgia, though, with some nice sea breezes blowing in off the gulf....

She was visualizing those breezes, along with white sand beaches and sparkling blue water twenty minutes later as she unlocked the door to the tiny two-bedroom apartment she'd shared with Yancy for the past three years. She opened the door and the fantasy winked out, snuffed by the sheer emptiness of the rooms beyond, the way a vacuum extinguishes a flame. She wasn't sure what it was that made the apartment seem so bleak and lonely now. She and Yancy weren't exactly joined at the hip; Yancy had her own life, and her job often took her away for several days at a time. Unless, Joy thought, it was the unaccustomed tidiness. Yancy was a sweetheart in so many ways, but she did tend to leave clutter in her wake, much the way the Charles Shultz character, Pigpen, scattered dust.

She waited, listening...waiting. But the feeling didn't come. It had just been that one time, two days ago, when she'd walked into the emptiness of the apartment—*knowing* it was empty, and yet...*Yancy had been there.* She'd *felt* her there. She'd heard her—no, not really heard, not with her ears. That, too, had been more a feeling than anything else. Something experienced, something perceived, though not with the usual five senses. But every bit as real.

After a moment, she gave herself a little shake, then closed the door and locked the dead bolt and chain. It had taken some getting used to for somebody who'd grown up in a place and a time where people seldom locked their houses, but those actions now came as automatically to her as they did to all New Yorkers. She plopped the dripping umbrella into the flowerpot she kept beside the door for that purpose and headed for her bedroom to get out of her wet clothes before she "caught her death," as Momma would say.

Hers was the smaller of the apartment's two bedrooms. That had been her choice; as one of seven kids, she was used to crowded quarters, and anyway, with her huge wardrobe, Yancy needed the extra closet space more than she did. Joy's clothes were few but precious to her; she collected vintage garments the way once upon a time she'd collected teddy bears—sparingly, and with a great deal of affection for each piece. The tiny room barely held a double bed and dresser, and one of the first things Joy had done was to have a shelf installed near the ceiling, around three of the room's four walls, to hold her collection of bears and family photos. They gazed down at her now: bears ranging from her tattered childhood companion, Boo, and the Pooh in graduation cap and gown she'd gotten when she'd graduated from Ogelthorpe High, to the genuine—and expensive—Steiff bear her second husband, Freddie the Bas—okay, the Rat—had bought for her on their honeymoon.

Photos included two of Momma and Daddy—their wedding picture, and a snapshot of the two of them standing in front of Daddy's first truck, Daddy standing behind Momma with his arms around her waist and his chin resting on top of her head. He'd liked to do that because she was so short. Joy and her oldest sister Tracy were the only ones in the family who took after Momma that way. There was a posed but inexpensive group portrait of Tracy and her husband Al and all the kids, most likely taken at the school where Tracy taught sixth grade. There were nice professional poses of her brother Troy and his wife Charly and their kids, and Jimmy Joe and Mirabella with theirs. And baby brother C.J. with his Caitlyn, that stunning fairy-like girl he'd married just last fall, and the little dark-haired, dark-eyed darling they were adopting. There was a picture of her sister Jessie with Sammi June, taken on Sammi June's graduation day, and next to it the formal portrait of Jessie's husband, Tristan, in his Navy dress uniform, with the American flag in the background. The family was still reeling from the shock of Tristan's return last month after being presumed dead for years and years. It turned out he'd been held prisoner in Iraq. Joy was sure that now that he was home and the two of them were together again, they'd be having a new picture made soon.

That's my family, she thought. *All paired up, two by two, like the animals in Noah's Ark. All but me.*

Well, and Roy, of course.

And she couldn't help but smile back at the face that grinned so irrepressibly down at her from its frame on the high shelf. Dark as a pirate, teeth white in a tanned and arrogant face, hair whipped by the wind as he stood on the deck of his boat like a buccaneer captain on the high seas... Roy, her "little" brother, seven years younger. Unlike Joy, he'd never been married, and the family had gotten used to the notion that he wasn't likely to, given his carefree attitude toward life. Joy thought that was just fine, as long as he was as happy being single as she was. Why shouldn't he be, living the kind of life every man dreams of? Captain of his own boat, making his living running fishing charters in the Gulf of Mexico....

Roy. Her jacket dropped onto the bed as she quickly turned her pocketbook upside down, dumping its contents onto the comforter. Snatching her address book and her cell phone from the pile, she turned on her heel, and minutes later she was in the kitchen with her laptop open on the table. On the screen in front of her was a map of the Gulf Coast of Florida. With unsteady fingers she thumbed through the address book until she found the entry she wanted. She peered at the map again. After a moment she sat back and let out a breath. Then she picked up her cell phone, checked the address book once more and dialed.

Scott Cavanaugh was washing the day's accumulation of fish guts and squashed bait from the deck of the *Gulf Starr* and didn't hear the cell phone ring. Ryan, who'd been hiding in the cabin on the pretext of "cleaning the galley," brought the phone out to him.

"It's Uncle Roy," he hollered over the noise the water was making. Scott noticed his son had a sort of hunched-up, unhappy look, but didn't mention it as he twisted the hose nozzle to shut off the water. He took the phone from him and said, "Hey, pardner, wha's up? Where'n the hell are you?"

The owner and occasional captain of the *Gulf Starr* chuckled. "You know I'd tell you if I could."

"Yeah…okay, so I take it this isn't to tell me you're on your way home?"

"'Fraid not. Sorry. And doesn't look like I'm gonna be for a while. So, how you holdin' up? How's the charter boat business?"

"Okay…picking up. Had a small group today. Ryan and I handled it ourselves. Got a pretty good bunch for tomorrow, half day—Jose's gonna help out since Ryan's mom's got something lined up for him to do."

"It's just baseball sign-ups." Ryan's tone was sulky. "I'd rather go out with you, Dad. I'm too damn old for Little League, anyway."

"Hey, you're not old enough to use that kind of language

with me,'' Scott said, arching his eyebrows and jerking his head toward the galley. ''Don't you have a job to do?''

Ryan muttered, ''Yes, sir,'' as he levered himself down the steps and into the cabin.

On the other end of the cell phone connection Roy was chuckling again. ''The kid's sure growin' up. Hey, tell him I was just kiddin' him, okay? I think I mighta hurt his feelings.''

''Oh yeah? What'd you say to him?'' Scott slid a sideways look toward the galley, where Ryan was helping himself to a soda from the cooler.

''Ah, I was just askin' him when his voice was gonna change, *you* know. I sure didn't mean anything by it, but I think he maybe took it the wrong way.''

Scott grimaced at a circling pelican. ''Yeah, well, he's a little bit sensitive about that right now.''

''Sorry, man.''

''Not your fault. It's a tough age.''

''Shows you what I know about kids.''

''It's not all that difficult to figure out. You used to be fourteen. Not all that long ago, actually. Don't you remember what it was like?''

''Hell,'' said Roy, ''all I remember about that age is being in this…sex fog, know what I mean? Only thing on my mind was—''

Scott laughed, then groaned. ''Don't remind me. I don't even want to think about it.''

''Yeah. Ryan's a good kid, though. I don't think you have anything to worry about.''

There was a pause, while Scott thought, *That's easy for you to say.*

Then Roy said in a different tone altogether, ''Uh, listen, buddy, the reason I called is, I need to ask you a favor.''

Eager to change the subject, Scott said recklessly, ''Sure. What's up?''

Roy sounded wary. ''It's kind of a big one.''

"O-kay," said Scott, wary himself now. "You gonna tell me what it is, or am I supposed to guess?"

It came on a rush of breath. "It's my sister."

"Okay, I know a little bit about those," Scott said, nodding amiably. "Got a few of 'em myself." He did, too—four of them. All older than he was. He'd about been mothered to death as a kid. He considered it a wonder he'd survived.

"Yeah, well, she's headed your way, and it's too late to stop her."

"Not a problem. You want me to meet her? When's she due in?"

"Uh…tonight?"

"*Tonight!* Jeez, man."

"Yeah, I know. Don't blame me. I just checked my voice mail and found her message. Must have left it yesterday. She's—"

"Yesterday! Okay… The impulsive type, huh?"

"Yeah, well, that's Joy Lynn," Roy said dryly, then hastened to add, "Hey, don't get me wrong, she's a terrific person, good-hearted as they come. It's just that she's, well, she can be a little bit ditzy, is all."

A ditz, thought Scott. *Great.* Just what he needed—another Beth. "I know something about those, too," he muttered, throwing a guilty glance toward the galley. It was his policy not to make negative comments about Ryan's mother within his earshot.

"Oh, hey, she's nothing at all like your ex," Roy tactlessly assured him. "For one thing, she's not helpless. Pretty independent, in fact. She'll tackle just about anything, whether she ought to or not."

"Great," Scott breathed. "I take it this is the sister who's not married, not the schoolteacher with all the kids who's married to the cop, or the one whose husband just turned up alive in Iraq?"

"Right. Joy Lynn's single, but you don't have to worry about her being a man-hunter, or anything like that—just the opposite. You wanna know the truth, I think those two divorces of hers pretty much soured her on the whole idea.''

"Great.'' Scott sighed again. "Okay, so, what is it that makes her such a ditz?''

"Well, for one thing, she's got this idea of tryin' to write a novel. A murder mystery, for God's sake. Like that's something she'd know anything about.''

"I don't suppose you need personal experience. Just a good imagination.''

"Yeah, well, she's got that.''

"Okay, that doesn't seem so bad. What else?''

"I don't know. She's kind of got this Shirley MacLaine thing going…'' Roy sounded vague. "You know, ESP and karma and reincarnation and all that psychic stuff. Not that she's a fanatic about it—says she just tries to keep an open mind.'' Roy paused, then gave a snort of laughter. "But you know what they say about open minds. You got one that's open at both ends….''

"Empty. Yeah, I know.''

"Not that she's an airhead—she's not. She's plenty smart. It's just that—''

"I get the picture,'' Scott said with resignation. "Don't worry about it. I'll take care of her. I've got a key to your house. I'll see she gets settled in, show her around, take her out on the boat. Show her a good time.''

"Hey, now, not *too* good a time. She *is* my sister.''

There was a pause, while Scott tried to think of something to say to that, then a gust of laughter from Roy.

"Jeez, I'm *kidding.* If anybody ought to have the word *trustworthy* tattooed on his forehead, it's you. You're what mommas everywhere have in mind when they tell their little kiddies to 'find a nice policeman.'''

"Thanks,'' Scott said dryly. "I think.''

"Anyway, I surely do appreciate you standin' in for me, man,'' Roy said, genuine relief in his Georgia drawl. "It's a load off my mind. I owe you one, buddy.''

"You bet you do,'' Scott said fervently. "Big time.''

He broke the connection, checked his watch, then stuck his head through the cabin door. "Hey, kiddo, come on, we have to go. Chop chop."

"I'm not done cleaning," Ryan protested, trying not to look guilty about the soda in his hand.

"I can see that." Scott untied his rubber apron and laid it across a table, then leaned against the cabin door frame for balance while he tugged at a boot. "Can't be helped. I'll finish up tomorrow. Right now I've got to—" he dropped the boot on the floor and went after the other one "—get you back to your mom's."

"Aw, Dad, what happened to pizza after?"

"Look, I know—"

"We *always* go for pizza. Come on, Dad. Mom thinks I'm eating with you. There's probably not even gonna be anything to eat in the whole house."

Scott squinted at his son, hoping that might cloud his vision enough that he wouldn't have to see the disappointment on the boy's face. It didn't work. "We'll stop for burgers on the way. How's that?" He reached out to rumple his son's hair, then hooked the arm around his neck and pulled him in for a quick hug. As he did so, he couldn't help but notice that the top of the kid's head still was an inch or so short of his shoulder. He felt a guilty twinge of fatherly anxiety about that, knowing how badly Ryan wanted to be tall, to take after his dad. But it's early yet, Scott reminded himself. After all, he'd gotten most of *his* height after he turned sixteen. Of course, the boy had his mother's genes to contend with, too. That could make a big difference. All that Aiken clan tended to be on the short side.

"Hey, I'm sorry," he said gruffly. "I'll make it up to you. Right now Uncle Roy's got something he needs me to do for him."

"Yeah, I heard," Ryan said in a derisive tone as he tried halfheartedly to extricate himself from the neck hug. "Some lady, right? His sister—the 'ditz.'"

"Hey, watch your mouth." Scott tightened his hold.

"Wha-at? 'Ditz'? What's wrong with 'ditz'?"

"You don't know she's a ditz, you've never met the lady. And even if she is, that's not something you get to say, you hear me? What are you, two years old—you have to repeat everything you hear? You know better than that."

"Yeah, I know…sorry," Ryan muttered.

Scott let him go and he clattered on up the steps, out of range.

"Roy really is in a spot," he said as he joined his son on deck. "His sister's coming in for a visit, doesn't know he's not here, he's got no way to get in touch with her to let her know… You can see why I've got to stand in for him, can't you?"

"Yeah, I know. It's okay, Dad, really—" Ryan angled a look up at him, blue eyes squinting against the last of the sun's light, and Scott felt a surge of emotion unlike any other, one only a father gets to feel when he gazes at his son's face and knows what a lucky man he is. "Anyway, it's only this one time, right? I can deal."

Scott snorted a laugh and resisted an urge to hug his kid again. Instead, he made himself settle for a quick hand-squeeze to the back of the neck and a husky "Attaboy."

He followed Ryan up the gangway and locked the gate. "Hey," he said as he caught up with his son on the paved walkway. "Roy said something about…he thought he might've hurt your feelings." Ryan threw him a puzzled look. "You know, about your voice changing."

Ryan looked away quickly and hitched up a shoulder. "Dad, it's *okay*. I knew he was kidding. Roy's always kidding around like that."

"You're not really worried about it, are you? You know, your voice *is* gonna change. It'll happen when it happens. From one day to the next, probably."

Ryan was watching his feet. He gave a dejected sigh and said, "Yeah, I know…. I just wish it'd hurry up."

"What're you in such a hurry for? Something I should know about?" Scott said it in a joking tone, trying to lighten

An Order of Protection

his son's mood. He was unprepared when Ryan stabbed him with a passionate blue gaze.

"Because then maybe everybody will stop treating me like a little *kid*." Ryan made a jerking motion as if he meant to break into a run, but after one lunging step, hesitated and came almost to a halt instead.

Following his son's gaze, Scott, too, found his steps slowing. Coming toward them down the long marina pathway was a woman. A stranger. She hadn't seen them yet; her attention was on the boats in their berths, and she had a hand up to shade her eyes as she tried to read the names painted on their shadowed sterns. She was wearing a white skirt made of something light that floated in the breeze and played peeka-boo with her legs, hitting her maybe halfway between her knees and the white tennis shoes on her feet. The skirt had a wide, snug-fitting waistband, and tucked into it was a sleeveless yellow blouse with a collar that was turned up in back. At that distance he couldn't be certain, but it looked to him like the yellow material had tiny dark-blue polka dots on it. Her hair, held back from her face by a bright yellow scarf of some kind, was a soft honey-brown, and it seemed to sort of *bounce* when it hit her shoulders. She reminded him of something from another time, another century, even. Something vaguely Donna Reed-ish or maybe a combination of her, Lucy Ricardo and the cheerleaders in *Grease*.

"Do you think that's her?" Ryan asked in a low voice.

"Dunno," said Scott. "Let's find out." He walked pur-posefully forward and sang out, "Hello, can we help you?"

The honey-hair belled outward as she turned her head to-ward them, and relief lit her face with a smile that just about took his breath away.

"Oh, yes, if you know your way around here you sure can."

Oh Lord, it was a Georgia accent, no doubt about it.

"I'm lookin' for my brother's boat. I b'lieve it's called the *Gulf Starr?*"

Ryan was looking up at Scott. Scott looked back at him.

Then he turned to the woman, held out his hand and said, "Yes, ma'am, we've been expecting you."

Which was a bald-faced lie. The woman standing before him wasn't at all what Scott had been expecting. Apparently there were one or two little things Roy had neglected to tell him about his so-called "big" sister.

Chapter 2

For starters, while Roy's sister may have been a few years older than he was, in Scott's opinion the only way she could ever be classified as "big" would be in relation to something extremely small, like, say, puppies, or kittens, or daffodils. Images of all three flashed through Scott's mind in those first few moments.

The puppy part may have had something to do with her eyes, the soft, golden-brown of them, like honey, and the heart-melting way they had of looking up at him through thick, dark lashes. A way that seemed to be begging him to pick her up and take her home with him. The kitten part— well, that was probably her voice. It had a certain quality, a soft raspiness about it, that set something to humming down in the center of his chest in response, like a cat's purring. As for the daffodils…

"Dad."

Ryan's hoarse whisper and the jab of a bony elbow in his ribs made him jerk his fascinated gaze away from honey-brown hair and the ends of the yellow scarf wafting in the gentle gulf breeze.

"I'm Scott Cavanaugh, and this is my son, Ryan," he said, thrusting out his hand. "Roy's out of town. I'm his partner—on the boat, anyway. At least, I try to run it for him when he's not here. And I guess I'm your designated welcoming committee."

While he was saying all that, she was gazing at him with parted lips and extending her hand in a hesitant, wondering sort of way. He watched it disappear into his as if it had been swallowed whole. He considered it a good thing that it was her turn to talk, because for the life of him he couldn't think of another word to say.

"Hi," she said. "I'm Joy."

And the thought popped into his head: *Yes, I think you just might be.*

Oh my Lord, he's big! That was Joy's first thought, as her gaze traveled up…and up…and up over a broad chest under a not-very-clean white T-shirt. Of course, she was used to people being taller than she was; most over the age of twelve were. This man, though, in addition to being tall, was simply *big.* Not fat, her mind hastened to clarify, not at all. Just solid muscle nicely arranged on big sturdy bones. And not in an intimidating way, either, but in a way that made her think of comfort and shelter and protection—like a bunker, maybe. Only cosier. *Like a giant teddy bear.*

"Nice meeting you, Scott," she said, smiling as she retrieved her hand from the warm nest that enfolded it. She transferred the hand and the smile to the boy standing loose-limbed and restless at his father's side. "And you, too, Ryan."

It didn't bother her too much that she got only a sullen mutter along with a reluctant hand from the boy. She was accustomed to adolescent males; in fact, her brother Calvin, who liked to be called C.J., now that he was a grown-up husband and father, had been a lot like that when he was the same age.

Not that she had much time to dwell on it, because the significance of what the boy's father had said finally hit her. Her breath made a whooshing sound, like a balloon deflating, which was pretty much what she felt like.

"You said Roy's out of town?" Weak in the knees, she looked for something to sit on. "Do you know when he'll be back?"

"Sorry, I don't. Not anytime soon, that's all I can tell you."

Scott's voice sounded sympathetic, but Joy didn't look to see if his facial expression agreed. She was gazing at nothing, chewing the inside of her cheek and thinking hard.

It's my own fault. I should have waited to hear from Roy before jumping on a plane. Of course I should have.

But waiting any longer to begin the search for Yancy had seemed impossible, once the idea had come to her that her own brother was *right here,* living within a few miles of where Yancy had been staying, and that he could help her with her search. She'd been counting on him. *Now* what?

She sighed. The answer to that was never in doubt. She'd have to do this by herself, of course.

"Hey, it's okay, don't worry about a thing," Scott was saying, naturally unaware of the cause of her distress or the scope of the disaster, and his hand was a firm but gentle pressure on her shoulder. "Everything's going to be fine."

Again, Joy looked up. Up into vivid blue eyes, reassuringly crinkled at the corners, and thought she could almost believe, even without him saying another word, that things *would* be fine.

"I have a key to Roy's house. He told me to tell you to make yourself at home, for as long as you want. I just need to take Ryan home, and then I'll see you settled in. Tomorrow, if you want, I can show you around…take you out on the boat—"

"Dad," Ryan said, in a warning sort of way.

Scott snapped his fingers. "Oh, right. I've got a charter tomorrow. But it's only half a day—morning. I'll be free later on, if you, uh…you know, if you'd like to go out."

"Thank you," Joy murmured automatically, in the Southern way. "That's just so nice of you."

Scott was curious as to why her brother being gone had hit her so hard. He'd watched her when the news hit her, and he'd swear her knees had buckled.

"How'd you get here?" he asked in a conversational tone as he was steering her, his hand barely touching her elbow, toward the marina parking lot.

"Flew," she said vaguely. "To Tallahassee."

"What'd you do, get a rental at the airport?"

She shook her head, still only half listening to him, the rest of her mind obviously churning away on whatever her problem was.

"No, I took a taxi."

"A *taxi?* From Tallahassee?" Scott said poetically, and Ryan snorted. Scott grinned at him, then turned to Joy again. "I didn't know you *could* take a taxi all the way here from Tallahassee."

"You can take a taxi anywhere if you pay enough," Joy said in a firm voice, and he could see she was back with him again, with her chin up now, and her eyes seemed a lot less puppy-like than they'd been before. "I didn't have any idea how to find Roy's place, so I thought I'd just let the cabdriver worry about that. Or—" her smile unexpectedly returned, along with a sideways and upward glance through her lashes "—it may just be I've been living in New York too long. We New Yorkers take taxis anywhere that's too far to walk. Anyway, as it turned out, he knew his way around this town quite well. At least, he didn't have any trouble finding the address, and I had no idea Roy lived right on the beach like that. My goodness, what that place must cost! And, anyway, when there was no one home there, I told him about the boat and he knew to bring me here."

"All the better," Scott said amiably. "This way you won't

have to follow me. You can just go with us while I drop Ryan off, and then I'll take you over to your brother's. If you want, I can take you to pick up a rental car tomorrow. In the meantime, I hope you don't mind riding in a beat-up old pickup truck.'' He smiled at her as he pulled a set of car keys out of his pocket.

''Oh, I've ridden in a few of those in my time,'' Joy said dryly, and he chuckled.

Then he stopped dead in his tracks.

''Where's your luggage?'' He was wondering how it could have escaped him all this time that she didn't have any. In his line of work he was supposed to notice details like that, and the fact that he hadn't caused his heartbeat to give a guilty kick.

''I left it in the harbormaster's office,'' she replied, with a breezy little motion of her head in that direction that made the soft-looking waves of her hair ripple and the daffodil-yellow scarf ends flutter. She angled *that look* at him through her lashes. ''So I wouldn't have to drag it all over the marina while I was looking for Roy's boat.''

''That was smart,'' Scott said, exchanging a look with Ryan.

Gee, he sounds surprised, Joy thought, with a sense of wry inevitability. She could guess what Roy must have told him about her. The words ''my sister the nutcase'' came to mind.

They'd stopped beside a white Chevy truck of a vintage familiar to Joy, since it predated her emigration from rural Georgia to the big city roughly twelve years ago. Scott unlocked and opened the passenger-side door and motioned her in. ''Excuse the mess. Shove that stuff off the seat—there you go.''

She climbed into the cab and hitched herself over onto the middle of the bench seat, moving a handful of assorted receipts, junk mail and unidentified papers over as she did so. Ryan sprang weightlessly into the cab behind her and slammed the door, then settled himself as close to it and as far away from Joy as he could possibly get.

"We'll drive by and pick up your bags on the way out," Scott said as he slid into the driver's seat, and just like that, the cab of the truck seemed very small. He reached to put the keys in the ignition while Joy fished around for a seat belt, and in doing that it was impossible for her not to brush against him. The heat in the truck grew stifling, and she gave up the seat belt search in favor of breathing.

"There's one there somewhere," Scott muttered, and he was poking a hand down into the space between his jeans and her skirt, sort of nudging the skirt out of the way. "Ryan, you got one over there, son?"

Ryan made an impatient sound as he jerked around to pull and tug at the buckle that was tightly wedged in the crack between seat and back. After freeing it, he handed it to Joy without a word and fastened his own three-way belt with a loud *click.* Then he went back to staring fixedly out the window.

With a murmured "Thanks," Joy took the long end Scott handed her, crimped and crumpled from being crammed underneath the seat. She fastened the belt and cinched it tight, then settled back, heart racing in an annoying way.

Scott started up the truck and backed out of the parking space, then drove slowly around the perimeter of the lot toward the entrance and the marina office, and with every move he made, though she didn't think he was doing it on purpose, his big, sun-bronzed arm seemed to shift and slide against some part of Joy. Even when it didn't actually touch her, she could *feel* it, as if all the nerves in her skin on that side of her body had set up remote outposts.

He smells like the sea, she thought. *Like fish, Joy—face it, he smells like fish.* Okay, but not at all unpleasantly. It had been a long time since she'd been this close to a man who didn't smell like designer cologne.

The harbormaster, a scrawny man with butch-cut gray hair and skin like leather whose age could have been anywhere from thirty-five to sixty, had evidently been watching for them. As the white Chevy approached, he emerged, grinning, from his office, towing Joy's big suitcase behind him with her carry-on slung over his shoulder. He gave her a nod and a wink, exchanged friendly greetings with Scott and Ryan through Scott's open window, then hoisted the bags into the back of the truck and gave them all a goodbye salute as he called out, "You enjoy your stay, little lady. And come on back."

Of course, he pronounced it "Come *own* back," which made Joy feel right at home. It had been a long time since she'd heard Southern accents.

They drove out of the parking lot and away from the just-set sun, and twilight came quickly, the way Joy remembered it did in the South. Scott drove with his window down and the air was warm and soft with humidity, and she remembered that very well, too. She couldn't hold back a contented sigh.

Scott glanced over at her. "Been to Florida before?"

She shook her head. "First time. But I grew up in Georgia."

With his eyes on the road ahead, he told her how the Panhandle of Florida was different from most of the state and more like the rest of the Deep South. "Like Georgia, we have seasons," he said. "Which makes this—summer—our high season."

Joy nodded. She turned to Ryan. "So, you must be out of school, I guess?" Accepting the boy's grunt for conversation, she went on in a friendly way. "It's nice you get to spend your summer vacation helping your dad out on the boat."

Ryan muttered, "I wish."

Scott laughed. "His mom has some ideas of her own on that score."

Ryan mumbled, "I don't even *like* baseball."

Scott didn't say anything more but rubbed a hand over the bottom half of his face as if he was holding something back. Joy would have asked Ryan why he didn't care for baseball, but before she could, the boy cranked down his window and turned his face to the wind in a way that plainly said he wasn't in the mood for polite conversation.

In that silence, the evening turned finally from lavender to indigo. Scott drove inland, away from sand and pine and palmetto groves and houses on stilts and into quiet streets lined with old trees and modest homes built in the Southern style, with steps leading up to wide front porches. Presently, he pulled the Chevy to the curb in front of one of them, a pretty red brick with baskets of flowers and waving Boston ferns hanging from the eaves of the white porch, and cement urns filled with pink and red impatiens flanking the steps.

Ryan was out of the truck before it had stopped rolling, slamming the door and calling out "'Bye, Dad," as he loped up the long brick walk.

A light on the porch came on. A woman had come to stand at the top of the steps, one hand resting on a vine-wrapped trellis rising out of yet another flowerpot. She was slender and no taller than Ryan, when he joined her, and pretty, with blond curls tied up high on her head so they tumbled haphazardly over her forehead and ears like a child's. She waved at the Chevy, and Scott leaned across the seat and Joy hunched out of his way while he ducked his head low to wave back at her.

Through the open window Joy heard the woman's childlike voice saying to Ryan, "Who's that with your daddy?"

And she heard Ryan answer in his adolescent mutter what sounded like "Uncle Roy's sister."

Joy moved over into the seat Ryan had vacated, fastened her seat belt and turned a questioning eye on Scott. "Uncle Roy?"

He looked over his shoulder and pulled away from the curb. "It's kind of an honorary title." She could see the shine of teeth in a wry smile. "Ryan's short on uncles. I've got four sisters and his mother's an only child—so he sort of borrowed your brother. Roy's good with the kid. I keep telling him he should be thinking about having a couple of his own."

"Good luck," Joy said, and Scott chuckled, a nice sound in the near-darkness.

It was odd, but she felt quite comfortable with him now that Ryan was gone and there was some space between them. Odd, considering they'd just met. Maybe, she thought, she'd known him in a past life....

After a moment, she looked over at him again. "Forgive me for asking—I know it's none of my business—but are you and Ryan's mother separated?"

"Beth and I are divorced."

He said it matter-of-factly, she noticed, and utterly without tension.

"For about, let's see…five years, now."

"You seem to be on friendly terms."

"We are."

"That's nice. For Ryan, especially."

Her voice seemed remote, and Scott looked over at her and saw that she'd turned her face toward the window. "Yeah, it is," he said. "Most of the time."

He didn't tell her there were times he wished the break could have been cleaner, that the way Beth was so dependent on him made it seem at times as though he had another child to deal with rather than an ex-wife. He just didn't know whether that was a good thing or a bad thing. As divorces went, he didn't have much to compare his to.

It occurred to him that the woman sharing the cab of his pickup probably knew a whole lot more about divorces than he did, and that maybe the reason she'd gotten so quiet was that the subject was a sore one for her. Much as he hated to probe, he didn't like leaving it like that, like the proverbial eight-hundred-pound gorilla sitting there on the seat between them. And she *had* been the one to bring it up.

So he said, "What about you?" And when he felt her turn her face toward him he threw a bold glance back at her. "Your brother told me about—"

"My two?" She laughed, but it had a brittle sound that didn't seem to fit with what he'd seen so far of her warmth and soft eyes and ready smile. "Yes, I'm sure he did. I think

I set some kind of record in my family. My brother Jimmy Joe has one, but so far that's it, except for me."

"You have my sympathies," Scott said, meaning it. "Divorces are tough, even the 'good ones.' I know I wouldn't want to go through that again."

"No," she said on a soft exhalation. "And I don't intend to ever have it happen to me again. Not," she added in a thoughtful way, "that I *intended* things to turn out the way they did the first two times, I suppose. It's just...well, I'm not taking any chances, that's all."

Her tone sounded final, and remembering what Roy had told him about his sister being "soured on the whole idea," he thought he probably ought to leave the subject right where it was. But again, for some reason, he wanted to know more about those two divorces of hers, and the marriages, too. From what he'd seen of her so far, it was hard to imagine anybody not being able to get along with her. Knowing it was none of his business didn't help. His curiosity was like a chigger bite he couldn't help but scratch.

Years of experience had made him good at asking questions of people who didn't care to answer them. He started out casual, his voice quiet...non-threatening. "How about you? You on good terms with your exes?"

Her laugh was brief, but he could definitely hear pain in it.

"No, 'fraid not."

Again that note of finality; okay, she really did *not* want to talk about this. At least, not to him. He couldn't blame her but still couldn't let it go. He wondered if it was because in his mind he kept seeing her as he'd first seen her—the generous curves of her body, the breathless lifting of her smile, the way her eyes had of looking up through her lashes. He kept hearing that furry quality in her voice, feeling the answering buzz in the center of his chest. As far as he was concerned, divorces, particularly two of them, didn't fit with that picture.

"I'm sorry," he said gently, trying the sympathy tack. He

rubbed the back of his neck and added, "I have to say, though, whatever happened, I can't imagine it was your fault."

He felt the look she gave him, and now her laugh held a note of surprise. And maybe a new and unspoken awareness? Did he want that? What the hell was he trying to do, here, anyway?

Then she did speak, and the pain and the sadness were still there, lurking behind the laughter. "Oh, who knows? I think every divorce is different. My two certainly were, and I'm sure yours was totally different from either one of mine."

"Yeah," said Scott, nodding thoughtfully. "I'm sure that's true. I know in my case it helped that it wasn't personal."

"Wasn't personal?" She was looking at him again, sounding puzzled.

"As in, it wasn't me *personally* Beth objected to. She just decided she didn't care to be married to a cop."

He heard a sharp intake of breath, and then, almost in a whisper, "You're a cop?" This was followed by a firmer statement of sheer disbelief: "Oh my God, you're a *cop?*"

Which wasn't quite the reaction he'd expected, or was used to getting from people when they first found out what he did for a living. Among law-abiding folk, that reaction was generally respect, curiosity or mild wariness, while the choice of those with less-than-happy associations with the law tended to vary from chagrin to dismay to drop-everything-and-run-like-hell. But he was pulling into Roy's driveway right then, so he had to wait until he'd stopped the truck and turned off the motor before he could investigate what it was that made the woman sound so…*awed.*

Yes, *awed.* That was the word that came to his mind, once he'd set the brake and could look over at her. In the wash of Roy's security flood lamps, her face looked unnaturally pale and her eyes, gazing at him, reflected the light like tiny stars. But he knew it wasn't the floodlights that made her look as if she were witnessing the Second Coming. The glow in her eyes, the wonder in her face came from within.

"You really are a cop?"

It was the third time she'd said it. While he was shaking his head in confusion and saying, "Yeah, what—" she held up a hand to stop him in mid-sentence. Then she put the fingertips of that same hand delicately to her own lips, and he heard her throat clear, saw her eyelashes drop, then lift again.

She fixed those incredible eyes on his and said huskily, "Scott, do you believe in Fate?"

"Okay, let me see if I've got this straight. You came down here because your roommate didn't come back from vacation and you think something bad's happened to her and you wanted your brother to help you find her." Scott was sprawled in a folding canvas deck chair, squinting hard at the woman who was sitting across the round glass-top table from him, looking as wholesome and innocent as it's possible for a woman to look with a long-necked bottle of Bud Lite in her hand.

She gazed back at him, golden eyes unblinking. "Right."

"Uh-huh. At the risk of stating the obvious, why don't you just go to the police and report your friend missing?"

She didn't answer right away, and in the artificial glow of the light attached to the ceiling fan circling above their heads he could see her cheeks turn pink and her throat ripple, though she hadn't touched the beer.

After a moment, she said, "I did," and there was frustration, even anger in that clipped reply. And something else—a certain wariness, maybe. She looked toward pale dunes furred with sea grass and beyond them the glittering dark waters of the Gulf of Mexico.

"They didn't believe me. You probably won't, either. But I'm sure I'm right about Yancy being in trouble. Don't ask me how I know, but I do."

Dammit, Scott thought, mentally rewriting the word *ditzy*—

he'd already crossed it out a couple of times—on the page in his mental notebook with her name on it. Remembering, too, what Roy had said about his sister trying to write mystery novels. Roy was *really* going to owe him for this one.

Pressing the thumb and middle finger of one hand against his eyelids and adopting the patient, gentle tone he normally employed with semi-hysterical crime victims and eyewitnesses, he said, "Joy, if the officers you talked to didn't believe your friend's absence was cause for concern, they must have had a good reason. What is it you're not telling me?"

After a repeat of the pause, swallow and blush, she closed her eyes and spilled it, along with a sigh of reluctant acceptance. "Okay. Apparently Yancy checked out of her hotel herself—paid her bill, signed the credit card receipt and everything—two days early. The desk clerk on duty at the time even remembers her." Her lips tilted into a wry smile. "Which isn't too surprising. Yancy's pretty memorable. Anyway, he says she was with someone—a man—and that she looked...happy." Her voice caught a little on that last word.

She lifted the beer bottle to her lips, discovered it was empty and abruptly rose, sweeping the bottle with her and announcing, "I'm going to have another one of these," as if defying anyone to stop her. She nodded toward the sweating can of iced tea Scott was turning in circles on the table top. "What about you?"

"No, I'm good," he said, then moodily let his gaze follow her as she slipped through the sliding glass door into the kitchen, opened the refrigerator and helped herself to another bottle of her brother's beer. She'd changed her clothes, which was only a matter of exchanging the skirt for a pair of knee-length white pants and tying the shirttail ends of the yellow-with-blue-polka-dots blouse at her waist and ditching her shoes, and the shape and sway of her hips was enough to make him reach for the can of tea and take a big gulp because his mouth had gone dry.

Memorable. As the word wrote itself across that notebook page in his head it occurred to Scott that he'd yet to see any evidence that Joy Starr had any idea how memorable *she* was.

By the time she rejoined him on the deck and sank into the chair across from him with effortless grace, tucking one leg under her, he was thinking it was way past time for him to be going home. He didn't like the way his thoughts were going, the way he kept noticing things he shouldn't: like the fact that she'd ditched the yellow scarf, and with her hair falling in soft loose waves to her shoulders she looked about sixteen, from a time when sixteen was still sweet. *Thanks a lot, Roy...*

"You don't drink?" She waved her bottle at him as she asked it, with a boldness he suspected was more the product of the beer she'd drunk than her basic nature.

He shook his head and forced himself not to stare at the shine of moisture glazing her lips. "Not in any twelve-steps sense, but...no. I figured out early in my life as a lawman that it's way too easy for someone in my line of work to take refuge that way. Watched a couple buddies get lost, scared myself bad enough a couple times to know I didn't want to go down that road. So, I quit. Cold. Figured in the long run it was easier that way."

Her golden eyes seemed to flicker with the shadows of the whirling fan as she sipped, then burped softly. "I admire your self-discipline."

"Oh, hey—" He jerked back, both surprised and discomfited by the remark. "It wasn't that hard. I don't need to crawl around in my own vomit to figure out when something's no good for me. I don't see how it takes self-discipline if it's easy."

"I meant that as a compliment," she said with exaggerated meekness. After a pause for his smile and snort of self-deprecating laughter, she added thoughtfully, "I don't think of self-discipline as being a virtue, so much, as a factor of being a grown-up. Which—don't take this the wrong way, I also mean it as a compliment—I believe you are."

"Thanks," said Scott in surprise and sincerity, and then he was silent for a moment or two. In his mind he was busy scratching out that word *ditzy* once again, and thinking that in the short time he'd known her, his ideas and impressions about Joy Starr had been crossed out, erased, written over and amended so many times, by now her page in his mental notebook was a confused mess he couldn't make head nor tail of. Maybe, he thought, he ought to just tear that one up and start fresh.

He cleared his throat, took a sip of tea and said casually, "Why do I get the idea the men in your life so far weren't?"

"My ex-husbands, I assume you mean."

She smiled and he saw just a hint of a dimple and that through-the-lashes look that shortened his breath every time.

"It's nice of you to give *me* the benefit of the doubt, but...no, I don't believe they were."

She settled back in her chair with an air of finality and a little shake of her head, and as her hair resettled into its graceful waves, he was thinking that whatever faint hope he might have had for personal revelations had fizzled once again.

Then she said, "Not that I don't have good men in my life to compare them to—I do. I don't have any excuse at all for having such poor taste in men. I think it's just bad karma."

Karma. Ignoring that, he smiled and leaned toward her, chin on the heel of his hand. "Such as who?"

"Well, my daddy, when I was growin' up—" she'd slipped unconsciously into a deeper Georgia accent "—but then I lost him when I was pretty young. In fact, I wonder sometimes if that wasn't why I..." To Scott's renewed disappointment, she shook that off, backed up and started again. "My brothers are great, of course. Jimmy Joe, especially, the way he took over Daddy's trucking business after he died, and raised his boy, J.J., alone, until he met his second wife, Mirabella. Troy, my oldest brother—he was in the navy, you know. The SEALs. Retired now, though, and married to

Charly, who's a lawyer in Atlanta. He's a private investigator, and has a stepson and then a little girl of his own. Then there's C.J., my baby brother. For a long time he was considered the family black sheep, because he dropped out of high school, I guess, but I never did think he was. He was always a good kid, just got lost for a while. Now, he's a lawyer, married and adopting a little girl. You can't get much more grown up than that.''

Scott laughed. "No, I guess not. So that leaves…'' He paused and she joined him in saying it, with the same little sigh: *"Roy.''* And they both laughed. It felt surprisingly good, doing that.

"So, what about Roy? Is he your family's black sheep, then?''

"No,'' she said, dimpling again. "I think I probably have that honor. Anyway, I think it's more like Roy's not *any* kind of a sheep. You know what I mean? He pretty much goes his own way, following his own rules. Always has.''

"True.'' And Scott was thinking, with a twinge in his belly, about the reason why Roy was off who-knows-where at the moment, and what it was he might be doing. Things not even Scott knew about and didn't care to know, and those he did know about he couldn't tell anyone, least of all the woman sharing a moonlit deck overlooking the Gulf with him right now. Not unless the worst happened, in which case it would be his unhappy duty to tell her lies.

"But about whether or not he's a grown-up…'' Joy continued in a musing tone, gazing at the shimmering water. "I think he is, in some ways. In others, it's like he's Peter Pan. Can't bear the idea of settling down. Thinks he's immortal…''

"I know what you mean,'' Scott said with a small shudder, shifting in his chair. "The man has the self-preservation instincts of a sixteen-year-old boy. Sometimes I feel more like his father than his friend, trying to look out for him, feeling responsible for him, you know?''

"Yes, I do,'' she said with soft emphasis, bringing those

eyes around and hitting him full force with their effect, which he was discovering was something akin to that of a battering ram. "That's *exactly* the way I feel about Yancy. So, I know you can understand why I simply *had* to come down here and find her. And why, since Roy's not here, I have to ask you to help me."

Scott sat back with a groan, thinking it was a little like chasing a perp through a swamp and coming around a clump of palmettos and finding the guy he'd been chasing was behind him instead of in front. In short, he'd been had.

Chapter 3

"Of course," Joy said, trying to hold her voice steady when all of her insides seemed to be vibrating, "I will understand if you'd rather not. Since you *are* a policeman—"

"Deputy sheriff," he said glumly.

"—and it *is* the official position of two different police departments that Yancy went wherever it is she did go of her own free will, and that she is an adult and therefore it is not the business—" She stopped, because Scott was silently laughing and shaking his head. *"What?"*

"What'd you say you do for a living? You're a psychologist, right?"

She bristled, not understanding what he was getting at. "I can't imagine why you'd think that. Actually, I write the news for a New York radio…" She stopped, the tempest in her insides picking up intensity. Scott was doing the silent head shake, and this time his smile wasn't as friendly.

"Or a con artist? Because if you're not, you should be. I've had experts try to manipulate me, but none of them could hold a candle to you."

Her breath caught, audible in the sudden silence. "Is that what you think I'm doing? *Manipulating* you?" Well, of course she *had* been, if that was what he wanted to call it. Joy preferred to think of it as making use of whatever tools she happened to have at her disposal. However, being so easily caught doing so made her unjustifiably angry—though oddly enough, the butterflies in her stomach had disappeared.

"I'm sorry," she said in her best Southern drawl, rising as regally as someone just a hair over five feet tall can. "I certainly did not intend to do that. And I *certainly* would not want you to feel I'd *conned* you into doin' somethin' you don't want to do." Well, she hadn't been raised in Ogelthorpe County, Georgia, for nothing.

With that, she marched into the kitchen, and she didn't know whether to be pleased or not when she heard the sliding glass door whisk open again, then shut with a gentle *thump*.

"Frankly, Miss Scarlet," came a deep-throated growl from behind her, "I don't believe you'd be capable of 'conning' me into anything, though I'd find it mighty entertainin' watching you try."

She whirled around, heart thumping from some unexplained infusion of adrenaline, and found that, far from seeming put out, Scott was grinning at her with what looked like delight. She didn't know, for a dozen heartbeats or so, whether she considered that pleasing or annoying. While trying to decide, she leaned back against the counter, closed her eyes and found laughter unexpectedly waiting somewhere inside her. Rather than fight it, she gave in to it.

"You're forgetting," he said gently, "I was raised in the South. I'm pretty much immune to that *Steel Magnolias* crap."

His voice should have warned her. When she opened her eyes she found the distance between them smaller than she'd anticipated, and tension leaping back and forth across the meager space like electricity seeking a way to the ground. She tilted her head back and her breath caught; even his eyes seemed infused with electricity, a vivid, intense blue in the bright kitchen light.

She shook her head, re-centering herself, and said quietly, veiling her eyes with her lashes, "Okay, but I meant what I said. No con. If you don't want to help me, I'll have to look for Yancy by myself. But I *will* look, until I find her."

Scott said under his breath, "Now, *that* works."

And Joy had no idea what in the world she could have said or done to make him look as though he'd been whacked upside the head.

Before she could ask for an explanation, he seemed to shake himself, like a cat who'd been sprinkled with water. Then he moved away from her, breaking the tension that had been between them. If, she thought, it had ever existed except in her own mind. She really didn't know which would be worse—having the tension be real, or having her mind play ridiculous games with her when she needed it focused on Yancy.

Across from her, Scott leaned one shoulder against the refrigerator and folded his arms across his chest. Brows lowered, cop-serious, he said, "I suppose you have a plan?"

A plan? Of course I have a plan. Except that for one panicky moment, she couldn't remember what it was. From where she stood, which put her head at a level more than a foot lower than Scott's, the part of him that most naturally met her eyes was the place where brawny, sun-baked arms, nicely furred with darkish hair, met the white cotton-molded mounds of T-shirt-covered chest. Half-forgotten images and associations and feelings careened through her mind with such speed and undirected force, she actually felt dizzy. "Plan." Her voice echoed oddly in her ears. "Well, of course. I intend to start at the place where Yancy was last heard from, obviously." She gulped air like a netted fish.

Scott was nodding. "Sounds about right. And that would be…"

"It's a big resort, golf courses and everything. Very posh.

It's not that far from here—fifty miles or so. It's called Spanish Keys.''

"Spanish Keys?"

Was there a leap of interest in his eyes? She'd thought so for an instant, but now it was gone and once again she didn't know if it had ever been there or had been only her vivid imagination.

He gave a low whistle and said mildly, "Well, that's definitely the high-rent district. You didn't mention your friend was loaded.''

Joy sighed. "She's not. That's her problem. She wants to be, in the worst way.''

She pushed away from the sink and moved restlessly toward the table, and as if following her move, Scott vacated his post against the refrigerator door. Now that it was accessible again without going through him, Joy thought about helping herself to another bottle of beer, but decided against it. Her mind was having entirely too much fun with the effects of the first two.

"Yancy grew up poor," she said, pausing in front of the sliding doors to gaze out at the view. Except that instead of dunes and sea out there, in the dark glass she saw the room behind her, and Scott, taking up a large part of it, leaning now against the countertop, watching her. A strange quiver rippled through her and she folded her arms across herself as if she'd felt a chill. What was it Granny Calhoun used to say? *A goose walking over your grave.* Which never had made sense to her.

"Her daddy was a preacher in some little town in New England—Maine, I think. She ran away from home right after high school, and he pretty much disowned her, which is something I cannot understand, how any father could...but anyway.'' She took a focusing breath and turned back to the room, finding it both warmer and less crowded than its mirror image. "Yancy got modeling work in New York, something that's easy to understand if you could see her, but she didn't really like it, and eventually she started doing spots for TV stations, reporting on fashion shows, things like that, and even writing articles for fashion magazines. She's good at it, too. Yancy's so bright and funny and talented, which I don't think she even realizes, which is sad—'' She broke off, aware once again that Scott was watching her, listening intently. He really was a very good listener.

"I'm sorry,'' she said, seconding the apology with a smile. "I suppose I'm talking too much. I've been told I tend to do that. I go off on tangents, now and then.''

Scott shook his head but didn't smile back, his eyes, unreadable, simply resting on her as if he'd found a comfortable place for them to be and had no intention of shifting their position anytime soon.

Which she certainly couldn't say for herself. *Her* eyes didn't feel comfortable anywhere close to him, and neither did the rest of her. She felt off balance, restless, itchy and self-conscious and longed, suddenly, to escape that confined and well-lighted room, to flee back out to the deck and the friendly night, where the workings of her capricious mind would be less easy for those keen blue eyes to read. *Coward,* she scolded herself. *You're forty-two years old—what's the matter with you?*

"Anyway—'' she went on when he still didn't comment "—the point is, Yancy gets to be right up close to the world of the rich and famous, without being a part of it. And she wants *so much* to be. And she thinks the only way into that world for her is to marry into it. Old-fashioned as it sounds, like something out of Jane Austen, I've always thought, what she's hoping to do is land a rich husband. Which,'' she concluded, worried enough by her own recital of Yancy's circumstances to override her nervousness about meeting Scott's eyes, "makes her vulnerable. Particularly to the wrong kind of man.''

"Yes, it would,'' Scott said, gravely nodding.

And she didn't know what she'd expected to see in his eyes, but the compassion and concern she did find there were

like a swallow of hot cocoa on a cold day. *So good…
so good.*

He straightened abruptly, all business. "Okay. Tell you
what. Like I said, I've got a charter tomorrow morning, a
half day, so I should be cleaned up and done at the boat by
two o'clock or so, and after that I'm free. Normally I work
the day shift, but I'm off this weekend. Don't have to go in
until Monday. So, if you can amuse yourself until then, and
promise not to go off half-cocked on your own, I'll drive you
down to Spanish Keys. We can… I don't know, maybe have
dinner. Something. How's that?"

"That would be great. Thank you…" And her eyes were
climbing the heights of him, scaling the masculine chest, sun-
reddened neck and substantial five o'clock shadow, to rest
with faint surprise on a mouth of a most appealing shape and
firmness. For a terrifying moment she feared the rest of her
might follow. Swept up on a wave of gratitude and relief,
she had an urge to kiss him, and might well have done so—
Joy was prone to such generous impulses—if she could have
reached that mouth. As it was, the only part of him accessible
to her, short of wrapping her arms and legs about his body
and hitching herself upward like a lumberjack scaling a tree,
was that massive and no doubt unyielding chest. So, she
made do with thrusting out her hand and concluding with a
breathless "…so *much.*"

As her hand vanished into his, her mind clicked, whirred
and spun into a giddy little song: *This feels so good, so-
goodsogood…*

He was mumbling something. Her mind tuned in at
"…pick you up tomorrow, then. About three?"

She nodded automatically, her mind still singing, *So-
good…sogood…sogood.*

"Well, good night, then." He let go of her hand and
walked away, and only after she heard the front door close
did she realize he'd had that poleaxed look again. What did
that *mean?*

* * *

Scott was on his way down the wooden stairs that led to the driveway when he discovered he was sweating. He was used to the local weather, having grown up in it, so he was fairly sure his state of dampness didn't have much to do with the warmth of the evening, or the humidity that was normal for Florida at this time of year. What it reminded him of was a time in his long-ago memory, that interminable adolescent period when he seemed to have spent his days in perpetual need of a cold shower. Clearly not a state he wanted to be in at his age and station in life—forty-five years old and an officer of the law, for Pete's sake.

So, why was there a spring in his step and a song in his heart at the thought of spending another evening in the company of his buddy Roy's allegedly ditzy sister, Miss Joy Lynn Starr?

He could have told himself he was planning to do so only to fulfill the promise he'd made to her brother, or to satisfy his own sense of responsibility as a lawman and protector of the innocent—which strangely enough, he was fairly certain she was. However, while he was willing to admit to being possessed of an average number of human weaknesses, self-delusion wasn't one of them. Miss Joy was turning out to be a whole lot of potent sex appeal packed into one tiny package, and when it came to sex he was as susceptible as the next man. Maybe more so, considering how long it had been since he'd had any.

Hey, man, forget it, she's too small for you. Why don't you find somebody you don't have to worry about crushing? He heard himself say that, way back inside his head. And he heard his self reply, *She's not that much tinier than Beth, and I managed that okay. There's Ryan to prove it.*

By the time his thoughts had progressed that far, he was back in the cab of his truck, and the images in his head made him glad it was dark and he was alone and sitting down. After taking a few moments to dispel the mental pictures of Joy's curvy little body tangled with his in tumbled sheets, he wiped sweat from his face with an unsteady hand and reached for his cell phone. He punched in a pre-programmed number, and when a voice answered in the usual policeman monotone, he said, "Hey, Duff."

Joe Duffy, manning the night desk down at the station, said back, "Hey, Cavanaugh. How they bitin'?"

"Not bad. How 'bout you? Things pretty quiet?"

"Couple disturbance complaints from the beach houses… fistfight up at the Oyster Bar. About usual for a Friday night."

"Yeah… Listen, Duff, I'm not gonna be in 'til Monday, and I've got a charter tomorrow, but I was wondering if you could do me a favor in the meantime?"

"Might as well—nothin' else goin' on. What can I do you for?"

"Could you check and see if any Jane Doe DBs have turned up in the last couple weeks, within, say, a hundred mile radius of Spanish Keys?"

"Spanish Keys, huh? Uh-huh, okay."

Scott could hear the piqued interest in Duffy's voice; suspicious DB's were a rarity in their jurisdiction.

"What you got goin', Cavanaugh?"

"Oh, you know, got a request from somebody. Friend of a friend… Worried momma, you know how it is. Probably nothing, but I said I'd look into it. Don't make a big deal out of it, just keep it quiet, okay? If you find anything, you know where to reach me."

Scott was sure Duffy would have liked to ask him a few more questions, but luckily another call came in just then, so the duty officer was limited to a drawled "Will do" as he broke the connection.

As he tucked away his phone and reached for the ignition key, Scott was hoping he hadn't just made a huge mistake. Like, maybe he was getting himself into something he was going to regret. But, he told himself, better to be on the safe side, right? Even if Miss Joy did turn out to be the ditz her brother believed her to be.

A sexy and lovable ditz, maybe, but a ditz nonetheless.

And on that score, as far as he was concerned, the jury was still out. Aside from that, Scott had a sneaking suspicion Roy's ''big'' sister didn't need looking *after* so much as she did looking *out for.* As in, Beware of Dangerous Curves Ahead.

There were several reasons why Joy had trouble falling asleep in the guest bedroom of her brother's small but hospitable beach house, in spite of the fact that she was shaky with exhaustion. She'd been up since before dawn to catch her flight, then there'd been a change of planes in Atlanta, followed by the long taxicab ride from Tallahassee and at its conclusion, the unanticipated complication of finding her brother out of town and a large stranger in his place. She'd expected to be out like a light once her head hit the pillow. Instead, even after a surprisingly comforting supper of microwaved SpagettiOs gleaned from Roy's meager larder and a shower that was blessedly and consistently hot, she lay awake tossing and turning until the wee hours.

Part of the reason, she was sure, was the quiet. But for the faint hum of air-conditioning, the night was utterly still. Having grown up in the Georgia countryside amid timber tracts and cow pastures, Joy was used to nodding off with the screeches, hoots and hisses of rural Southern nightlife in her ears. Later, she'd grown accustomed to the nightlife of big cities, where the screeches, hoots and hisses came from cars and police sirens and squabbling neighbors. Here, not even surf sounds penetrated the shingled walls and double-paned windows. The Gulf was calm, the dunes a buffer against the gentle lapping of the tides and the occasional slap of a jogger's footsteps on wet sand. The silence was a vacuum, one her overcrowded mind couldn't wait to fill.

Old worries and new concerns jostled and elbowed one another for center stage in her thoughts. Yancy, of course: *What's happened to her? Where could she be? Why hasn't she called? Something must be terribly wrong, because she wouldn't do this to me!* And this new person Fate had seen fit to drop into her life, seemingly out of the clear blue sky: Scott Cavanaugh. *Why is he taking up so much space in my head? And what am I going to do about him?*

She tried telling herself his intrusion into her mind was understandable, even natural. He was the new dog in the yard, as dear old Granny Calhoun would have said, rest her soul. Joy was only thinking about Scott the same way she'd thought about Sam and Frida Macklinburg when they'd first moved in next door, because they were an unfamiliar element to be incorporated into the normal order of her life. *Sure, Joy, and you lost sleep imagining what Sam would look like under that gray plumber's uniform, wondering whether his chest is hairy or smooth, and whether the rest of him is as tan as his neck and arms. Right.*

Sweaty and annoyed with herself, she stared at the ceiling fan circling silently above her head. *Why should I have to do anything about Scott Cavanaugh? He's a temporary necessity in my life, that's all* was the obvious answer to the nuisance question, but Joy was too honest a person to find any comfort in it. She knew that was *not* all. Scott was a cop and Roy's friend, he could help her find Yancy, and since Fate had given him to her, she would make use of him. But that was definitely not *all.*

Her panicky mind shied away from the looming thoughts like a nervous horse, but even another flip-flop couldn't keep them from invading: his hand engulfing hers...the brush of sun-warmed skin against her arm...the bulge of tanned biceps against the bulge of white T-shirted pecs...blue eyes resting on her with the ease of old friends... *That mouth.*

A groan surprised her. It seemed to come from a place inside her that she hadn't even known about, and that convinced her it was time to call in the big guns. *Zack,* she thought grimly. *Frederick.* And as she'd known it would, forcing the faces of her two ex-husbands onto the giant TV screen in her mind was the next best thing to a cold shower. *Never! I'm not going there, ever again. No, sir!*

She lay quietly, then, while subdued echoes of remembered fear, anger and shame shivered through her in chilling little waves. But as the ripples died and warmth gradually returned to her body and calm to her mind, she heard a timid voice way back in there somewhere saying, *Okay, I'm with you on the marriage thing, no problem, but what about sex? Sex is good. Are you sure you want to go the rest of your life without that?*

She knew the answer to that question, and it brought her no peace. Just an old ache and a new restlessness, and it was a long time more before she slept.

In spite of that, Joy was up at dawn and on the deck with a cup of coffee in time to watch the fishing boats heading out into the Gulf. She knew one of them must be the *Gulf Starr,* with Scott at the helm, and in her mind's eye she saw the white boat rocking gracefully through a gentle swell, outriggers aloft like gossamer wings, a warm breeze riffling through dark hair—or no, he'd be wearing a cap of some kind, of course. A captain's cap? She smiled at the thought. Oddly enough, Scott's presence in her mind didn't seem troubling or ominous this morning. Instead, it brought her a rather pleasurable warmth.

She went for a long walk on the beach and saw fresh turtle crawls, and horseshoe crabs and jellyfish and seashells, and then sat on a sand dune and watched flotillas of pelicans glide their stately way back and forth along the shore. There were other people on the beach, but to Joy, accustomed to the crowded busyness of New York, the world seemed vast and unpopulated, a quiet, peaceful place. Last night the quiet had been a dangerous vacuum, an abyss filled with monster thoughts. Today, it felt more like a blank page labeled Opportunity, a fresh canvas, an open line to…whoever might be Out There. *Yancy?*

Maybe, she thought, she hadn't "heard" from Yancy after that one time because there'd been too much distance between them, and there'd been too much interference, too much noise, too much bustle. Maybe here, close to where Yancy was, in the silence and solitude and open spaces...

What could it hurt? Resolved to try anything, Joy recalled remnants from the yoga classes she'd taken a few years back and coaxed her legs into the lotus position. She closed her eyes and lifted her face to the sky. Sun warmed her eyelids as she drifted, senses honed, her mind an empty vessel...but, except for the muttering of complaints from her forty-two-year-old body, nothing came to fill it. Then she tried forming a thought. Yancy's name...Yancy's face, and sent it outward with all her concentration, imagining it like a bright beam of light arcing out over the water. She concentrated until her neck muscles began to ache, and then waited, quivering inside, for a reply. But she heard only the distant chirping of children romping in the surf, building castles in the sand.

Oh, well. Evidently, ESP wasn't something that could be turned on and off at will. In her case, anyway. Feeling vaguely silly, Joy untangled her protesting limbs and made her way stiffly back to the beach house, thinking that its tall and narrow silhouette, gray shingles and stilts reminded her of a heron standing up straddle-legged among the dunes.

Scavenging for breakfast, she found an open box of instant grits in Roy's cupboard. It was enclosed in a zipper bag to protect it from roaches, which, given what she knew about her brother's personal habits, led her to believe he must currently either have a steady girlfriend or employ the services of an efficient housekeeper.

She couldn't remember the last time she'd eaten grits. She microwaved herself a large bowlful, which she topped with butter and strawberry jam, both of which she found in the refrigerator in reasonably good condition. They were neither as good as she remembered Momma's being, nor as bad as she'd expected the instant version to be, but eating grits in any form made her think of home and family. She thought to herself that she needed to remember to ask Scott what her little brother Roy was up to these days—where he'd gone off to and how long he'd been gone and when he was expected to be back.

That led to some unexpected homesickness, though it may have been the emptiness of the house and that awful silence that made her think nostalgically of her crowded and noisy childhood, growing up with four brothers and two sisters in a house with one bathroom. Whatever the reason, after she'd washed and put away her bowl and spoon, she settled herself on the deck with the cordless phone from the guest bedroom, her traveling address book and her prepaid long-distance calling card, intending to spend the rest of the morning making calls to her mother and as many of her brothers and sisters as she could get hold of on a Saturday morning.

After punching in the endless series of numbers required to make the first call, while waiting for someone to pick up, Joy turned the card over and rubbed her thumb across the picture of the teddy bear on the front. She'd bought the card at the post office, and it was a commemoration of the hundredth birthday of the teddy bear. She'd bought two, and she'd given one to Yancy and had made her promise to use the card if she wanted or needed to call. Yancy had promised faithfully to call often and tell her *everything*.

The phone was on its fourth or fifth ring—she'd lost count—which meant Momma'd gone out somewhere and forgotten to turn on the answering machine again. She let it ring awhile longer before punching the "star" key for another call, still gazing at the teddy bear and stroking it with her thumb. She felt a quivering deep down inside her chest, and waited, her mind whispering, *Yancy, are you there?* But that strange yet unmistakable feeling of her friend's *presence* that had come to her that day in her apartment in New York didn't return.

If only, she thought, it could be that easy. *E.T. phone home.*

Joy was ready and waiting for him when Scott pulled into the driveway of the beach house. That in itself was a surprise to him since Beth, his ex-wife, always managed to be late no matter how much advance notice he gave her, but he was completely unprepared for the jolt he got just seeing Roy's sister again.

Part of it had to be the way she was dressed. He didn't know what he'd expected. More of the G-rated, *I-Love-Lucy*-slash-cheerleader look she'd sported the day before, he supposed, but as it happened, for today's foray into the habitat of the rich and famous she'd chosen a different role model altogether. Who, exactly, he couldn't have said—one of those impossibly gorgeous, glamorous movie queens from the same era. Ava Gardner, maybe? Anyway, she had on slacks... pants...trousers? None of those words seemed adequate to describe the article of clothing that draped over her hips and rounded behind and swirled around the tops of her open-toed high-heeled leather sandals. Whatever it was called, it was an iridescent tawny gold in color, something soft that shimmered when she moved. The top was made of the same material, a halter affair that left her arms, shoulders and most of her back bare. It had long tapering pieces of material at the sides that crisscrossed in back and tied off-center at the waist, molding snugly to her waist and outlining breasts that made a man's mouth go dry. In direct contrast to the voluptuousness of her clothes, her hair was drawn sleekly back into an elegant knot at the nape of her neck and held in place by some sort of comb or clip made of tortoiseshell that made him think of Spanish dancers. Aside from that, her only jewelry was a pair of simple gold hoop earrings, and sunglasses with a retro cat's-eye shape and tortoiseshell rims. The whole effect was an incredibly intoxicating blend of cool glamour and hot sex.

But the most incredible part was that from the open and uninhibited smile that lit her face and the artless and eager way she skipped toward him down those wooden stairs, Scott was certain Joy had absolutely no clue.

Chapter 4

He had himself under control by the time she'd made it down the stairs and was opening the door of the Chevy. At least, he hoped he did. *Yeah, I'm cool and flinty-eyed, thinking Clint Eastwood thoughts.* He knew he should have gotten out and opened the door for her—basic good manners, if not the Southern gallantry he'd been raised on, dictated that much—but he seriously doubted his self-discipline would have stood the test of watching Joy's bottom moving around underneath that slithery, shimmery gold material as she negotiated the climb up into his pickup truck. Most likely even Clint Eastwood had his limits.

"Hi," she said, breathless as a girl, bouncing a little as she used the tips of her toes to push herself back in the seat. *Damn* but she was short. He thought again what an amazing thing it was that so much style, elegance and pure, unadulterated sex appeal could be crammed into such a little bitty package.

"You look nice," he said, using the clever device of glaring over his shoulder while backing down the driveway to give himself the excuse to let his eyes slide across her body one more time.

"Thanks." She clicked her seat belt into place, then threw him a look—a wry little smile—and briefly touched the tortoiseshell comb in her hair. "I hope I'm not overdoing it. Yancy showed me pictures of this place—brochures and things—and it looked *very* posh. I don't want to be overdressed, but I don't want to stick out like a sore thumb, either."

He didn't tell her she was pretty certain to stick out no matter what she was wearing, though not anything like a "sore thumb." More like a rose in a patch of weeds. What he did say was "I think you look fine."

"Thank you."

He could feel her eyes appraising him as he drove.

"You look nice, too," she added.

Well, he had to snort at that, his smile as crooked as hers had been. Next to her, in his standard, summer dress-up uniform of khakis and knit shirt, he felt about as sophisticated as Joe College—maybe even Joe High School—proudly squiring his date to the drive-in movies in his dad's old pickup.

He glanced over at her. "Hope you don't mind going in the truck. Other than a patrol car, this beauty happens to be my only set of wheels. It's a gas guzzler, but it'll haul anything, pull anything, go anywhere and do anything I ask of it. Don't see any reason to change."

He couldn't read the look she gave him, not in the few seconds he allowed himself, but he felt vaguely chided when she quietly said, "No, of course I don't mind."

"I did wash it," he said, his smile going wry once again.

Solemnly, she said, "I'm honored."

"I should hope so. It *is* a classic, you know."

She laughed, and he didn't have time to examine the feeling that husky sound fostered inside him, a pool of warmth that began somewhere in his chest and spread like whiskey-fire, because just then his cell phone, tucked in the pocket of his khakis, began to shiver against his thigh.

He muttered a mild swear word and then, "Excuse me," as he pulled it out and glanced at the caller ID, then punched the "on" button. "Hey, son, hang on a sec, okay?" He handed the phone to Joy and nodded toward the dashboard. "Do me a favor, would you? Plug in that doo-hickey there and hand it to me, then stick this in the cradle...yeah... perfect. Thanks."

Watching Scott adjust the hands-free headset gave Joy a nice little buzz of approval, and yes, admit it—pleasure. Was it because he was a cop, she wondered, or simply an honest-to-God grown-up, that he paid attention to such a simple and common sense safety precaution? Either way, she liked it. She liked that he'd said "doo-hickey," too; her daddy had used that expression, and it had been a long time since she'd heard it.

She liked the scrubbed, just-shaved shine of his jaw and his hair, still damp from the shower, the little-boy look of it, so at odds with the gray streaks and the craggy, granite-like grown-man's features. She liked the way his cheeks creased and a fan of wrinkles appeared at the corners of his eyes when he smiled.

Face it, Joy, you like him. You're attracted to him, more than you have been to anyone in a long, long time.

Something knotted inside her, and the feeling of pleasure vanished, leaving a formless fear in its place. Lord, she didn't *want* to be attracted, not to Scott Cavanaugh, not to anyone. Not at the best of times, and particularly not *now.* Besides which, she thought gloomily, if I'm attracted to the guy it can only mean there's something wrong with him.

She stared at his wholesome-as-grits, shiny clean hair and polished jaw and thought, *I wonder what it is. Wife beater? Corrupt cop? Compulsive gambler? Secret racist? No, too nice for that. Could he be gay?* Scott peeled off the headset and glanced over as he handed it to her, blue eyes crinkling, mouth smiling, and two thoughts collided inside her head like runaway locomotives on the same track: *Oh God, that mouth—I forgot about his mouth!* And, *Gay? Oh, I hope it's not that!*

Which made no sense at all, considering she didn't want to be attracted to him anyway, right? So, why should she care what his sexual orientation was?

"That was Ryan," he told her unnecessarily.

Joy, too busy putting the cell phone away and mopping up after the train wreck inside her head, didn't reply.

After a moment, he shifted as if he'd grown uncomfortable in his seat and elaborated. "I guess he had a bad day at the ballpark."

Remembering the misery on the boy's face when he'd said "I don't even *like* baseball," Joy limited herself to a sympathetic "I'm sorry." Well, it wasn't her business, after all.

An opinion Scott apparently didn't share, because he went on, staring straight ahead. "Which is not too surprising. He isn't crazy about the game of baseball, even to watch. And he downright *hates* Little League." He lifted a shoulder. "But…it means a lot to his mother. Her daddy used to coach, probably to compensate for the sons he never had."

"That's very perceptive of you." Joy was gazing, fascinated, at a little muscle working in the side of his jaw.

He threw her a self-deprecating grin. "Lord, it's not that hard to figure out. I mentioned, didn't I, that Beth is an only child? Anyway, there's obviously some issues involved, so I try not to say anything." His eyes returned to the road ahead and the smile disappeared. "I don't know, though. I think maybe I'm gonna have to step in at some point. The kid's having a tough enough time right now, what with the hormones kicking in. Well, you know."

"I remember how it was with my brothers," Joy said. "The youngest ones, anyway, C.J. and Roy. Troy was older, and I don't believe Jimmy Joe ever got a chance to be an adolescent. He went straight from being a kid to being a daddy."

"You don't have any? Kids, I mean. Roy didn't mention."

"No." Normally, when she had to answer that question, that was as far as she was willing to go, and most people got that message from the flat way she said it. But she could see the short answer wasn't going to satisfy this man, and for a scary moment she thought she might tell him the things she almost never told, about the miscarriages and the disappointment and pain and other stuff that went with them. For a moment.

But that was ancient history, and Joy wasn't one for dwelling on the past, much less burdening other people with it. And she'd come to terms with being childless long ago.

Her voice was steady when she added, "It wasn't in the cards for me."

She hadn't asked for sympathy, but it was in his voice anyway when he replied softly, "I'm sorry." Then, with a dry chuckle, he amended it. "At least, I think I am. Funny how people always assume not having kids is a bad thing. Right now, I'd almost have to consider maybe you're the lucky one."

She smiled, knowing it was what he wanted, and gratefully took the opportunity he'd given her to return the conversation to safer ground. "What is Ryan, about thirteen?"

"Fourteen. He's small for his age, which is part of his problem. He's worried he's going to take after his mother's side and end up—well, you saw Beth. Both her parents were—" He broke off as the cell phone began to dance in its holster, making a rattling sound. He squinted at the readout, then exhaled and muttered something under his breath. "I'm sorry, could you—"

Wordlessly, Joy unhooked the headset and handed it to him, then hit the cell phone's "on" button for him.

"Hey, Beth. Yeah, he did. I just got through talking to him...." He spoke in a low, private voice, and she couldn't help but notice it had a certain softness, a gentleness that hadn't been there before. And that there was something in his eyes she couldn't read at all.

Okay, probably not gay, she thought as she concentrated

on tuning out the conversation, though Scott's side of it consisted mostly of wordless murmurs and meaningless mutters of acknowledgment anyway. *Just lots and lots of baggage: like a teenaged son and an ex-wife he's not quite gotten over.*

Definitely not the worst a man could have in his character debit column, but enough to warn any sane woman to steer clear.

"Sounds like you have your hands full," she said lightly when, sometime later, Scott handed her back the headset and reached over to disconnect the call. And she wondered at the ironic little chuckle he gave her in return.

Oh yeah, Scott thought, *I have my hands full, all right.* Ryan *this close* to open rebellion against his mother, and Dad on his way down the coast to a resort so far out of his price range it wasn't funny, riding herd on a middle-aged lady who thinks she's Nancy Drew.

And the instant that thought formed in his mind, he could hear a whole chorus of jeers and laughter and all sorts of thoughts chiming in. *Middle-aged? Riding herd? Who're you kidding, Cavanaugh?* And other comments more X-rated than G.

The truth was that he mostly had his hands full with keeping himself on track and his mind on what he needed to be doing, which, he reminded himself, was keeping Roy's sister out of trouble, *not* getting himself into it.

The Spanish Keys Resort was every bit as posh as advertised. It rose out of the sand dunes and golf courses like a Moorish palace, gleaming white in the sun, standing out in sharp relief against a dark backdrop of palmetto and pine groves. Arched colonnades framed lush gardens and manmade lakes and provided an elegant gateway to sugar-sand beaches. Even the gulf waters, dotted with bright Windsurfer sails, seemed clearer and bluer off the resort's private shores.

The parking valet was so well-trained he didn't blink an

eye when Scott handed over the keys to his battered pickup in the arched pavilion paved with mosaic tile that fronted the hotel's main entrance. Joy didn't bat an eye, either, bestowing her knock-'em-dead smile on the doorman as she alighted from the old truck with all the regal aplomb of a grand duchess. Scott couldn't decide whether it was confidence she had in such abundance, or the kind of cluelessness that supposedly shields drunks, fools and children. All he knew was she could have walked into the place—or, for that matter, the Waldorf or the Ritz—wearing blue jeans and a T-shirt and she'd have looked like she belonged there.

He'd been hanging back a bit, observing her from a distance and taking in the surroundings with a cop's peripheral vision. Not that he believed there was any reason to do so, he told himself, it was more force of habit than anything. A little smile of pure masculine appreciation hovered around his mouth as he watched Joy march up to the reception counter, peel off the cat's-eye sunglasses and lay that smile and one of those patented champagne gazes of hers, filtered through charcoal lashes, on the nearest desk clerk. Scott's smile grew broader as he watched the clerk, a young male of apparent Hispanic ancestry, aloof and immaculate in his burgundy blazer, melt like an ice-cream cone left out in the sun.

"Yes," the desk clerk purred in a sultry Latin accent. "How may I help you today?"

She didn't flirt, that was the magic of it. As an observer rather than the recipient of that particular brand of sorcery, Scott could see that all she did was stand there and look the guy in the eye—in her special way, of course—and say what she wanted to say, just as she'd planned to say it. And the poor guy never knew what hit him. Small wonder, Scott reflected; it was pretty hard to defend against something you never saw coming.

The woman really didn't have any idea what potent weapons she possessed, and Scott couldn't decide whether that was a terrifying thing, like a monkey with a machine gun, or the sexiest thing he'd ever run across in his life. Most likely it was both.

Clearly, though, sexy or not, not even Joy could get blood out of a stone. The desk clerk was peering at a computer screen, shaking his head and looking so disappointed at not being able to supply the magical creature before him with the answers she wanted, Scott decided to take pity on him.

"No luck?" he murmured as he joined her at the counter, and without thinking, put his hand on the back of her waist.

It sort of just *happened*. Came naturally to him. Except that when he felt the warm flesh underneath that slithery-soft material, like the glossy coat of some magnificent animal, he felt the jolt of it all the way through his body and right down into his groin. He snatched his hand away as quickly as he could, but the damage was done. The way her head snapped up and her eyes slammed into his, he knew she'd felt some kind of a jolt, too. The only thing he didn't know was whether it was the same one he'd felt, or something altogether different.

"Oh, Scott," she said, breathless and husky, as if surprised to see him there. "He says he doesn't remember Yancy at all. And the person I talked to on the phone, the clerk who remembered checking her out—Carlos, right?" She bestowed another dazzling smile upon the desk clerk. "Anyway, he isn't working today."

The desk clerk, whose manner had cooled considerably since Scott's arrival on the scene, didn't return Joy's smile. "Even if he were here," he said, drawing himself up stiffly, "it would not be appropriate for an employee of this resort to discuss one of our guests. I am sorry. I can tell you only that the person you asked about—Miss LaVigne—is not currently registered as a guest with us. Beyond that I cannot help you."

"Oh dear," Joy murmured as the desk clerk waited politely, hands on the countertop, coolly arched brows at odds with the Latin smokiness of his eyes "I know I should have

called first. As usual.'' Again her eyes lifted and collided
with Scott's.

The disappointment in them would have made any man
forget his better judgment, and before he regained his senses
he was on the verge of hauling out his badge and making
official noises. The time might come when he'd have to do
that, he acknowledged, but not now. Not yet. And preferably
not with Joy beside him.

''We can always come back,'' he heard himself say to her
in an undertone as they were turning away from the reception
desk and the now-watchful eyes of the clerk.

''He wouldn't even tell me what room she was in,'' Joy
said in the same hushed way. ''At least I could have talked
to the maid…*somebody*.''

She was furious, he realized, or anyway, extremely upset.
Her voice was shaking with emotion.

She'd paused in the middle of the vast lobby, the stained-
glass domed skylight raining down sunshine and a Moorish
fountain splashing nearby, and was turning in a vague sort
of way, like someone adrift in a calm sea. He knew how it
felt to find himself stalled in an investigation, so he didn't
tell her he'd known she wasn't going to find out anything
from a personal visit to the resort, nothing she couldn't have
gotten over the phone. Oddly enough, he didn't feel like saying anything to her in the way of I-told-you-so's. What he
wanted more than anything else was to find a way to erase
the panicky look from her eyes.

''What am I going to do now?'' She was asking it of
herself, not him, but he answered it anyway.

''Well, since we're here, we might as well have a look
around,'' he said, earning himself a quick, stabbing glance
from those golden eyes. He shrugged and smiled. ''Have a
bite to eat, too, while we're at it—it was part of the package,
remember? And you brought pictures of Yancy, right? Might
try showing 'em around, you know…waiters…bartenders…
You never know what you might turn up.''

The tight, frustrated look on her face relaxed into a ghost of a smile. She took a breath and said, "That's a good idea."

But she still looked lost, and again it seemed natural to put his hand on her waist, this time to guide her across the lobby toward a glass wall that looked out upon a tropical garden paradise. He was prepared for the jolt, now, so it didn't come as so much of a shock. In fact, it was amazing how right it felt to be touching her, a warm and simple pleasure with a secret kick to it, rather like port wine. He had a college history professor to thank for introducing him to that vanishing tradition, and the more he thought about the comparison, the more it pleased him. *Warm, sweet, potent...a little bit retro... And if you're not careful it'll knock you for a loop.*

Across from the wall of glass, two sets of quarry-tile steps lead down to a lower level. Between the stairways, a waterfall cascaded down an artfully assembled rocky slope that was heavily planted with tropical greenery and dozens of varieties of blooming orchids. The effect was dazzling, even to Scott, who, unlike his ex-wife, wasn't much of a flower person, while Joy, who he'd have been willing to bet money *was,* barely seemed to notice. Probably, he told himself, she was too wrapped up in the mystery of her missing roomie to notice much of anything. Such as his hand on the small of her back, or the fact that he very nearly had her body nicely tucked into the crook of his arm. He found that mildly and irrationally annoying.

Joy was in a mild and irrational state of panic. *This is not supposed to happen. I'm not supposed to feel like this. I came down here to look for Yancy. I'm worried sick about Yancy. So, how come this guy's hand touching my back feels so good? And how can he be touching just my back, when I can feel it inside my chest and my stomach and the soles of my feet and the palms of my hands and all those other places I don't even let myself think about because nobody's touched me there in so damn long?*

She went down the steps carefully, not saying anything, not looking to the right or to the left, barely even breathing, all her concentration focused on putting one foot in front of the other and not stumbling or tripping over her feet or any similar stupid move that might invite that big strong arm across her back to tighten around her like a safety line. In her present state, she truly did not know what she would do if that happened. She only knew the prospect was way too seductive to take a chance on finding out.

"This place is huge," she said when they were outside and she could allow herself to breathe and talk again, more to assure herself that she still could than to make a serious attempt at conversation. In the process of opening the glass door for her Scott had taken his hand away from her waist, and under the guise of pausing to don her sunglasses she'd been able to put some distance between them. Still, what felt like runaway electrical charges skated joyously around under her skin, as if she'd been hit by a bolt of summer heat lightning. If he touched her, she was certain her skin would sizzle.

She could feel Scott's eyes on her as she moved away from him, strolling along flagstone paths that skirted an enormous meandering lagoon. The sultry Florida heat was stirred by cooler eddys—man-made mists and tropical breezes that felt like caresses on her skin. Swaths and patches of tropical landscaping lapped the edges of the lagoon in places and swooped away from it in others, creating shady grottos and glades where people with beautiful tanned and toned bodies sipped exotic-looking drinks served by waiters in tropical costumes reminiscent of the Spanish Caribbean.

"Yancy must have loved it here," she whispered, her feet slowing unconsciously. That was a mistake—like a homing pigeon, Scott's hand found the small of her back again. Breathless and jittery, too weak to object to that dangerous pleasure, she let him steer her to a table in a palm-shaded nook next to a waterfall. From somewhere nearby, a marimba played in soft, evocative harmony with the music of the water.

"Something to drink?" Scott asked, as a waiter hovered.

"Something with pineapple," she said with far more force and defiance than the question warranted, and then, with a whole chorus of warnings clamoring in her head, she grimly added, "and *rum.*" Given the direction in which her thoughts had been going, she felt as daring and illicit as a teenager with a fake ID.

Scott ordered iced tea for himself, and when the waiter had gone, leaned back in his chair and gazed at her in that way he had, neither smiling nor frowning, but simply as though his eyes felt comfortable resting on her. The rest of him looked comfortable, too, completely at home even in those posh surroundings. It had very little to do with the clothes he wore, she realized, and a lot to do with…self-confidence, maybe? And something less easy to define, though the word that had come before and still persisted in her mind was *grown-up.*

"This is quite a place," Scott said, just before the silence became too long.

Joy nodded. Her gaze slid away from him. "It's everything Yancy hoped for and more. That's why—" her eyes lashed back, and he saw a fierce little flame in their depths "—I can't understand why she would have left early. It makes no *sense.*"

"I can think of one reason she might have." She waited, poised for rebuttal. "You said she was looking to find somebody, a rich husband. Maybe she did."

She was already shaking her head. "Then, why wouldn't she call me?" Her hand, resting on the tabletop beside her sunglasses, curled into a fist. "I know Yancy. The first thing she'd do if she met somebody is *call* me. She'd be *dying* to tell me about it. I was like her big sister. When she'd come home from a date, even if it was late and I'd already gone to bed, she'd knock and ask if I was awake, loud enough to make sure of it if I wasn't already. And she'd have to come in and sit on my bed and tell me all about it, every detail—"

Her voice broke slightly and he could see her struggle to control it.

After a pause she drew a breath and went on, speaking too rapidly. "I even gave her a phone card, one of those prepaid long distance cards, because I knew she wasn't taking her cell phone with her. She had the least expensive plan, just local area, everything else was roaming. Yancy could be a cheapskate when she needed to be, and she'd been saving up for this trip for ages. So, when I saw the cards at the post office, it struck me that it was the perfect solution for Yancy, especially since it had a teddy bear on it and I used to collect teddy bears.... Anyway. She'd been using it. She *had*. Then, all of a sudden, nothing." She stopped for breath, and her fist struck the table with a force so controlled it seemed almost gentle. "Why is it so hard for anyone to believe something bad might have happened to her? She was looking for Mister Right, yes, but what if she met Mister Wrong, instead? Those things happen all the time. You, of all people, must know they do."

He nodded and cleared his throat but didn't say anything right away, knowing she wasn't going to buy more reassurances, from him or anyone else. And he didn't want to add to the worry that was already tying her in knots by telling her what he knew about Spanish Keys and about the uneasy feeling that had begun to nibble at the backside of *his* belt buckle.

"Suppose you're right," he said, then leaned back and watched the waiter arrange their drinks on the glass tabletop in front of them—a tall sweating goblet of iced tea for him, and for Joy, something that looked too pretty to drink even if you could find it under all the fruit and flowers.

He paid for the drinks, tipped the waiter and asked for dinner menus, then took a grateful swallow of his tea. And shuddered. *Damn. Unsweetened.* He should have known a resort catering to "foreigners" wouldn't automatically serve it sweet. After looking around unsuccessfully for sugar, he sighed to himself and, because he was thirsty, took a manful gulp of the stuff and nodded at Joy.

"How's your drink?"

She let go of the straw and murmured, "Delicious."

And he couldn't help but think that her lips, moist and tempting, should have worn a sweet, sexy smile when she said it, her eyes a sultry golden glow looking with invitation into his. Instead, she sat hunched and tense over the fruit and flowers, eyes fierce, like a small but hungry hawk. "You said, 'Suppose you're right.'"

"Yeah." Clearing his throat again, he pushed aside his iced tea glass and leaned forward, resisting the urge to take her small clenched fist and cuddle it in his two hands. Gently, as if talking to a child, he said, "Joy, you know that if Yancy did meet Mister Wrong, percentages will tell you it's already too late. And even if she's alive, the chances of you being able to do anything to help her, or find her, are just about nil. You know that, don't you?" He paused, and she glared past him and said nothing. "Leave it," he said softly but firmly. "Some things are beyond your control. Let the pros take over."

Her head jerked toward him, a spare but ominous motion that reminded him of the flicking tail of an angry cat.

"Like you?"

Still watching her, fascinated, he nodded before he thought, then hastily amended, "Well, probably not me personally, it's not really my jurisdiction. I can help you, though. Get things rolling—" The waiter interrupted, presenting them with enormous menus, and Scott, with obvious relief, beamed at her over the top of his and said, "Well. We'll talk about it. Let's have dinner, shall we?"

"I'm not very hungry," Joy muttered, and as she studied the menu, frowning at prices that seemed high even by New York standards, Scott leaned toward her and said in a low voice, out of one side of his mouth, "Don't worry, in places as expensive as this, the portions are so tiny it won't matter anyway."

She gazed back at him, worried, tense, angry, wanting so much to take it out on someone. And the only person within range had eyes the sparkling blue of the ocean on a sunny day and a smile so sweet she couldn't help but smile back. And she did smile, but reluctantly, giving up her anger almost with resentment, as if he'd robbed her of something she wasn't ready to part with.

"Do you suppose they'd have a BLT?" she said, putting down the menu with a sigh.

Scott laughed and said, "Somehow, I doubt it." When the waiter came back, he didn't wait for her decision but ordered steak fajitas for both of them, then leaned back in his chair and watched her in that relaxed way he had, idly turning his sweating iced tea glass on its coaster.

Joy gulped her drink—it really was delicious, and she was probably going to order another one after this—and tried to think of something to say. Without her anger she felt vulnerable and uncertain, as if she were walking on shaky ground without any support, and the urge to reach out to the strong, quiet man sitting across from her was impossible to resist.

"I know Yancy's alive," she said at last, poking through the fruit and floral arrangement in front of her with her straw, the rum making a warm sunny place inside her chest. When he didn't reply, she flicked a glance at him through her lashes. "I know you'll think I'm crazy, but I *know* she is." Then she closed her eyes and sighed. "I might as well tell you. You think I'm a nut, anyway. The reason I know is that…something *happened* to me, okay? Yancy…contacted me. Back home, in New York."

Scott leaned forward, frowning. "I thought you said—"

"Not by phone—not in any way I can explain." Pushing aside her drink, she leaned toward him, too, her hands almost touching his, and told him about coming home to her empty apartment that day and *feeling* Yancy there. "It was so weird. It was like, I could hear her…feel her…even smell the perfume she wears, and it was so *real*. And yet, it wasn't, and

I knew it wasn't. Can you understand what I mean? Frankly, I'm not sure I do—understand it, I mean. Nothing like that has ever happened to me before, or since, and I've been really trying. Especially since I've been down here. But...nothing. It hasn't happened again, not even a smidgen.''

She leaned back and reached for her drink and took a thirsty, rather defiant drag on the straw. The straw made a loud rattling sound, and she looked up guiltily to find Scott studying her, his chin propped on his hand.

''Well, what are you waiting for? Go ahead, make fun of me. It's okay, really. I know you want to.''

''I don't,'' he said quietly. ''And even if I did want to, I don't think I would.''

''Why not?'' She looked at him curiously. ''Don't tell me you believe in ESP.''

He shrugged. ''I don't believe or disbelieve. Hey, police departments and even the FBI have been known to use psychics to help solve cases.'' A wry smile carved a crease in one cheek. ''Anyway, I like to think I'm smart enough not to ridicule something even science doesn't understand.''

Joy gazed at him, a sense of wonder shivering inside her, like something newly born. ''That's just how I've always felt.''

''It occurred to me, though...'' Once again he had to sit back to allow the cat-footed waiter room to arrange the various dishes of fajita makings on the table between them.

They both watched in anticipatory silence while the waiter—barely more than a boy—skillfully stir-fried strips of tender seasoned and marinated beef in a small shiny pan over an open flame, then transferred the still-sizzling meat to a platter which he placed in front of them with a flourish. When he had departed with a crisp ''Enjoy your dinner,'' Joy looked back at Scott and found that for no apparent reason, her heart was beating fast.

''What occurred to you?'' she prompted, almost in a whisper, but the nervous skittering inside her chest and the cold hollow feeling in her stomach had already told her it was something she didn't want to hear.

Scott was frowning at the array of food spread out in front of him, and she thought with growing dread, *He doesn't want to say it.*

But he did say it. "You say you got that strong 'feeling,' and ever since then, nothing, right?"

He cleared his throat, and she could see it was an effort for him to meet her gaze focusing on him with laser-like intensity.

"Joy, from what I've heard…read, these kinds of… 'communications' usually happen at times of profound emotional stress. And since you haven't felt anything from her since, maybe that's because she was…that she's—"

"No," Joy said flatly. "She's not dead. I know it. *She's not…*"

Chapter 5

"**Y**ou have to at least consider the possibility," Scott said.

Joy shook her head and said implacably, "No. I don't. And I won't," and he let his breath out in exasperation.

Much as he wanted to humor her, the sheer bullheadedness of the woman was wearing his patience thin. "Look," he said reasonably, helping himself to a warm tortilla, "it seems to me there are only a couple of likely scenarios here. One, your friend Yancy found herself a candidate for rich Mister Right and went off with him and even as we speak is somewhere preparing to live happily ever after. I know, I *know*—" he held up the fork he was using to build his fajita "—she didn't call you. But people in love sometimes do incomprehensible things. Believe me, I know. It's a *possibility*. Two— and I know you don't want to consider this one, but you have to—she met Mister Wrong and is no longer able to phone anyone. Either way—"

"Three," Joy said evenly, selecting a tortilla from the covered dish, "she met Mister Wrong and is being held against her will and prevented from contacting anyone." Having made that absurd pronouncement, she veiled her eyes with her lashes and proceeded to fill her tortilla and fold it neatly. Then she lifted her lashes just enough to allow her to gaze through them. "Or, she could have been taken out of the country, or both of them could have been injured..." She picked up the fajita and took a bite, chewed, swallowed, then shrugged. "There's all sorts of things that could have happened. And I intend to find out what. But I'm simply not ready to believe she's dead. I won't abandon her."

"You're very bullheaded, you know that?" Scott said conversationally as he chomped into his own fajita.

She didn't reply and her eyes were solemn and golden as she took another bite and licked an errant dollop of sour cream from the corner of her mouth. Watching her, he was finding it hard to remember to be annoyed with her for her ridiculous fantasies, or that he was a cop who knew better. He polished off his fajita and reached for another tortilla, and his stomach growled with a hunger that had nothing to do with food.

"Excuse me?" A smiling young woman was standing beside their table. She was wearing a flowered skirt, a low-cut, off-the-shoulder blouse, and a flirty yellow hibiscus flower in her shiny black hair. A pretty girl, but Scott's mind had only so much room for erotic fantasies, and right then that was all taken up by a short, sexy lady with honey hair and golden eyes.

Then he saw that the black-haired girl was holding a camera, and there was a large camera bag hanging awkwardly from one tanned shoulder.

"Would you like to have your picture taken? It makes a lovely souvenir of your evening."

He said an automatic "No, thanks." Then, belatedly aware of how abrupt, even curt that sounded—the lady was only trying to make a living, after all—he smiled up at her and added, "Sorry, not right now, okay?"

And instantly he wished he'd stuck with rude and hostile, because the photographer, evidently taking her cue from the smile and ignoring the words that went with it, struck a coy pose and purred, "Oh, come now. Handsome guy…beautiful lady…romantic evening… Don't you want to take the memory home with you? Hmm? Make all your friends jealous?" She winked at Joy, who gazed back at her in curiously intent silence.

Oh, hell, he thought, why not? It seemed the quickest way to get rid of the interruption, and what would it cost him? A tip? He knew how these things worked; he didn't have to buy the picture, after all.

"Okay, sure," he said, giving in. He glanced at Joy. "If…you don't mind?"

Joy shook her head.

"Oh, good," the photographer trilled, shimmying a little as she backed into position. "Okay, scooch in close, you two. That's right put your arm around her, big guy, don't be shy. Okay…heads together…nice smile… *Perfect.*"

The flash went off, and he was sure he'd blinked, as usual, but who cared? At the first contact his fingers had made with Joy's bare arm, his heart had given a lusty lurch and his temperature had shot up several degrees. Now he was doing his best to bring everything back in line, which would have been hard enough under the best of circumstances—like trying to rein in a fired-up racehorse after a false start—but next to impossible with her hair brushing against his cheek and her scent, like old-fashioned roses, in his nostrils.

He barely noticed, while he was peeling his fingers away from Joy's arm and shifting his chair back to its original position, that the photographer had whipped a brochure out of her bag and was writing a number on it with a marking pen, and at the same time explaining how and when and where the picture would be available for viewing and how to go about ordering copies and enlargements.

He didn't notice because he didn't care about the damn pictures, he only wanted the intruder gone so he could be alone with Joy again. He wanted to go back to looking at her across… No, that wasn't true, either. What he wanted was to go back to where he'd just been, with his arm around her and… No, wait. Okay, the *real* truth was, he wanted *both* of his arms around her, some place private, and her naked, and probably him, too, and preferably, though not necessarily, in a bed.

Okay. There you have it. Wow.

"Thanks. Enjoy your dinner," the photographer sang, and was moving on when Joy shoved back her chair and cried out, *"Wait!"*

That got Scott's attention, along with the photographer's. Joy was half out of her chair, and Scott could almost see her vibrating, like a just-released bowstring. As the photographer turned back, eyebrows raised in polite inquiry, Joy sank back into her chair, though he could see that she was still tense and riled.

"I'm sorry. I have a question. Several, actually. First, do you photograph everyone who comes here to the hotel?"

The photographer laughed gaily. "Well, we sure do try."

"How long do you keep the pictures you take?"

"Well…"

"You said they'd be on display. I was wondering how long you leave them up, in case someone wants to order copies. Because—" Joy rushed on before the photographer could answer "—I have this good friend—she's the one who recommended this resort to me—*us*—" she threw Scott a quick and unexpected and completely false smile "—anyway, she was here about a week ago, and I know she didn't order any pictures, and I was thinking, if you still have hers, I'd love to get some for her, as a surprise. What do you think, honey?" And she was gazing at him, all smiling, dewy-eyed, counterfeit eagerness.

What did he think? How *could* he think? Right then his brain was completely tied up trying to figure out how someone could sound so completely loopy one minute, and be so damn smart the next. She was amazing, she really was. He wondered if it was the mystery writer in her.

"Good idea," he murmured.

"Well, gee." The photographer considered, balancing camera and bag on one canted hip. "You know, I've never had anybody ask me that before, but I don't see why you couldn't. If it was last week, your friend's picture might still be in the display case. Sure, just check, and if it's there, you can order the same way you would your own. Just put the number you want on the form and leave it at the front desk along with your payment. They'll send it to whoever you want."

"Thank you," Joy breathed.

"Anytime. You folks have a nice evening." The photographer wandered off, hips swaying, in search of fresh prey.

Joy looked at Scott. He looked back at her, trying to think of something appropriately admiring that wouldn't also sound condescending. He settled on "Good thinking."

"Thank you." She was pushing back her chair, laying her napkin on the tabletop.

"Hey," he said mildly, "don't you think we should finish dinner first?"

"I've had all I want. I told you I wasn't very hungry." She paused, looking at the half-eaten fajita on his plate. "It's okay, you don't have to come if you aren't done eating. I'm sure I can find this display case by myself."

"Oh, hell." Muttering to himself, Scott signaled the waiter. Joy was already on her way down the winding pathway that bordered the lagoon, heading back to the hotel lobby. "Sorry, something's come up," he said when the waiter arrived, trying to do the mental math and hauling what he hoped were enough bills to cover dinner and a generous tip out of his wallet, at the same time doing his best to keep track of his rapidly disappearing "date." He remembered to add "Keep the change" as he loped down the shallow flagstone steps after Joy.

"I told you, you didn't have to hurry your dinner," she said when he caught up with her, just inside the glass wall entry to the lobby. "I'm sorry. I couldn't sit there, when—"

"Yeah, yeah, Nancy Drew, when you're hot on the scent.

I know, I know.'' He was out of breath after practically running up those damn stairs; he couldn't figure out how come it was so hard to keep up with somebody whose legs were half as long as his. Frankly, and to his own surprise, he was beginning to get a little ticked off at her again. "Tell me something," he panted. "Are you always this…this—"

"Bullheaded?"

She, he noticed, didn't seem at all short of breath.

"I was going to say, independent. Self-sufficient…"

"I haven't always been, no," she said evenly, throwing him a look. "But I've learned to be."

He waited, willing himself to breathe slowly and deeply and willing his heart to resume a normal rhythm, while Joy approached the concierge's desk. After a conversation that included lots of smiling and gesturing, she turned and headed off toward a distant corridor without so much as a glance his way. Fine, he told himself. Obviously, he'd been the only one having overheated adolescent fantasies, and that was just as well. What had he been thinking? And it wasn't as if he hadn't been warned. Sworn off men—wasn't that what her brother had told him? So be it. He didn't need the aggravation.

And no sooner had those thoughts flashed through his mind than he was feeling thoroughly ashamed of himself. *Come on, Cavanaugh, what are you, a whiny little boy? She's not paying you enough attention? She's worried about her friend, she came to you for help, and you want her to be making puppy-eyes at you with lust in her heart?*

Well, to be honest, that's exactly what he wanted, and if that made him a poor excuse for a human being, he couldn't help it. It made him feel better, though, to tell himself it probably wasn't personal on her part, that he could have been…oh, whoever the latest Hollywood heartthrob was, and she still would've paid him no mind. Not a *lot* better, but a little.

By the time he caught up with her, she was standing in front of a glass display case, peering at the photos of smiling vacationers that were pinned to the corkboard-covered back wall.

"There she is," she said without turning. Her voice was pitched low, almost hushed, but it quivered with emotion. She looked up at him, one hand still resting on the glass, index finger tapping. "She *is* here. That's her. That's Yancy."

Her face was so pale, he wondered if she was going to pass out on him. It was on the tip of his tongue to ask her if she felt okay, if she needed to sit down, but he thought better of it. He had an idea it wouldn't go over well with this particular lady to be treated like a fragile flower. Trying not to think about how vulnerable she looked and how much he wanted to put his arms around her and lend her support, he leaned over so he could get a line on where she was pointing, and peered through the glass.

"Which one?"

"Right there. Third row down. The one with the red hair. She's with somebody. A guy."

Third row down. He followed the direction of her finger. Then…the word, one he didn't allow himself to say in front of Ryan, was out of his mouth before he could stop it. The redhead was with somebody, all right. Somebody Scott recognized.

"What?" Joy was staring at him, her brown eyes for once wide open, unveiled by lashes.

"Nothing," he muttered, convincing no one.

"There is too something. What is it? Is it the guy? Do you know him? What do you know about him? Tell me, dammit."

"I'll tell you," he said grimly, making a decision he hoped he wasn't going to regret, "but not here. Come on, let's get out of here." Once again, his hand found its way to her waist. Not saying a word but obeying its guiding pressure like an automaton, as if she had no will of her own, she turned with him and they walked together unhurried, back down the wide corridor, across the vast lobby with its splashing fountain and out onto the hotel's tiled and covered entryway.

Walking like that, he thought how they must look, to anyone watching, like honeymooners. Almost certainly lovers. Lovers who'd just had a spat, maybe, from the tension in her body and her pale, unsmiling face, and the grimness in his. He'd got the feeling, though, that she didn't seem to *mind* him touching her. She didn't move closer to him, but she didn't move away, either.

He gave his ticket to the parking valet and they waited in silence for his truck, neither of them making any pretense at small talk. Silent or not, Scott had never been more aware of anyone's presence than he was of Joy Lynn Starr's right then. Though it was late in the evening the sun was still up, low in the sky and bright as polished brass—so bright she'd put on the sunglasses again—and it hit him with a jolt that it had been about this same time yesterday that he'd first set eyes on his buddy Roy's allegedly ditzy sister. Twenty-four hours. And how—tiny as she was, even in high-heeled sandals she barely reached the top of his shoulder—had she come to be such an enormous factor in his life?

It wasn't all about sex and lusting after her luscious, curvy little body, either, though that was definitely a factor. There was something about her, eyes hidden behind those retro glasses, the contradiction of that elegant hairstyle and outrageously sexy outfit, an air of mystery, of exciting things going on behind closed doors, that piqued his curiosity. Piqued, hell. He was on fire with the desire to know all there was to know about her. Sure, he wanted her body. But he wanted her secrets, too.

"It's bad, isn't it?" Joy said. She'd waited as long as she could. She'd waited until they were outside the hotel, and then she'd waited while the parking valet was bringing the pickup around, in a silence so fraught with suspense, she could hardly breathe. Except for a brief argument she'd lost over who should pay the parking fee and tip the valet, Scott hadn't spoken a word to her since he'd promised to tell her about the man in the photograph with Yancy. Now, after finding their way back through the palm and pine groves, they were out on the open highway heading north.

Enough was enough.

"No." Without looking at him she could see his head turn toward her briefly. "I never said that."

"You *know* him," she shot back at him. "That man in the picture with Yancy. Don't you?"

There was a pause, and then he said, "I don't...*know* him. Let's just say, I thought I recognized him, that's all."

Joy closed her eyes and inhaled sharply. "Oh God. You've seen his picture. You probably have it plastered all over police headquarters. He's a serial killer, isn't he?"

"Where do you get these ideas? He's not a serial killer. At least, not that I know of." After a moment he said reluctantly, "Look, the guy's name is Diego DelRey. That's Spanish, and it's shortened from a whole bunch of stuff that basically means an ancestor of Diego's got a big chunk of the New World as a gift for being a right-hand man to the king of Spain several hundred years ago. What I know about *Diego*—better known as Junior, by the way—*all* I know, really, is that he's got a reputation for being a playboy and the spoiled brat youngest son of a family that still owns a big chunk of the New World, several dozen chunks, actually, spread over half a dozen different countries. Including—" he jerked his head toward the rear of the pickup truck "—that resort we just left. Spanish Keys."

Staring openmouthed at his profile, Joy saw his cheek crease with a smile that wasn't the least bit pleasant.

"I'll say this. If your friend was looking for a rich man, she definitely found one."

Joy closed her mouth and swallowed. "What else is there? What aren't you telling me?" He was silent so long, she finally prodded on a rising note of alarm, *"Scott?"*

He rubbed a hand over the lower half of his face and exhaled through his nose. "Dammit, I shouldn't be telling you any of this."

"Scott...please." She made a valiant attempt to smile. "What do you think I'm going to do, run to the nearest TV station with the news? I want to find Yancy. If you know something…"

He glanced over at her. Had his face softened, just a little?

"Okay. What I know, what I will tell you is this. The feebs have been quietly looking into the DelRey family for a long time—FBI, ATF, DEA, the whole alphabet soup, all under the umbrella of Homeland Security. They work closely with the state organized crime unit and keep us lowly locals pretty well informed, most of the time, as a courtesy, I suppose. Anyway, from what I understand, the DelReys have got a lot of legitimate businesses in a lot of different countries, and they come and go between them by private jet. Nothing criminal's ever been proven against them, but the potential is there. The feebs are trying—"

"Potential?" Joy said faintly. She felt cold...queasy. Her own voice sounded far away, beyond the ringing in her ears. "For what? You mean...drugs?"

"Just about anything. Drugs, arms, money laundering—you name it, at one time or another the DelRey name has come up. The problem right now is, nobody can get to them. In spite of the new Homeland Security laws, you still have to have more than a sneaking suspicion before you can go searching around through private homes and legitimate businesses." He threw her a crooked grin. "The price we pay for living in a free country."

She didn't return the smile. She was trying to absorb what she'd just heard, which was difficult because there was something very unreal, she decided, about having your imagined scenario come true. She kept thinking, *This can't be happening.* And how could that be, when she'd been sure all along that it had?

"So," she said slowly, to see whether saying it out loud

would make it more real, "Yancy has gone off with the son
of the owner of the hotel she was staying at—"

"You don't know that."

"No, but it makes perfect sense. No wonder nobody
wanted to tell me anything. She went away with the son of
a family that's probably involved in terrorism and organized
crime—"

"Unproven, remember."

"—and nobody's heard from her since," Joy finished,
grimly triumphant.

"Are you sure?"

"What do you mean?"

"Just because she didn't call you doesn't mean she might
not have called somebody else. What about her family?"

She shook her head. "I told you, remember? Her daddy's
a preacher in some little New England town, very strait-laced.
They pretty much disowned Yancy when she went off to the
big sinful city and took up modeling. Can you imagine what
they'd say about something like this? They're the last people
she would've called." She chewed her lip for a moment,
trying to rake some order into her thoughts. Order, that's
what she needed. Not panic.

"Okay. This guy—Diego, Jr., you said?—convinces
Yancy to check out of the hotel and go with him…where?
Where would he take her? Someplace even fancier? More
exotic?" Eager now, she tugged some slack into her seat belt
and turned half around on the pickup's bench seat, tucking
one foot under her. "You said the feds have been watching
the family. Do you mean, like, surveillance? Cameras?
Maybe they saw something. Maybe they even know where
Yancy is. You could find out, couldn't you? You said they
keep you informed. Scott?"

"Joy." He couldn't look at her while he was shaking his
head. Those big brown puppy-eyes… "It's not that simple.
Anyway, I said they keep us informed *as a courtesy,* I didn't
say they let us look at their surveillance tapes and sit in on
briefings. Look, I'm not about to go blundering into an in-

vestigation involving half a dozen different government agencies and God knows how much of the taxpayers' money, on the basis of a resort photographer's snapshot, okay? I can't, not if I value my job. Which I do, believe me. Skippering your brother's boat wouldn't begin to cover my alimony and child support bills.''

''You don't have to,'' Joy said tightly, breathing hard. ''I'll take care of it. Just tell me where this Diego guy lives. Is that too much to ask? I'll go and see if Yancy's there myself. Why not? Why would they think anything of it? I—I'll… I'll pretend to be the Avon lady.''

He burst out laughing; he couldn't help it. The vision in his mind of Joy with her little sample case in one hand and her pocketbook over the other arm and a little pillbox hat, ringing somebody's doorbell and singing out, ''Avon calling.' It was just so retro. So…Joy.

''Sorry,'' he said, before she could get words out. Riled up as she was, he was afraid to think *what* she'd come up with next. ''Won't work. Not unless you have a boat. The DelRey estate is on an island—not too far, actually, it's between here and Spanish Keys—called, appropriately enough, King's Island. It's a private island, and it's accessible only by boat or helicopter. Nobody gets on that island without an invitation or a warrant.''

''We have a boat,'' said Joy.

Scott looked at her and swore under his breath. ''No. No way. Out of the question.''

''Why?''

''I told you why. I'm not getting into the middle of an ongoing federal investigation. My boss would have my ba— uh, my head on a platter.''

''I told you, you don't have to be involved,'' she said evenly. ''I'll go myself. I'll hire somebody else to take me.''

''Joy…'' He forced himself to breathe deeply and count slowly to ten. He was a patient man. Easygoing, most people would have said. A rock. But this woman would try the patience of a saint. "You don't seem to be hearing me," he said carefully. "Maybe I'm not making it clear to you."

"Don't patronize me." Her voice was even softer than his.

Surprised, he glanced at her and saw that she was looking steadily at him, her face unnaturally pale and set as stone.

He let out his breath in a low hiss. "I didn't mean to."

"I'm not a child," she said. "Just determined. From the beginning, nobody would believe me when I said something had happened to Yancy. *Now* I find out she was seen in the company of a member of an organized crime family. I came here to find her, and I believe there's a good chance she's on that island, and I won't be patted on the head and told to be a good little girl and ignored again."

"I'm not ignoring you," Scott said fervently. "Believe me, I'm not. What I'm trying to tell you is, you will not be able to get onto that island. Not unless somebody invites you. The whole place is ringed with security. You breach it, and the best you can hope for is that they'll pick you up and escort you back to wherever you came from." He glanced over at her and added quietly, "I'm sorry. I really am. But there's nothing more you can do."

She didn't reply. After a moment she reached up and pulled off the cat's-eye sunglasses, folded them and tucked them away in her purse, then went back to gazing out the window in the direction of the vanished sun.

Headlights came on and replaced the sun's glow. Scott drove with one hand, the other covering the lower half of his face, and thought unhappy thoughts as the Chevy plowed steadily into the dusk.

"I'd like to see it," she said, her voice coming unexpectedly out of the silence and near-darkness.

He glanced at her and her eyes gazed back at him, pinpoints of light caught from somewhere sparkling in them like stars in a moonless sky.

"The island, I mean. Can you take me there in Roy's boat?"

Huh, he thought. He didn't know whether she'd done it

on purpose, mentioning *Roy's boat*. If she had, she was way too smart for him, that was for sure. Because what that did was remind him that she wasn't just an uncommonly beautiful woman who was threatening to crawl under his skin like a chigger bug and drive him crazy. She was somebody who'd been entrusted to him by the closest thing he had to a brother. And although the word didn't sit at all well with him, given the feelings he'd been having about her, the charge he'd been given was to watch over and protect Joy Lynn Starr like he would his own *sister*.

He couldn't smother a groan, which, of course, she misunderstood.

"Please, Scott." Her voice had the tiniest bit of a break in it. "I just want to get close enough to see it."

And even in the dark, even looking straight ahead, he could see her puppy eyes pleading with him.

What could he do? "All right," he said. "All *right*. Tomorrow's Sunday..." He didn't have a charter booked, and Ryan was going to the water park with his buddy Chip Tucker. He'd planned on spending the day wiping down the boat and, since Beth was out of town, doing some of the handyman chores around her place that she'd been pestering him about. But what the hell? "I guess we could make a day of it, cruise on down that way. But only to look, and only from a distance, you understand?"

"Yes," she said softly. "I understand."

"No getting me down there and then trying to con me into doing something stupid."

He heard a little openmouthed gasp, and felt her big eyes swing his way. "*Con* you? There you go again. I thought we agreed I couldn't."

"Miss Joy," he said, and his growl wasn't meant to be the least bit menacing, "I think our track record together speaks for itself. I'm almost afraid to think about what you'd be able to con me into, if you really put your mind to it."

"I wish you wouldn't say 'con', it makes me sound devious. Which I'm not."

Her voice had a new breathlessness, a suspenseful quality that made his own heartbeat lurch and stutter, then settle down to a solid hammering against the backside of his breast-bone.

"No," he said after thinking about it, "you're not. Maybe *con* isn't the right word. Maybe *entice* is more like it."

"Entice?" Her voice was so faint he barely heard it.

"Yeah, as in *lure, tempt, seduce—*"

"Seduce? *Me?* I've never seduced anyone in my life. I wouldn't even know how."

The Chevy bucked and lurched to a stop. Joy gave a startled gasp and jerked around to look out the window. Apparently she hadn't realized they'd arrived back at Roy's beach house.

Scott put the truck in neutral and set the hand brake, then turned to face her. "Lady, you were *born* knowing how. You don't even have to think about it, it just comes naturally to you. You probably couldn't stop yourself from doing it even if you wanted to, any more than you could tell your heart to stop beating."

She was slowly shaking her head, gazing at him in what he'd swear was genuine awe.

She whispered, "I have no idea what you're talking about."

He laughed low in his chest. "You know, you probably don't. That's what makes you so dangerous."

"*Dangerous.* My God, now you make me sound like… like some kind of weapon."

"Weapon?" Was it the fact that they'd stopped moving and the humid heat of the semitropical night was pouring into the cab of the truck that made the air seem too thick to breathe? The scent of roses felt like liquid in his sinuses. He could hear his pulse whomping in his ears like someone pounding on a bass drum. "You've got weapons you don't even know about."

"What?"

The pale oval of her face seemed to swim toward him in the viscous darkness, a mask portraying bewilderment.

"I don't— Nobody's ever said such a ridiculous thing to me before. What…weapons?"

And he was touching her, laying his hand alongside her face and cradling her jaw, his hand so big that his fingers curved clear around and burrowed under the bundle of her hair and found the warm, moist nape of her neck while his thumb was busy caressing the plump velvety pillow of her lower lip.

"Most I couldn't describe if you paid me," he said, and his voice was husky, way back in his throat. Because he knew he was about to kiss her. God help him. "Part of it's your eyes, the way you look at people, kind of through your lashes—" She closed her eyes and tried to shake her head, tried to smile, her lips sliding against the ball of his thumb, and he said, "Yeah, and that's another one, right there—the way you smile."

"What's wrong with my smile?"

Her whisper, the breath from it, bathed his lips.

"Not a damn thing…"

She closed her eyes, and so did he.

And he jumped just about out of his skin when his cell phone, which he'd left sitting in its cradle on the dashboard, went off like a live rattlesnake. He fumbled for it, his nerves too adrenaline-jangled even to swear.

"*There* you are! Oh, thank God, I finally got a hold of you. Scotty, where in the world have you been? I've been trying to reach you all afternoon long."

"Hello, Beth," he murmured with a silent sigh.

Several long minutes later he disconnected the phone and looked over at Joy, sitting quietly in the shadows. Her face was turned away from him—ever courteous, she was trying, in that confined space, to give him his privacy, he thought— and he allowed himself a second or two…or three…to treat his eyes to the graceful line of her throat, dark against the lighter sky, to remember the softness of her skin and the old-rose scent of her hair... To think about what had almost happened and what might have been. To wonder whether he'd been saved in the nick of time, or robbed of something special.

Then he cleared his throat and said gruffly, ''Well. Slight change of plans.''

Chapter 6

Considering it wasn't the way he'd planned to spend the day, Scott couldn't figure out why he felt so cheerful about the way things had turned out. Other than the fact that it was Sunday, the weather was fine, he had the day off, and, instead of policing rowdy vacationers or pressure-washing the siding on his ex-wife's—formerly his—house, he was on the bridge of a hell of a nice boat out on the Gulf of Mexico, which was sparkling in the sunshine like a lounge singer's sequins. On the landward side, gulls wheeled and pelicans dove in the wake of a shrimper heading back to harbor with its catch, and far out in the other direction, sailboats floated like wind-blown flower petals on the deep blue horizon. And down below him on the deck, his son was talking with a beautiful woman. Yes, things had turned out just fine. In fact, he couldn't think of a thing about the day that could have been better.

Okay, he could, but every time that thought came into his head he felt so guilty he pushed it right back out again. *Scotty and Joy...alone together on the boat...all day...oh man.*

Dammit, he liked having Ryan around. Besides, the kid needed him right now. Scott didn't mind having him along for the day, he really didn't. Especially since the kid was probably the only thing keeping his old man from making a complete fool of himself.

Although, at the moment it was hard to remember those sultry moments last night, sitting in the dark cab of his pickup in the driveway of Roy's beach house, when it had seemed certain he was going to kiss his buddy Roy's ditzy sister, Joy. Today... Hell, today she looked more like Ryan's sister than she did Roy's, in those knee-length white pants and a navy-and-white knit top that hung kind of loose on her, like a kid's T-shirt. In addition to that, she was wearing a white baseball cap with a ponytail that stuck out through the hole in the back and a pair of big plastic dangly earrings in the shape of daisies. She looked fresh and clean as a daisy, and about sixteen years old.

Until she picked up the pair of binoculars hanging around her neck and leaned way forward with her elbows planted on the railing so she could get a better look at the island shimmering in the heat waves off the starboard bow, thereby banishing any and all doubts that she was in fact a beautiful, curvy, full-grown and uncommonly sexy woman.

As if she felt the warmth of his gaze, she straightened up, turned and looked up at him. Seeing him watching her, she smiled and waved, completely without self-consciousness.

Something kicked him hard under his ribs. Which unsettled him so much that he got mad, first at himself, and then, because he needed someone else to blame for his foolishness, at Joy.

"Hey," he called down to her, and when both Ryan and Joy pointed to themselves and mimed *Me?* added, "Joy, come up here a minute." And he tried not to see the disappointment on his son's face as he turned back to the rail.

A few minutes later, when Joy's head, ridiculously cute in that baseball cap, topped the ladder and she joined him, breathless and smiling, earrings swinging, in the cramped space of the bridge, he knew he'd made a tactical mistake. And he tried his best to ignore the voices in his head telling him it was what he'd wanted all along.

"Oh, hey," she said, looking around, "it's nice up here. And you can see much better, too." And up came the damn binoculars.

He swore under his breath and reached over and yanked the glasses down. "Would you at least *try* to be a little bit subtle with those things?"

Joy looked at him, surprised by the edge in his voice. He'd always seemed so laid back, easygoing, even when he was annoyed with her. Even when he was accusing her of conning him. Or…what was it he'd called it? *Enticing. That was it.* Last night, he'd accused her of enticing him…seducing him. And he'd been about to kiss her, she was sure of it. If his cell phone hadn't rung…

And what if he had? What would I have done?

And why, oh why did she have to remember that *now?* When she was standing way too close to him, she'd gone hot and tingly all over, her lips felt swollen, and she couldn't seem to take her eyes off of his mouth.

"I'm sorry," she murmured, "I'll try." And she could feel her cheeks burning.

"I'd rather not have it be too obvious we're interested."

She nodded and licked her lips, then couldn't resist arguing, after a small breath, "Well, I'd think people must *look* at them, all the time. Just out of curiosity." But she let the binoculars fall on their cord and turned her eyes forward.

Down on the bow, she saw Ryan looking up at them. She smiled and waved to him, but he turned his back to her and leaned both forearms on the rail while he squinted unhappily into the breeze. Joy sighed, and although she didn't think she'd done so out loud, Scott glanced over at her.

"Don't let him get to you. He's disappointed, that's all."

Joy nodded and said in a low voice, so Ryan wouldn't hear, "It's nice he could come with us. That must help a little."

Scott gave her a look. "I think you mean that."

"Well, of course I do. Poor kid. He told me about his friend Chip swiping his sister's bike and riding it into the canal and getting himself grounded so they couldn't go to the water park. It's a shame he has to be punished when he didn't do a darn thing. I told him life isn't fair, but I don't think he wanted to hear it." She was silent for a moment, then smiled wryly. "I'm sure Ryan would much rather it be just you and him, today, without some strange lady along for the ride."

"Yeah, he probably would. He's a little jealous of my time and attention right now. I'm thinking it's most likely an 'only child' thing. His mother's the same way. That's why she didn't want to be married to a cop, you know. Jealous of the job."

Joy studied the horizon, the island shimmering in the haze. "Excuse me for saying so, but your social life must be the pits." He made a snorting sound. She glanced up at him, then down at his hands, lightly resting on the boat's shiny chrome helm. She thought of the way one of those big hands had cradled her jaw, caressed her neck last night. *Social life?* She thought, no, she *felt* the way it had felt then—warm and gentle and strong. She'd wanted to cuddle up to it and purr. *You mean sex life—admit it.* Something contracted inside her, making her emit a barely audible gasp that she rushed to cover with "I know, it's none of my business. I just have to wonder how he reacts to the women you spend time with." *Sleep with.*

"If you want to know whether or not I'm seeing anybody," he said out of the side of his mouth, like a gangster in a bad B-movie, "all you need to do is ask."

She stiffened and drew herself up. Or in. Away from *him,* however minutely. "I was wondering about *Ryan,*" she lied. "Wasn't that who we were talking about? I was wondering if he hates all the women you spend time with, or if it's just me."

The sideways tilt of his mouth quivered into a smile. "It

is and it isn't.'' She looked at him and waited. He let out a breath he'd apparently been holding. ''The truth is, I haven't really 'spent time,' as you delicately put it, with anybody, not for the past few years, anyway. You're the first, so... yeah, I guess you're the first one to get the royal treatment.''

''But,'' Joy said, and her throat felt thick and her words sounded muted to her own ears, as though she were talking in a dense fog, ''we aren't 'spending time' together. Not really. Not...in that way. You're just helping me look for Yancy.'' *But last night you almost kissed me, and there's a good chance—a certainty, even—I'd have kissed you back. And after that, who knows what might have happened? I probably would have invited you in, and maybe we'd have spent the night together, and right now we'd be having a whole different conversation.* ''Doesn't he know that?''

''To tell you the truth,'' Scott said, ''I haven't discussed you with him.''

He sounded grim, almost angry, but she couldn't bring herself to look at him in order to see if he was. She felt as if she were vibrating inside. Her skin, her face, her body, *everywhere,* felt hot.

''Well, maybe you should,'' she said tightly. ''He needs to know he doesn't have anything to worry about, at least where I'm concerned.''

''Yeah, maybe I should do that.''

Breathing as if she'd just lost a foot race, Joy lifted her binoculars and was appalled to feel her hands shake. Setting her teeth firmly together, she focused the glasses on a nearby boat, and gave a sharp yelp of surprise.

Scott tensed and said, ''What?''

''Somebody was looking back at me! With binoculars! Can you believe that?''

''On the island? That's impossible, we're not close enough.''

''No, not the island. That boat over there. See it? The one—''

"Okay, that's it, that's enough. Give me those things."

"What?" She lowered the binoculars just enough to stare at him over them.

His hand was reaching for the glasses. His eyes glinted like the sun on the water as he transferred his gaze from her to the horizon and back again. "Come on, hand 'em over." And he snapped his fingers twice in quick succession.

It was the finger-snapping that did it. Joy's temper erupted only once in a blue moon, but when it did it went off like a geyser. "*What?* I will *not*. Just because somebody else had the good sense to take binoculars out on a boat trip? And by the way, don't you ever snap your fingers at—hey!"

He'd let go of the helm and taken hold of the binoculars with both hands, and was about to lift them from around her neck. The eyes gazing down at her no longer looked as much like deep sea water as they did flint, and the mouth she'd been contemplating kissing a moment ago had hardened to a thin, determined line. Just as determined, Joy grabbed hold of the strap with both hands and held on, with the result that, when Scott tugged on the binoculars, instead of coming off over her head, they acted like a lasso. Jerked off balance and without hands to steady herself, Joy said, "Oof!" and fell heavily against his chest, which turned out to be every bit as solid and unyielding as she'd thought it would be.

For several seconds, neither of them moved or uttered a sound. Then they both spoke at once, muttering incoherent "Excuse me's" and "I'm sorry's," as he let go of the binoculars, she tried to push herself upright, and he tried to steady her, and in the process, somehow, his hands came to be holding her arms and sort of gliding up and down her bare skin from elbows to shoulders and back again.

Joy's heart banged violently against her rib cage, and her temper-geyser subsided back into a seething, boiling cauldron of embarrassment and secret lust. She didn't dare look at him. Focusing on the center of his chest and hoping she had enough self-control left to keep from flinging herself right back against it, she lifted the binoculars strap over her head and handed them to him. "Here. I'm sorry. They *are* yours."

"Joy…" It was almost a groan.

Against her better judgment, she let her gaze climb upward past his chest to his eyes. No longer the least bit flinty, they seemed bewildered, almost vulnerable. She felt a peculiar aching, squeezing sensation where her stomach met her chest, and turned her head, ripping her gaze away from him the way she used to pull off a bandage when she was little— quickly, because it hurt less that way.

And what she saw when her eyes had managed to focus again was Ryan, standing in the bow of the boat, staring up at them with hurt and hostility in every line of his body.

She might have made some sound, said something, but in any case, Scott had already followed her gaze. He didn't say anything and neither did she. They stood together, much too close together, frozen, staring back at the boy's sullen, unhappy face. And after a moment, Ryan hitched a shoulder and with elaborate unconcern, made his way along the side of the boat, swung past the outriggers and disappeared into the cabin.

Scott let out a breath. Joy closed her eyes. Taking a small step back, she once again held out the binoculars. This time he took them without a word, and she slunk to the ladder, climbed down from the bridge and left him there.

What she wanted to do was keep right on going, over the side of the boat and into that giddily sparkling, cool blue water. What had she been thinking?

Well, she *hadn't* been thinking, that was the problem. No way could she apply that word to the activities her brain had been engaging in lately. My goodness, running around in circles like the mind of a lovesick teenager, indulging in fantasies she thought she'd put behind her long ago. Poor Scott. He hadn't asked for her to come along and cause trouble between him and his son. And that poor little ol' Ryan. Wasn't adolescence tough enough without her making it worse?

And while she was at it, poor Yancy. What if Yancy had been trying to get in touch all along, and couldn't get through to her because Joy was too distracted thinking about sex, and Scott—or, to be more accurate, sex *with* Scott? *If something terrible happens to Yancy because I didn't find her in time because I was too wrapped up in myself, I'll never forgive myself. Never.*

But how in the world do I turn it off?

How was she supposed to tell herself not to be attracted to someone? Telling herself that only made it worse, it seemed to her. Made her think of him all the more, puzzling about it, asking herself why, of all the times, did it have to be now? And of all the people, all the men she'd met in the years since her last divorce, why *him?*

Because he's different.

Well, yeah, he was. At least, he seemed to be. But that didn't mean anything. Frederick had been about as different from Zack as it was possible for a man to be, and look how that had turned out. Face it, she had lousy taste in men. Case in point: Scott Cavanaugh might be a nice enough guy, but he was a man with baggage. Plus, he was a cop, and everybody knew cops made lousy husbands.

So, who says you have to marry the guy? He's nice, you're attracted to him. Why not just go for the sex and be done with it?

There was an idea. And it made her stomach lurch and her pulse thump in the usual places, just thinking about it. Maybe she *should* go for it, get it out of her system. That way she could go back to concentrating on the search for Yancy without all this sexual tension getting in the way. That might work.

Except…there was Ryan. The kid would know. He would *feel* it, sense it. She was sure of that. He might wind up hating his dad because of her. He sure as heck would hate *her,* even more than he already did. And she wasn't sure why she minded that so much, if it was only going to be a short-term thing. It came to her with a sick, achy feeling around her heart that she minded very much what Scott's son thought of her.

Scott wished Joy could have found someplace else to run off to and brood besides the bow end of the boat. From where he was and had no choice but to be—at the helm, steering the damn boat—it was impossible not to see her there. Impossible not to think about her. Both of those things made him feel lonely and sad, and he didn't need to be a rocket scientist to figure out why. He wanted her, and he couldn't have her. Simple as that.

Thing was, he was pretty sure he'd get over her, once this search for the missing roommate was over and done with and Joy had gone back to where she came from. She'd leave, and he'd return to being who he'd been before she came into his life: a pretty good deputy sheriff in a fairly quiet corner of the world; part-time skipper of a hell of a nice boat; a guy trying to be a good enough dad not to ruin a really great kid. That was it. It was enough. Or it had been.

You must have a really lousy social life.

Hah. That thought almost made him laugh out loud, except it wasn't funny. Because it was true. He told himself it was because of Ryan, that he'd needed to concentrate on his kid, on making sure the divorce didn't damage him too much. But it had just hit him that in a few years Ryan was going to be over that adolescent hump and on his way to his own life, and where did that leave dear old Dad? Alone, that's where, if you didn't count running errands and playing Mr. Fix-it for his needy ex-wife. Maybe he'd meet somebody then, when he was free to do something about it, but maybe he wouldn't. And meanwhile, what if he met somebody *now?*

What if he'd already met her?

His gaze came to rest once more where it felt most at home, lately, on the small, ridiculously cheery-looking woman standing in the bow of the boat, honey-brown ponytail peeking through the back of her baseball cap, flipping

in the breeze. *Forget it,* he told himself. *She's not for you.*
She had issues with men, way too much emotional baggage,
not to mention she wasn't interested in him. Nothing personal, just that her mind happened to be on more important
things at the moment.

Nothing personal. Yeah, and wasn't that what he'd told himself when Beth left him? Nothing personal, it's just that you're
a cop. Now Joy. Nothing personal, she's just got other things
on her mind. Was that coincidence? What if it *was* personal?
What if it was something basically wrong with *him?*

Well, shoot. If it was, how would he know? The one person he could have asked wasn't available, and though he tried
to be objective, he couldn't think of anything right offhand.
He knew he wasn't handsome, but he was nice-enough looking, he thought. Small children didn't seem to run screaming
when they saw him. Healthy, in pretty good shape, not over-
weight. He kept himself clean, didn't smoke or drink, and
was respectful of women—all people, really. Hey, he was a
pretty damn decent guy! So, how come he had, as Joy put
it, such a lousy social life?

I'm going to have to have a talk with Ryan, he thought.
Not just about the birds and the bees, either. They'd already
done that one, but it looked like maybe he needed to cover
the more complicated stuff. The emotional stuff. The stuff
about even great dads needing somebody to be close to now
and then. Somebody reasonably close to his own age to talk
to, laugh with, hold on to and snuggle with. Yeah, he'd better
do that, and soon. Maybe today, right after he'd dropped Joy
off. Beth wouldn't be back from that sorority reunion of hers
until late—they could pick up a pizza, go back to the house
and have a good old-fashioned father-son evening together.
Ryan would like that. And when the time was right…

He rehearsed his speech all the way back to the marina,
making sure to include some stuff about how, even if he ever
did find someone to have a relationship with, it was never
going to change the way he felt about Ryan; he was always
going to be his dad, they were still going to spend time to-

gether, and he was always going to be there for him and so on. He about had it to the point where he was pretty sure he wouldn't forget anything important, but it was still occupying a good part of his mind as he guided the *Gulf Starr* through the crowded marina, busy with Sunday afternoon boaters and noisy with screeching, swooping gulls.

He brought the boat around and was preparing to back into the slip the way he always did—easier to load and unload both catch and passengers that way—and Ryan was at the stern, ready to jump out and secure the lines. Joy was there, too, watching, probably trying to help but mainly getting in the kid's way. None of which sat well with Ryan, who'd been crewing on the *Gulf Starr* since he was twelve. He was bustling and elbowing his way around her, managing to be both sullen and officious and taking up a lot more room than he really needed to get the job done.

Scott didn't feel like he ought to interfere, since he'd have to holler down from the bridge, and considering what had happened just before she'd left him there a while ago, there was way too much tension floating around as it was. He didn't want her to think...hell, he didn't know what he wanted her to think, or what she was apt to think. The woman was a damn mystery to him is what she was.

Best leave it alone, let the two of them work it out, he told himself as he turned back to the console. He cut the engines and waited for the *bump* of the stern against the back of the slip, followed by a gentle rocking motion as Ryan jumped out of the boat. That's what should have happened. Only what did happen was he felt the rocking motion first, followed in very short order by a loud squawk, a splash and a bellow from Ryan.

"Dad!"

A quick glance over his shoulder confirmed Scott's worst fear. He could see Ryan back there, gripping the aft railing and leaning over the side, but Joy had disappeared.

"Throw her the ring!" he yelled as he lunged for the ladder. Swearing, he made it to the deck in about two seconds flat, just in time to hear the *splat* of a life preserver hitting the water. He peered over the railing, and his heart just about stopped when he saw a white baseball cap floating and bobbing in the widening space between the boat and the slip.

"I didn't mean to, Dad—"

Ryan's chalk-white face and shimmering blue eyes hovered briefly in Scott's peripheral vision as he tugged at his deck shoes, but his mind was in emergency mode and he didn't reply. He felt no emotion at all, not anger, not even fear.

Then he was poised on the side of the boat, arcing downward toward the water. And the first thing he saw when he surfaced was Joy's face, three feet from his. Her hair was plastered to her skull and she was brushing at her mouth and eyes with one hand while she fanned the water with the other.

"*Yuck,*" she said, spitting and brushing disgustedly, "I think I swallowed a feather."

"Are you okay?" God, he couldn't believe how calm he sounded, considering he felt like he'd just been to the bottom of the Gulf and back.

"Oh, I'm fine. Except..." She bobbed for a moment, taking stock. "My shoes are gone. Dammit."

"You're sure you're not hurt?"

"Well, maybe my pride. Oh God, I'm sorry. This is so embarrassing." She added that last with a sputtery grimace.

Somebody up above them hollered, "You folks okay? Need any help down there?"

"Yeah, Doc, as a matter of fact. Give her a hand up, would you?" His neighbor in the next slip, a plastic surgeon from Panama City, was standing on the dock holding a life ring. He and Joy side-stroked the remaining few feet over to him, Scott guiding her along like a crippled ship. He took hold of her waist and lifted her up as high as he could reach, and maybe it was because he was still so blasted with adrenaline, but she weighed nothing at all. The doctor grabbed her hands and pulled her the rest of the way up and onto the dock, rather like landing a big fish, Scott thought, only Joy was being a lot more cooperative than the average marlin.

Treading water, he looked up at her, huddled there at the doctor's feet like a half-drowned kitten in a spreading puddle, and something inside him started to shake. He didn't know what it was, whether it was the fear and anger he hadn't had time for, building up steam, or something entirely different. He'd never felt anything like it.

"Scott? Where are you going?" she called down to him in a suddenly frightened, quaking voice.

He was already swimming with powerful strokes after the *Gulf Starr,* which was drifting, slightly turned, just outside its own slip, Ryan, wide-eyed and pale, still hanging on to the stern rail as if he'd been welded to it. With nasty marina water lapping against his chin, he muttered grimly, though no one could hear him, "I'll be right back. First, I have to go kill my son."

He was definitely going to have that talk with Ryan tonight. It was just going to be a different talk than the one he'd planned.

Joy would have given just about anything to be able to edit the events of that afternoon. Starting with that episode on the bridge with Scott, but especially the last chapter. Not the falling overboard part. That had simply happened too fast to produce any real trauma, and except for a certain amount of embarrassment—by no means the worst she'd ever experienced—and discomfort due to wet clothes and bare feet, and the thought of what might have been swimming or floating around in that water, she hadn't been hurt at all. No, the part she wished with all her heart she could erase was now, being driven home in the pickup, wrapped in a musty blanket and sandwiched between a silent, steely-eyed father and his mutely miserable, red-eyed son.

Is there anything in this world more painful to see, she wondered, than a humiliated child?

She wished she could put her arms around him and give

him a big ol' hug, and tell him it was all right, and no harm done. But it wasn't her place to do that, and given what she knew about teenage boys, most likely he wouldn't want her to, even if it had been. If he'd just look at her so she could give him a smile, let him know she didn't blame him for what happened…

But Ryan kept his face resolutely turned to the window, and when the pickup pulled to a stop in the driveway of the beach house, he opened his door without a word, got out and waited for her to do the same, then climbed back into the truck and shut the door, so closed against her she didn't even have the courage to tell him goodbye.

As she was toiling up the stairs, blanket hiked up around her like a queen's robes, she heard the pickup door slam. A moment later the stairs creaked with the weight of a heavy body, and she shivered as she felt Scott come behind her. She threw him a quick, jerky look.

"You don't have to see me in."

"Yeah, I do." He showed her the keys in his hand as he slipped past her. "You forgot these." He unlocked the door and held it for her, then followed her inside and closed it after him. He put the keys on the kitchen countertop, then opened the refrigerator and frowned at its contents. "What can I get you? Something to drink?"

"No, really, it's okay. I'll be fine. I think I'd like to take a bath first, anyway, and get into some dry clothes."

"There's nothing to eat in here." He closed the door and turned to her. "After I get Ryan squared away, I'll come back and pick you up and take you somewhere and feed you. We can stop at the store, pick up a few things—"

"You don't need to do that. There's soup in the cupboard, that's all I need. I'll be fine."

"What about clothes? Do you need anything? Beth would probably have something you could borrow. You're about the same size."

She assured him that she had all the clothes she needed, but thank you anyway, and then he just stood there and glared at her with eyes that looked burned around the edges. He was like a grounded hawk, she thought, hunched and helpless but trying his best to look fierce in spite of it.

There was that squeezing sensation again, somewhere low in her chest. She wondered if this was what people meant when they said their heart turned over. Whatever it was, it was powerful enough to make her breath catch and empathetic tears rush, stinging, to the back of her eyes. Impulsively, she pulled her hand from the blankets, reached out and touched his chest. His shirt was clean and dry. He'd changed into some spare clothes he kept on the boat.

"Scott, you don't need to worry about me. I'm fine. Really. No harm done."

His eyes stared over her head. "Luckily."

"And please, don't be too hard on Ryan. I don't believe he meant—"

His mouth formed a grim line, and his eyes flicked toward her. "Oh, he's sorry as he can be now, but he knew exactly what he was doing when he did it. It may have been an impulse, and I know he regrets it, but that's not good enough. In my line of work I see the results of bad choices every day. All it takes is a second, one uncontrolled impulse, to ruin somebody's life. Maybe a whole lotta lives." He let out a breath. "Look, I have to make sure he sees how serious this is, do you understand? I mean to make sure this is the first and last time he ever pulls a stunt like this."

Joy whispered, "I feel so terrible at being the cause of trouble between you and your son."

He covered her hand with his. She felt his heart beating and the warmth of his body seeping into her palm. It was all she could do to keep from crawling closer, putting her arms around him and snuggling up to that warmth like an orphaned kitten.

Above her head his voice rumbled gruffly. "He's my son. I'll deal with him."

"He's a good kid, Scott."

His gaze dropped suddenly and made contact with hers,

and his face, which had resembled something carved on Mount Rushmore, softened with a smile. Something about that smile made her heart ache.

"Yeah, he is," he said. "That's the hell of it, isn't it?"

Then there was silence. They stood there, her with her hand flat against his chest, his hand completely covering hers, like someone saying the Pledge of Allegiance. Looking at each other. Not saying anything.

I should say something, Joy thought. *Southern women always have the perfect polite thing to say at times like this. Why can't I think of a single one?*

Seconds ticked by. *He's got to leave,* Joy thought. *Ryan's out there in the truck.* But he didn't leave, and he didn't move, neither toward her nor away.

Then, like a seismic tremor, a shudder passed through his body. His voice sounded like something erupting out of the earth. "If you only knew how much I—"

"What?"

"Nothing. Never mind. Call me if you need anything." He made it to the door in about two strides, opened it and was gone.

In a daze, Joy followed him, closed the door and locked it automatically, in true New Yorker fashion. She wandered, like someone sleepwalking or lost, into the kitchen and out again. She climbed the stairs to the bedroom, where she dumped the blanket and her wet clothes in a pile on the rug, then went into the bathroom. Arrested by her scraggly image in the mirror, she stared at it in surprise and some alarm, as if she'd come upon a complete stranger in her house. As, in a way, she had.

After a moment she spoke to the person in the mirror with rueful sympathy. "Well, Joy, could this day possibly be any more of a disaster?"

Chapter 7

His message light was blinking. That was the first thing Scott saw when he finally made it back home after dropping Ryan, much chastened, at his mom's house with orders that he was to be grounded for a month. And getting off easy, at that.

He almost never got messages on his home phone. Ryan, Beth and Roy all preferred to call him on the cell. The land line number was unlisted, and the only people who ever called him on it were his sisters or somebody from work. The sisters seldom called unless it was his birthday or some holiday or other, which last time he'd looked, it wasn't.

He punched the "play" button with a sinking feeling in his gut. When he heard the quiet, angry voice of the duly elected sheriff of the county he worked for, he closed his eyes and uttered one succinct, sibilant cussword.

"Cavanaugh, I wanna know what the hell you think you were doing. Cavanaugh? You there? Okay, I want you in my office. *Now*. Or preferably sooner." *Click.*

Well, damn. The fact that he'd half expected it didn't make

it any better. He cussed himself silently all the way down to the station, telling himself he should have brought his own department into the picture the minute he'd heard Spanish Keys mentioned in conjunction with a missing woman. Telling himself he for *darn* sure ought to have mentioned it to the feds when Junior DelRey turned up in a photo at the resort, keeping close company with that same missing woman. Instead, he'd let himself get talked into taking the missing woman's Nancy Drew wannabe roommate for a boat ride, so she could personally scope out the DelRey's private fortress with a pair of high-powered binoculars. *His* high-powered binoculars. What had he been thinking?

What were you doing, Cavanaugh? That was the question he was going to get asked the minute he walked into Sheriff Johnny Dolittle's office, and right at the moment he didn't have an answer. Not one he cared to share, anyway. *Well, you see, sir, there's this slightly ditzy, very sexy, way-too-independent lady I'm supposed to be looking out for, and have just incidentally started to care quite a lot about, and I was trying my damnedest to keep her out of trouble.*

Next question: *Okay, Cavanaugh, and exactly when did you stop being a public servant and officer of the law, and start being Ms. Joy Lynn Starr's personal and private body-guard?*

And not doing all that great a job of it, apparently. He still got cold chills thinking about this afternoon, and all the things that could have happened when Joy went over the side of the boat. Things that would have made the outcome a lot worse than it had been. And what that might have meant, not just to his future and Joy's, but to that of a certain much-chastened, *very* sorry fourteen-year-old boy.

With all that on his mind, he must have been looking pretty grim when he walked into Sheriff Dolittle's private office a few minutes later. If he did, he fit right in with the half dozen or so people already there. In addition to the sheriff, in uniform and behind his desk on a Sunday evening, which was unusual enough by itself, there were four guys in suits and ties conservative and inappropriate enough to brand them instantly as feds, and a couple more that looked like Cuban street people, who Scott thought were most likely undercover DEA agents. None of them looked friendly.

Sheriff Johnny Dolittle, whose appearance matched his name about as much as a pit bull fits the name Fluffy, said "Cavanaugh" by way of a greeting, and didn't invite him to sit.

Scott said, "Sir," gave a brief nod to the other occupants of the room, and waited.

One of the suits, perched on the corner of Dolittle's desk, cleared his throat. With a loud *creak,* Sheriff Johnny leaned abruptly back in his chair and folded his arms across his chest, which hadn't lost much in girth or toughness since his football playing days at Florida State.

He fixed Scott with a cold stare and said softly, "You wanna tell us what you were doing out there today, buzzin' around King's Island?"

The suit on the corner of the desk cleared his throat again. "Our sources also tell us you were down at Spanish Keys yesterday. That's a bit out of your jurisdiction, isn't it?"

The sheriff gave the guy a quelling look, one that clearly said, *Back off. This is my boy, I'm gonna take care of him.* Then he transferred the look back to Scott and drawled, "These boys here are concerned their investigation might be compromised if it became known to the DelReys that one of our deputies was observed taking an undue interest in their, uh, activities. You understand what I mean, son?" He didn't wait for a reply to that. "Now, Scotty, since I know you to be one of my best deputies, not the kind to go off half-cocked on his own, I gotta think you had a good reason for being where you were, doing what you were doing, and that there's an equally good reason why you didn't see fit to tell us about it first. Am I right?"

"Yes sir," said Scott, devoutly hoping it was true.

"Well, son," said the sheriff, in that soft voice of his that could raise the fine hairs on a brave man's neck, "if you'd care to share it with us, now's the time."

It was dark when Scott pulled into his own driveway for the second time that evening. He was in a black and jumpy mood from the excess of nervous tension that had been flying around in the room he'd just come from, sore from being called to account in front of strangers by a man he respected and deeply troubled by all the stuff he hadn't been told. He'd given the feds everything he had, beginning with the phone call from Roy asking him to look after his sister. In return, he'd been asked for a detailed description and a photograph of the missing woman from New York, warned to steer clear of anything having to do with the DelRey family, and sent on his way.

He was in no mood for unexpected developments or drama, and when he nearly stepped on a small somebody huddled in the dark on his front steps, he just about jumped out of his skin.

"Good God. *Joy,*" he said, after he'd stuffed his heart back down where it belonged and could produce sounds again. "What the hell are you doing—"

She was already on her feet, hands extended. He felt their touch on his arm.

"Scott, I'm sorry—"

"How did you get here?"

"I took a taxi. Scott, listen. I've been thinking, and I have an idea how I can get onto that island. I tried calling, but you didn't answer, and I didn't think this was something I should leave on your answering machine. I mean, you never know who might be around when you play it back, right? Anyway, I really wanted to talk to you about it, so I came."

"Taxi." The word emerged as a wheeze. His heart was still pounding, and in order to keep her from finding out how badly her being there had unsettled him, he frowned and said sharply, "What, you just had the cab drop you off? Just like that? What would you have done if I hadn't come home?"

In the darkness he couldn't see her face, but he could feel her withdrawing subtly, her natural warmth cooling several degrees.

"I was pretty sure you'd be back sooner or later. You told me you had to work tomorrow, right? And given your personal, uh, situation, I didn't think you'd be out *too* late."

Scott was muttering as he went up the steps. "You always have an explanation, don't you. You make it sound so damn *reasonable*. No wonder I wind up doing things I know damn well I'll regret."

He unlocked the door and opened it, reached inside to turn on the light, then held it for her, frowning down at her as she slipped past him. And he was thinking, *No way am I falling for this woman. Uh-uh, absolutely no way.* But a hint of old roses had drifted up to his nostrils and excited little currents were scurrying around under his skin, looking for a place to land.

Joy's heart was flopping around inside her chest like a dying bird. *Something's wrong. I should have called first. Okay, I probably shouldn't have come at all, but it's important I tell...*

Liar, she whispered to herself. *You know that's not why you came. It's just an excuse, and a lousy one. You wanted to be with him. And you have no explanation whatsoever for that!*

She followed him up the steps and halted just inside the door. Swallowing the worst case of butterflies she'd experienced since making the finals in the sixth grade spelling bee, she said, "Scott? Is something wrong? Is Ryan—"

"Ryan's fine. Grounded for life, but...fine."

"If I've come at a bad time—"

"Wrong?" He threw her a look, eyebrows raised, taken aback but in an exaggerated way. "What makes you think anything's wrong?"

Without waiting for her answer to that, he pocketed his keys and made his way purposefully across a cluttered living room and down a short hallway. A moment later a light came on in the kitchen beyond.

Trailing along after him, Joy found him peering into the open refrigerator. She watched in silence, heart pounding, while he took out a can of iced tea, frowned at it and put it back, then took out a jug of milk instead. He set the jug on the counter, opened a cupboard and took out a glass, which he proceeded to fill with milk.

As he returned the milk jug to the refrigerator and picked up the glass, Joy stepped eagerly forward. "Oh, is your stomach bothering you? You know, Momma always used to take buttermilk when her stomach—"

"Why would you think my stomach is upset?" he interrupted. His eyes glittered at her across the top of the glass, a fierce and burning blue.

Oh dear, thought Joy. But it had been a long time since she'd let herself be intimidated by a man, even one as large and attractive as the one presently looming over her like the wrath of God.

"I don't know," she said evenly, bracing herself to meet his eyes. "I thought maybe…you do seem upset—"

The glass met the tile countertop with a soft *click,* and he smiled at her in a way that involved his mouth hugely, and his eyes not at all. "What reason could I possibly have to be upset? Sure, I've just come from getting chewed out by someone I greatly admire and deeply respect, who also happens to be my boss. Oh yeah, and my son nearly killed somebody today, somebody I'm supposed to be responsible for, and on top of that, I've got a woman with more imagination than sense running around like some middle-aged Nancy Drew trying to take on the whole damn Central American mob. But other than that, I can't think of a thing to be upset about."

Middle-aged? Okay, that hurt. She'd sucked in air when he said it, and been somewhat gratified to see him wince in acknowledgment, however slightly. Now, stretching herself up to every smidgen of height she could muster, she said calmly, "I'm sorry you got chewed out, I never meant for that to happen. If you'll recall, I did tell you I'd get somebody else to take me out to the island, but you insisted on doing it yourself. And Ryan didn't come anywhere near killing me, he just bumped me a little, I got wet and it could very well have been an accident. And besides *that*—" okay, so calm had been an unrealistic goal in the first place, and her voice was now developing pretty good volume and a bit of a quiver besides "—what do you mean, *you're* responsible for? *You've* 'got a woman'? As you so tactlessly pointed out, I'm a *middle-aged* woman, completely responsible for my own actions. Who put you in charge of me?"

"Your brother did," he said, watching her somewhat warily.

She gave a hoot of laughter. "Roy? My little brother? Oh, that's funny. I used to change that boy's diapers."

"Nevertheless." He drank milk, shrugged and said mildly, "He asked me to look after you, and that's what I've been *trying* to do. Believe me," he added darkly, "you haven't made it easy."

She couldn't help but notice his temper had simmered down considerably, in inverse proportion to hers picking up steam. Somehow, that calm, quiet manner of his only served to stoke her fires all the more. "I don't need you 'looking after' me," she said, seething, which was something she almost never did. "As a matter of fact, I've come up with a way of getting onto the island that doesn't need to involve you at all. All I need—"

"Joy, let me make this as clear as I possibly can. You are not going to that island." He spoke softly and with a look of infinite patience, as if he were dealing with a stubborn kindergartener. She felt a fleeting desire to hit him over the head with something large and heavy. A frying pan came immediately to mind.

Meeting his eyes with an unwavering stare, she said, in a voice as soft as his, "Excuse me, but unless you intend to arrest me, I don't see how you can stop me."

Oops, Scott thought. *Bad move.* Recognizing that perhaps a change of tactics was called for, he turned with his glass to the sink, dumped the last swallow of milk and filled the glass with water. Buying time, that's all it was. He was far from being a neat-freak. When he turned back to her once more, he had himself in hand, he thought. His expression was concerned, his voice calm and reasonable. He felt mature and in control.

All of which lasted maybe two seconds once he had her in front of him again, and he was seeing, really seeing, her for the first time since he'd found her on his doorstep. For once she didn't make him think of some bygone era, or a long-dead glamour queen. She had her hair twisted up on top of her head in a haphazard knot, like women do when they're getting ready to take a bath. And though she was dressed all in white, in the skirt she'd worn the first day and a plain sleeveless tank top, the effect wasn't even remotely virginal. More than anything, standing there in his kitchen, steaming almost visibly, she reminded him of a small white teapot about ready to blow.

He could feel his pulse quicken and his whole body clench in anticipation of the eruption. He couldn't remember the last time he'd felt like this—a deep-down inner excitement, as if there was a low-level electrical current running through him.

"Joy," he said, still striving for reasonable, at least, "even if you did manage to get onto the island, what do you think that's going to accomplish? If your friend was there, and free and able to move around, don't you think she'd have called you? You said yourself—"

"Maybe she's being closely watched. Or held prisoner." She glared at him, riled. "Maybe she's found out enough about the people she's with to be afraid for her life, and she's playing along with this Diego guy, to save herself. Maybe—"

Scott had been watching her in amazement. "Where do you *get* these ideas? Dammit, this isn't a plot for a mystery novel."

There was an instant and deafening silence. Then she closed her eyes and exhaled through her nose. "Oh, great, let me guess. Roy told you, didn't he? About my book."

The change in her face was so sudden that it hit him like a slap in his. The naked vulnerability in her eyes contrasted with the combative set of her chin and shoulders made him think of a tiny kitten with its fur all fluffed up, trying to look bigger and braver than she was. A dazed and unexpected tenderness filled him, and he crumbled like a cookie in hot cocoa.

He moved toward her and put his hands gently on her arms, ducking his head so he could look into her eyes. "Yeah, he did. And I think it's great. I admire you for having the imagination and the guts to do it, I really do. But look, isn't it just possible your imagination *is* working overtime here? That you might be seeing mysteries where there aren't any?"

There was a long pause, and he heard a voice inside himself say, *Uh-oh.* She was no longer seething. Her face was pale, her breathing quick and shallow, and her skin felt chilly to his touch. He thought it might have been the first time he'd ever actually *felt* someone's cold fury.

"So, you think I have trouble telling the difference between fiction and reality, is that it?"

"Joy—"

"No." She held up a hand and backed away, jerking out of his grasp. "Let me tell you something." Her voice sounded brittle and words formed quickly, as if she were afraid she wouldn't get them all out before it broke. "I'm forty-two years old. I grew up with four brothers and two sisters and a schoolteacher for a momma, and lost my daddy when I was barely grown. I've lived through two lousy marriages, three miscarriages and two divorces. I married my first husband, Zack, right out of high school, for the usual reason. I lost the baby, but it was too late to get out of the marriage. Things went along okay and I thought it might actually work out, until Zack lost his job and couldn't get another and

started drinking more and more. I'd had a couple more miscarriages before it got bad enough to where he actually hit
me, and that was when I left him for good, moved up to
Virginia, got a part-time job and a student loan, and went
back to school. That's where I met Frederick.'' She caught
his expression and snapped, ''And don't you dare laugh. It
was Frederick Vincent O'Conner III, which is an old family
name. Freddie is from a very old family, most of whom were
lawyers and rich as sin. Which Freddie thought meant he was
entitled to sin as much as he pleased with anyone he wanted
and act like a spoiled frat boy even after we were married
and still come out ahead in the divorce. Fortunately, his father and grandfather disagreed with him, so I got a decent
settlement. I used some of it to go back to school and get
my degree. The rest got me moved to New York and kept
me going until I could find a job and start supporting myself.
I like my job okay, but creatively it's not very fulfilling, so
I started looking around for other writing outlets. I like to
read and I'm a pretty fair writer and I have imagination, yes,
but I also have a logical mind and I'm pretty good at solving
problems, so I decided to write mysteries. I've taken—''

''Not romance?''

''What?'' She looked confused, as if she'd been barreling
along so fast she'd lost track of what road she was on.

He took a step toward her, smiling, folding his arms on
his chest to keep from putting his hands on her again. ''I
said, why didn't you decide to write a romance novel? Aren't
they the big thing now?''

She held her ground and her head tilted back so her eyes
could keep their hold on his, which gave her a belligerent
look she may not have intended. ''I don't know. Maybe because I don't believe in it.''

''But you do believe in murder and mayhem?'' Her throat
moved with her swallow. He watched it and found himself
wondering how it would be if he kissed her there.

''I know they exist.'' Her lips twitched into an ironic
smile. ''You think I don't know the difference between fan-

tasy and reality? I was in New York when the towers fell. I know the world's a scary place most of the time, and not very fair, and that in real life things usually aren't tied up in neat little summations like Hercule Poirot's. I think people want to believe in the *hope* that the bad guys will get caught and all the questions will be answered. Maybe people write mysteries for the same reason, I don't know. I know *I* didn't think about all that when I started, I just thought it was something I could *do*. But one thing I do know—you sure as hell have to know what's real before you can write about what *isn't*—'' Her voice broke then, but it was with anger, not tears.

And that made the vulnerability she tried to hide from him by closing her eyes and pressing her lips together that much harder to watch. Scott could feel his resolve becoming harder and harder to maintain, and he knew *he* was about to become way more vulnerable than he wanted to be. He knew he should step away from her, take a deep breath, count to ten. Instead, after a long pause, he heard himself say, ''I'm sorry.''

For several seconds after that, Joy just looked at him. It was as if he'd said something to her in a foreign language. Even though she knew they ought to, the words had no meaning for her. Then, all at once, understanding hit her, and the sensation was appalling, unlike anything she'd ever felt before—a loosening, melting feeling, as if every single one of her defenses had suddenly collapsed. She wondered if this was what the old novels meant when they said someone had ''come undone.''

She pressed her fingertips to her lips and turned quickly, so he wouldn't see how upset she was. ''Oh brother,'' she muttered, desperately trying to make light of it. ''You had to go and do that, didn't you.''

''Do…what?''

She didn't dare look at him. With her back to him, she waved a distracted hand. ''Just when I was starting to think you were… Just when I was starting to feel *safe* with you.''

"Safe? You're not making sense."

He sounded half angry, half bewildered, and she didn't blame him. She felt that way herself.

"Of course you're safe with me. If you don't know—"

His hand brushed her arm, and it felt like an electric shock. She jerked around awkwardly, like a broken windup toy. "No, I'm not," she whispered. "I'm not."

"Dammit, Joy—" The hand he'd touched her with flailed in the air helplessly, then raked backward through his hair. His eyes looked bright and angry. "You mind telling me what I've done to make you think that? All I said was—"

"'I'm sorry.'" Her lips felt swollen and trembly, so she licked them. "You said, 'I'm sorry.'"

"Okay, guilty. I guess I'm having a hard time figuring out how that's a bad thing."

His chin was set pugnaciously, which, far from making him intimidating, gave him the rather endearing look of an embattled little boy. Gazing at him, she could feel her heart melt, like a chocolate bar in the sun. "It's just that... I don't think any man has ever said that to me before."

"Oh, come on."

"No, it's true." It was hard to look at him, but she couldn't make herself look anywhere else. Her eyes devoured his face feature by feature, beginning with those burning eyes and ending with that undeniably, unexpectedly appealing mouth. She shook her head slowly. "Zack never apologized, even for hitting me. Neither did Freddie, when he'd been unfaithful to me. Nobody did. Ever. You're the first."

"Sounds to me," he growled, "like you have pretty damn lousy taste in men."

"I do," she agreed, staring at his chest in a dazed and wondering way. "Either that or terrible karma. Which is why—"

"Why...what?"

She closed her eyes. How had she gotten herself into this? There was no way out, now, except to tell him. Which was no big deal, after all. He probably knew anyway, by now.

And it wasn't as if she was a vulnerable girl with her ego to protect by refusing to admit it out loud. She was a forty-two-year-old, twice-divorced, *middle-aged* woman living in the twenty-first century. Definitely not a big deal. Except, somebody had forgotten to tell her heart, which was probably as retro as the rest of her, and beating so hard right now she could feel her whole body moving with it.

She let her breath and the words out in a single gust. "Why I can't figure out why I'm so attracted to you."

"You're...attracted to me?"

His face was a study in conflicted emotions, along with hints of some of the sweeter weaknesses suffered by men. Finally, it settled into a tenuous and rather goofy smile. Under different circumstances, she would have been tempted to giggle.

Instead, she said, "Like you didn't know. And like you said, I have terrible taste in men. So, what does that say about *you?*" She scrunched up her face in exasperation. "You know, I keep thinking there must be something wrong with you, and everytime I think I've found out what it is, you go and do something...something..."

"Nice?"

His lips were twitching. She glared at him, trembly inside.

He shrugged and murmured somberly, "What can I say? I'm a nice guy."

She closed her eyes again in utter defeat. "Yeah, sometimes I really think you are. I don't know what to think, or feel—" she shook her head and finished in a whisper "—I don't know what to do." And then there was silence.

Unable to stand it any longer, she opened her eyes and found that he was staring at her intently, as if she were a fascinating puzzle he was determined to solve. Unnerved, she licked her lips.

"What?"

He cleared his throat, but his voice was still raspy. "Okay, I think I've got this thing figured out."

"What thing?"

"This—you and me." He waggled a finger back and forth in the space between them. "You being here, me being an idiot. I think I know what it's all about."

"Oh yeah?" She looked at him warily. "And what's that?"

He shook his head, and his frown deepened. "I'd like to try a little experiment, to see if I'm right. Are you game?"

"Experiment?" Her brain was completely fogged. Her heart, however, had leaped right on ahead to its own conclusions and was thumping its approval like mad.

"Here—"

He put his hands on her waist, and the next thing she knew she was sitting on the kitchen counter with her knees pointed at his belt buckle and the tile cold under her bottom and her eyes were on a level with his. More important, so was her mouth.

"Now," he said, and leaned slowly toward her, watching her closely to see whether she'd object.

She didn't, so he kept coming. Except he had to lean quite a bit and rather awkwardly because her knees were in the way, and naturally, without even thinking, she moved them apart to make room for him.

He stepped into the space she'd made as if he belonged there. His hands—both of them this time—held her face as if it were some precious treasure he'd found. His mouth brushed hers, and what a sweet, sensuous pleasure it was, like rubbing her lips against fine silk. She caught her breath in the wonder of enlightenment, because in that moment she knew she'd been wondering all along what his mouth would feel like...taste like. Maybe she'd been wondering all her life. And somewhere in her head, as if a coin had dropped into a jukebox, a happy and familiar little song woke up and began to sing: *Thisfeelsogoodsogoodsogood...*

She didn't know when the ache began, but all at once it was there, all over inside her. As his lips, slightly parted, embraced and cuddled and sweetly sandwiched hers, she held herself utterly still, not breathing, afraid to move lest it spill over in embarrassing ways. And the happy little song in her head had taken on a raspy Janice Joplin sound, edgy with passion, heartbreak and pain.

He drew away, thank God, just before she began to shake in earnest. His exhalation blew its intimate warmth across her lips, and he said, "Well?"

She whispered, "What?"

"Was that it?"

"Was that what?"

"What all the tension's been about. What you came over here for. What I've been barking at you about."

"Oh. Mmm... I don't know." She licked her lips. "I'm not sure." She opened her eyes and looked up at him through the curtain of her lashes. "Maybe we should experiment some more."

He gave a brief little huff of laughter, all he had time for before he closed the gap between his mouth and hers once again. But that joining was brief, too, only a springboard to a joyous headfirst dive into really deep waters. Mouths shifted, gasped open and hungrily found each other again. No longer afraid to move, she explored his face with her hands and reveled in the raspy feel of stubble on her palms and fingertips. His arms came around her and lifted her completely off the countertop so that her face was above his, and it was as exhilarating to her as the upward sweep of a Ferris wheel. Her legs, already spread to make room for him, found it completely natural to spread wider, and then to wrap around him, exposing sensitive parts of her to sensations they hadn't felt in a very long time. The happy song in her head picked up again, now with a full symphony orchestra behind it.

Then her skirt was twitched impatiently aside and instead of cold, clammy tile she felt warm, masculine hands cradling her bottom, skin separated from skin only by the thinnest and most inconsequential of fabric barriers.

The *feelssogoodsogood* song in her head ended with the wild screech of a needle skidding across vinyl, and instead someone was hollering, *Wait! Have you lost your mind? You've known this guy what—two days?* All the usual, *sensible* arguments.

She peeled herself away from him just far enough to free her lips and feebly mumbled, "Wait."

That was all. Just "Wait," which she wasn't even sure she meant. But it was enough, and just like that, she felt cool fabric replace warm hands, and the cold, solid countertop supporting her bottom again instead of resilient masculine muscle. Not that he'd let go of her completely, thank God, and she kept her hands on his shoulders to make sure he didn't.

"Too fast?" he said, gently sympathetic.

"Yeah...a little." And then, to her surprise and annoyance, she heard a voice in her head hollering, *What, are you out of your mind?* She wished those voices would either get together or shut up. She looked at him and found that he was smiling at her, not in a triumphant, masculine way, but almost tenderly. She laughed softly as she leaned forward to brush his mouth lightly with hers. "Just a little."

"Okay, we'll slow it down," he said, then used his lips and tongue to tease hers until every nerve in her body felt raw and her skin was on fire with goose bumps, and her nipples hurt and she was shaking so hard she thought she'd fall apart.

Then he laughed, low in his chest, and said, "Are you sure you don't believe in romance?"

"Absolutely," she said, her voice as firm as she could make it, considering all the quaking and pounding it had to get past. "Anyway, this isn't romance, it's sex."

"Oh, hell," he muttered, kissing her throat, the side of her neck, "I'm just a guy. I don't know the difference."

She clung to him, laughing, head thrown back to give him clear pathways to wherever it was he was going with that unbelievably talented mouth of his. The voices in her head were silent, evidently either in awe or thoroughly chastened, and without their interference her body was like a puppy let off its leash—wanton, shameless, uninhibited, giddy. Her legs coiled themselves around his waist as if they had minds of their own, and her body felt simultaneously weightless and sinuous, humid and heavy. *This feels so good…so good.*

Something vibrated against her inner thigh. At almost the same moment, the telephone began to ring.

Scott swore and muttered, ''Ignore it.'' Then, after swearing some more, he returned Joy's bottom carefully to the countertop, plucked his cell phone from his belt and squinted at the caller ID. Another short descriptive word followed. He snatched up the ringing telephone just as the answering machine clicked on.

''Cavanaugh,'' he growled, glaring at Joy and trying not to breathe hard.

She smiled ruefully back at him. She watched his face as he listened to the voice on the telephone, and felt the passion drain from her body, leaving her weak. Then, when his face hardened and his eyes flicked toward her, and he abruptly turned his back so she could no longer see his face, she felt herself go clammy and cold. Though oddly enough, her heart was still pounding hard enough to hurt.

''What is it?'' she whispered, when he'd cradled the phone.

She could see him brace himself before he turned. ''We have to go,'' he said, almost brusquely.

''Go? Where? I don't—''

He seemed to pause then, and his hands were gentle on her waist as he lifted her down from the countertop. His voice was even more so, as if he were speaking to a frightened child.

''Joy, I'm sorry. That was the county medical examiner. They've got a female DOA. A Jane Doe. They need you to see if you can identify the body.''

Chapter 8

"That's something I hope and pray I never have to do again in this life." Joy gave a violent shudder as she dropped her pocketbook onto the couch in Roy's beach house. Making a beeline for the refrigerator, she opened it and took out a can of iced tea, which she handed over to Scott, then snagged a bottle of beer for herself. But when she tried to open it she discovered her hands had no strength in them, so she passed the bottle on to him, too.

Without a word he opened it and gave it back to her, and his eyes were somber and watchful. "Yeah...sorry we had to put you through it." He paused and took a drink of tea before he added, "I'm just glad it was a false alarm."

She glared at him, holding the cold wet bottle in her hand because she still felt too shaken to lift it to her lips. Unfairly, she was angry with him, wanting to blame *someone* for the fact that there was death and violence and tragedy in the world and finding no one else handy.

"I *told* you it wasn't Yancy, the second I saw her hair. Yancy's hair is *red*."

His eyes rested on her, not comfortably now, but thoughtful and somber. "Hair color can be changed."

"*Now* who's makin' up wild scenarios?" She was in no mood to be reasonable.

"They have to have you look at the face," he said quietly. "If at all possible. Otherwise—"

"I know. I know. Oh God—" Strengthening anger deserted her and as a sob welled up inside her she clamped a hand over her eyes. "That poor girl. I can't get her face out of my mind."

She felt his warmth come close to her, and then the beer bottle was eased carefully from her grasp. She heard a soft *thump* as it met the tabletop, and then strong arms were around her. Warm breath gusted into her hair.

"At least it wasn't your friend."

"Yeah…" She gave up trying to hold back the sob. It rippled through her, and she turned her face into his chest and whispered, "But she's *somebody's,* isn't she? Somebody's sister…daughter…wife…best friend. Somebody somewhere's gonna get their heart broken." He didn't reply, and after a moment she turned her head so her ear rested against the steady and comforting thump of his heartbeat. She sniffed, then softly asked, "What happened to her, do you know?"

She felt him shake his head. "The autopsy will have to determine that. Then we'll go from there."

"I can't stop thinking about her. She was so young…"

"Hey—" His voice was gruff. He leaned back, and his knuckle found the underside of her chin and tilted her face upward. "You have to put it out of your mind. Forget about it."

For some reason it had become hard to look at him. Maybe because of her vulnerability, her weakness, her embarrassing desire to snuggle right down in the shelter of his arms and stay there forever. It was to hide both the desire and the weakness that she straightened, brushed impatiently at her cheeks and said with mock grumpiness, "Well, I was fixin' to do that, but then you took away my beer."

A frown made pleats between his eyebrows. Below them his eyes held a teasing gleam. "That's a bad habit to get into."

"You got a better idea?" She sucked in air as she realized what she'd said and wondered how he'd take it. Snappy repartee and sexual innuendo were not her style. Her heart quickened as she saw the gleam in his eyes kindle into flame.

"Yeah, I do." He folded his arms on his chest, making biceps bulge against pecs, and gazed down at her in a superior, uniquely masculine way. "I've heard sex is a good way to forget your troubles. Since we've already established the fact that we both want it."

"Hmm." She'd meant to say more, along the lines of that witty repartee, hopefully, but discovered her tongue was glued to the roof of her mouth. Where was that beer when she needed it?

Frowning, she managed to say in the softly slurred accents of Oglethorpe County, Georgia, "I s'pose we did. Am I to assume you're suggestin' we pick up where we left off?" And by now her heart was whumping so hard she felt clumsy and off balance, like a car limping along with a flat tire. "As…therapy?"

"I am." Then his head was blocking out the light, and there was his mouth claiming hers again, his amazingly skilled, incredibly agile, unbelievably sensitive mouth.

Where, she wondered, did such a big, brawny, macho guy *get* such a mouth? And if the rest of him was anything like as gifted as that mouth… The bottom dropped out of her stomach, and she had to hold on to his arms to keep from falling.

It was sometime later when he murmured, "What d'you think?"

"Mmm. Yes. That'll do." She felt drugged—or drunk. She could feel herself swaying. It was hard to open her eyes. Looking at him was like trying to look at the sun. "But isn't this just as dangerous as drinkin'?'' *Oh, more so. Much more so.*

One of his hands was lightly stroking her arm. The other had crept along her shoulder to the back of her neck, and she fought the desire to let her head sink into its warm and sure support. It had been so long since she'd been touched the way this man touched her. Had she *ever* been touched like this? If she had, she couldn't remember. Longing filled her, along with a peculiar sense of having been cheated. *I'm forty-two years old. Why haven't I ever felt like this before?*

''Not as long as both parties agree and are absolutely clear on what it's all about,'' he said solemnly.

''Well, we pretty much established that a while ago, at your place. Just sex, right?'' Her fingertips were delightedly exploring the shape and textures of his arms, like children turned loose in a new playground.

''Right.''

''Which I definitely am,'' said Joy, nodding her head and going a little cross-eyed with the effort it took to focus her eyes on his face, so close to hers. ''Clear on. Just sex.''

''Mmm-hmm. And I'm a guy, so I don't know the difference anyway. Right?''

''Right. So, I guess…we're on.'' Her hands eagerly scaled the slope of his shoulders and found purchase on his neck, just before his mouth claimed hers again and her sane and reasoning world disappeared in a fog of sensation, of desire, of *feeling*.

A few concerns and cautions still flitted about in the golden haze of her mind, like butterflies too drunk and giddy to light. Except for one, more persistent than the rest…

''Wait.'' Her mouth was free again. She felt herself being lifted…carried. Groggy and breathless, she repeated, ''Wait.''

He halted, breathing as heavily as she was. ''What?''

''Do you have whatever you need to… Because I sure don't.''

''No.''

There was a long pause, while his heart banged against her side and her stomach went hollow and cold with impending disappointment. Having so bravely committed herself to the idea of sex with Scott, she almost couldn't bear the thought of *not* doing it. Then he was moving again, with a firm and purposeful step.

"But I'm sure your brother does."

"Oh Lord," Joy said, laughing feebly, burying her face in the hollow of his neck. "That's a dampening thought."

"Put it out of your mind."

"Uh-uh, that's your job." She lifted herself, not waiting, this time, for his mouth to find hers. And when it did, sure enough, all thoughts of her brother's sex life went right out of her head, along with most everything else. Everything except those happy little songs about how good she felt, how good his mouth felt, sliding around all over hers…inside and out…and how good his tongue felt, tangling with hers in delightful and interesting ways.

The next time he separated his mouth from hers he was sitting on the edge of the bed—Roy's, not the guest-room bed she'd been using—and she was sprawled wantonly across his lap. She felt him reach, and heard the nightstand drawer open, then close.

"Nope," he said, breathing hard.

Lying back against his arm, one of her arms hooked around his neck, she gazed up at him, and he looked back at her, though in the near-darkness she was sure he couldn't see her face any better than she could see his. Minutes passed while she listened to their syncopated heartbeats, plus every argument that had ever been made for why a condom wasn't *really* that important.

"Wait," Scott said. "Don't go 'way."

He shifted her onto the mattress and left her shivering and hugging herself. She heard his footsteps thump across the floor and into the bathroom. She heard drawers open, and then the medicine cabinet, and then a soft, "Bingo."

When he came out of the bathroom, she was waiting for

him, huddled like a lost kitten on the edge of the bed. Seeing her like that, the relief he'd felt a moment ago, when he'd known he wasn't going to have to deny himself the pleasure of her body after all, softened into something he hadn't felt since his divorce. Since quite a while before that, if he were completely honest. *Tenderness. Is that what I'm feeling? It can't possibly be love.*

He thought, *How can it? I haven't known her long enough!*

Probably just sex, he thought, trying to reassure himself. Like he'd told her, he was a guy, so he probably *didn't* know the difference.

And it sure as hell better *not* be anything more complicated than that. Because if he knew one thing for sure, it was that he wasn't eager to have his heart ripped out and stomped on again.

But in spite of all that going around and around like a dogfight inside his head, he found that he was sitting beside Joy with his hands on her upper arms. And his fingers were stroking her skin, which was like the softest, warmest velvet he'd ever imagined, and his heart was pumping fast and hard, and he was trying to decide whether he was about to do something wildly, unbelievably wonderful, or incredibly, unbelievably stupid. Like skydiving.

Considering how confused *he* felt, he wasn't surprised when Joy said, "Scott..." and put a restraining hand on his shirt.

His belly knotted with regret, which at least settled the question of what his own desires really were, once and for all.

"Second thoughts?" he asked gently, searching her face as his eyes slowly grew accustomed to the darkness.

She shook her head and gazed fixedly at his chest and her hand. "I think I feel guilty. We just came from..." She swallowed. Her fingers moved in slow circles on his chest, and he wanted to tear his shirt away so he could feel them on his skin.

But he reined himself in, limiting himself to that small

contact, her hand on the front of his shirt, his hands on her bare arms—and how could so little be so erotic? The way he was feeling right now he thought seeing her naked might kill him, while he told her it was a natural instinct, that being around death often aroused in people a compulsion to create life.

"There's probably a name for it. I don't know what it is, but I know it's nothing to feel guilty about. Happens all the time."

He heard the accepting sigh of her breath. "I don't want you to think—to feel like I'm just using you because I'm upset."

He leaned down and kissed the side of her neck, laughing softly. "Well, of *course* you are, darlin'. Using me, I mean. For therapy. I volunteered for the purpose, remember?"

"As long as you know," she said, her voice growing faint and rapid as he eased her over onto his arm and his hand nested the ripe, round fullness of her breast, "that it is just sex. Because I do have abs'lutely, *oh dear*, terrible taste in men, and—" she squirmed against his hand, beginning to pant a little "—I know there must be something wrong with you, I just—" the rest was only a whisper, because his mouth was covering the place on her throat where her voice came from "—haven't found out what it is yet."

"No problem," he murmured, kissing his way back to her lips and finding them open and hungry for him. "Just sex…" When he could speak again, he added, "And since it is, or is going to be, sex, don't you think it would be a good idea if we got rid of some of these clothes?"

The nice thing was, in his opinion, that since it was…sex, there wasn't any need on either of their parts to try to be graceful or romantic about it. The clothes came off. Quickly. Sometimes he did the work, sometimes she did, and sometimes they tried to help each other and only succeeded in getting their hands in each other's way and their clothes tangled up together, and both of them were shivering and laughing like excited children by the time they were through. And then, naked at last, they lay crossways in a tumble of hastily thrown-back bedding, facing each other with galloping pulses and dying laughter.

He wanted to look at her, was hungry to feast his eyes on the roundness of her hips and bottom, dying to gaze upon the full-blown lushness of her breasts, and to do that even while his hands and mouth explored them. But it would have been like throwing gasoline on an out-of-control fire. He was already so primed. In fact, he couldn't remember ever being so sensitized, as if he'd been holding himself back for hours. How long had he been lusting after this woman, anyway? He felt as though the entire time he'd known her had been one long episode of foreplay.

Promising himself those rich and erotic indulgences later, he leaned slowly toward her, and even though she rose up to meet him, it seemed an endless, bottomless plunge before he felt her mouth under his. And for some reason, there was no hurry now, no sense of urgency at all. The kiss was languid and deep. Her scent, her heat, her essence enveloped him. He lost track of time and space; all he knew was the feel…the taste…the smell…the *pleasure* of her.

He'd never known anyone so completely, uninhibitedly female. It was in the joyous, earthy little sounds she made, happy sounds that somehow made him feel earthy and uninhibited and happy, too. It was in the way she moved…with him and under him and over him, and there was no counting or accounting for whose hands and mouths did what and what body parts went where, just an all-over merging and melding and pleasuring that seemed to go on and on until he was sure he couldn't stand it a minute more, and then, somehow, found out that he could.

Inside her at last, he had a hard time remembering how, exactly, he'd gotten there. He only knew it was the best place he'd ever been. And then he heard her murmur something he couldn't understand and felt her settle herself more fully around him, felt himself sinking deeper into her still—and he found that was an even better place.

Nestled deep inside her, he felt her body do something wonderful and mysterious, and realized she was laughing. Braced and quivering, he whispered, "What?"

"I said, you feel so good," she whispered back. "So good."

Dazed, in awe, he looked down at her, searching for her face in the darkness, and was shaken to realize he was on the brink of saying something that was probably going to ruin everything. To forestall the dangerous words, he quickly lowered his head and kissed her, and the saving thought flashed into his mind: *Heck, it probably* is *just sex. What do I know?*

Then, once again he lost track of time and space. He knew that he was moving and so was she, in such perfect sync with him that he no longer gave a moment's thought to when or how the climax would come, so sure was he that whenever and however it did, it would be the best he'd ever known and that she'd be right there with him. He knew he'd never felt so good in all his life, and yet, in contradiction to that, he felt as if he'd been making love to this woman all his life. How could that be?

"You feel good, too," he whispered. "So good…" And they laughed together again.

He kissed her until he couldn't anymore and when he pulled away from her mouth with a gasp, he heard her gasp, too, then whisper, "Oh," and begin to arch and writhe in his arms. He felt her body clench and pulse around him, and in a burst of sheer happiness, as if a flare had ignited right over his head and was bathing him in its warmth and brilliance, he gave up the self-control he didn't even know he'd been using till now and simply let it come.

It was a short while later—he still hadn't gotten a handle on time, though he thought he had the space thing pretty well worked out—he was lying on his back with Joy beside him, drenched in sweat and breathing hard and feeling about as good as it's possible for a man to feel, considering he was drained and empty as an old sock. He was glad the lights weren't on so she couldn't see the silly grin on his face. And at the same time he wished they were, so he could see if she was wearing one just like it. He didn't know what to say. He didn't want to say anything, because he had an idea that the moment he spoke, or she did, the magic would disappear like smoke in the wind.

"Well," she said in that husky voice of hers, like a cat's purr. "That was definitely…sex."

"Yeah," he said, smiling because the happiness hadn't gone away after all, "it sure was."

He could feel her body tense, and her head tilt back to look at him. "I thought it went quite well, didn't you?"

He was opening his mouth to reply in a similar vein when the suppressed laughter in her voice got through to him, and instead he growled, "Not bad," and rolled her into his arms and kissed her a long and tender time that was prolonged by gusts and snickers of surprised delight.

By the time they were finally quiet again, he was back in the real world enough to be aware of certain discomforts. "Don't go 'way," he said as he left her in the tumbled nest of bedding and made his way to the bathroom. When he returned, he found that Joy, in a housewifely way he found touching, had tidied and smoothed the bed and was folding the sheets neatly back, her nakedness an enticing silhouette against the faint light.

"I wasn't sure," she began, her voice echoing her uncertainty. "Can you stay? I thought, since we've already…that we might as well…"

For an answer, he flicked away the towel he'd knotted around his hips. She reached for him at the same time he held his arms out to her. Her arms came around his middle and she nestled her cheek against his chest with a contented sigh.

"You do feel so good," she murmured, nuzzling like a kitten in his chest hair, "whichever way you touch me."

His eyes smarted unexpectedly. He laughed and said, "Ditto" as he peeled himself away from her. Holding her hands, he sat on the edge of the bed, then stretched himself between the sheets. "Come 'ere, you," he growled, lifting the covers, and she came against him as if she'd always done so.

"Still seems weird to be doing this in my brother's bed," she said, sounding grumpy as she snuggled against his side. And then, trying unsuccessfully to suppress a yawn, she added, "Oh well, like you said, guess I'll just have to put it out of my mind."

"That's my job, remember?" Scott said, resting his chin on the top of her head and getting it bumped as she lifted up to look at him in surprise.

"Can you?"

He considered, then chuckled ruefully. "To be honest, probably not right now. But give me a minute."

She laughed, and he thought it the warmest and most delicious sound he'd ever heard. His skin had begun to tingle with the first stirrings of new arousal when he felt her body relax and her breathing slip into deep and heavy rhythms. He tensed his stomach and lifted his head so he could see her face, just to be sure, and yes, she was. She was sound asleep. Just like that, from one second to the next.

As he mouthed the word, "Wow," he was wondering what in the world he was going to do if he'd fallen in love with his best friend's sort of ditzy sister, Joy.

The next thing he knew, he was waking up to a strange rattling sound. A second or two later, having identified the sound as his cell phone jumping around on the tabletop beside the bed, he groped for it, found the "on" button and mashed it, then brought it to his ear as he rolled onto his back and muttered a groggy, "Yeah…"

"Scotty? I didn't wake you up, did I?"

"No, Beth, that's okay, I've been up," he lied, eyes closed and breathing deeply and silently through his nose. There was an indentation in the pillow next to his head that still smelled, faintly, of old roses. "What's up? Everything okay?"

"Well, I'm sorry if I did, but I don't like to bother you at work, and I needed to ask you…"

"I said, it's okay. What is it?"

"Ryan being grounded…you know Little League practice starts today. Does that include—"

"No, Beth, he can go to practice." Not wanting to hurt her feelings, he didn't tell her Ryan would likely consider skipping baseball practice more of a reward than a punishment.

He scrubbed a hand over his eyes and got them open just in time to see Joy coming through the door with a coffee mug in each hand. Her hair was wet and she was wearing a man's bathrobe eight sizes too big for her, and at the sight of her, pleasure squirted through him like adrenaline, so that he was instantly awake, every nerve and sense humming in high gear. The smile on her face alone was ten times more effective than caffeine.

"Well, you're gonna have to tell him that, then, because he won't listen to me. Scotty, I really wish you'd talked to me before you went and grounded him for a whole month. You know, I do have some things comin' up I just can't postpone, and I was countin' on Ryan sleepin' over at—"

"Well, I'm sure we can work something out. Listen, I'm kind of in the middle of something—"

Joy, in the process of setting the coffee down on the bedside table, threw him a frown and a quick head-shake, forming the word *No,* with her mouth.

"Well, Scotty, I'm sorry to be a bother, but I really need to talk to you about something. Remember Sybil, my friend from school? Well, I saw her at the reunion, and she's—"

"Beth, I'm gonna have to call you back in a little bit, okay?" He disconnected the phone and caught hold of Joy's hand just as she was turning to leave. "Hey, where you off to?"

"I thought you might want some privacy."

"Nah, that was just my ex-wife. She usually calls about

this time. It's never anything important. I'll call her back later.''

''You don't need to do that on my account.'' She disengaged her hand from his and folded her arms across the overlapping halves of the giant robe.

''Well, I do on mine,'' he said, swinging his legs around and remembering to pull the blankets across his lap as he sat up. All the natural modesty and constraint he hadn't felt last night had returned with the wariness and reserve he sensed now, in her. The surge of delight he'd felt on opening his eyes and seeing her smile was fading fast. Then, all he'd wanted to do was tumble her, laughing and breathless, back into the place she'd left empty beside him. Now, all he was remembering was what she'd said, what he'd said, too, last night: *It's just sex.* If it was just sex, where did that leave them this morning? What was he supposed to say to her?

''I'd offer you breakfast,'' she said, ''but all there is in the cupboards is instant grits.''

''Coffee'll do for now. Thanks,'' he said, watching her, holding on to her eyes. What he wanted to say was, *Forget about breakfast. Come here and kiss me.* Why couldn't he? Last night the words would have come easily, naturally, between gusts of intimate laughter. This morning they seemed impossible. Out of place and out of line. How come, when what had happened between them last night had been, to him, anyway, the most incredible sex he'd ever enjoyed in his life?

It's just sex.

Yeah, well, that explained it all, he supposed.

''I need to be getting home, anyway,'' he said. ''Need to get showered and changed, get to work.''

''You can shower here, if you want.''

''That's all right, I'm gonna want to change my clothes.''

''Oh, of course.'' She picked up her coffee cup and turned away, and this time he didn't stop her. ''Well, I'll, uh…let you…'' She went out of the bedroom and closed the door.

I guess there's a good reason why I don't do this very

often, Scott thought to himself. No matter how good the sex was, the morning after felt just plain lousy.

Downstairs in the kitchen, Joy sat at the table, vibrating with leftover tremors, the coffee mug warm between her cold hands. *No wonder I don't do this sort of thing very often,* she thought. *Well, okay, never.* But...how could the night feel so wonderful, and the morning after so awful? She hadn't felt awful at first. All she'd wanted to do when she woke up was kiss Scott awake and go on kissing him until more of last night's wonderful things happened. Why couldn't she have done that? Why, instead, had she crept out of bed like a thief, dreading to wake him?

It's just sex.

And that was it in a nutshell, she supposed. Kissing and cuddling and making love in the morning light were things lovers did. People who'd just "had sex" got up and put their clothes on and went their separate ways, being overly polite and careful not to look at one another. And, she thought, as she heard Scott's footsteps on the stairs, in her case, feeling all hollow and sad and foresaken inside.

He came into the kitchen, hooking his cell phone onto his belt. Her heart did a little dance as she watched him come toward her, then lurched wildly when he passed behind her chair, and she thought he might put his hand on her neck, bend down to kiss her good morning. But he didn't, and her heart thumped a disappointed little dirge while he went on to the sink, drained the last swallow of coffee from his cup, rinsed it out and left it sitting on the countertop. He turned to her then, and she saw him take a breath as if to fortify himself.

"Wish I didn't have to leave like this," he said. His eyes glittered blue beneath his frown. "I have to get to work."

"I know you do. Don't worry about it." She was pleased to hear how calm and cheery she sounded. "I guess I should thank you, though," she added, and as soon as she said it, a bubble of remembered delight rose up and burst inside her, like the burp after a too-big gulp of champagne, spreading warmth through her chest and a smile across her face. "For...everything."

An answering smile lit up his face, and his body seemed to relax, as if, she thought, he felt relieved.

"No thanks necessary," he said modestly, and this time he did drop a kiss onto the top of her head and touch her shoulder as he passed her. "Call on me any time."

Just like that, the tension and the awkwardness between them dissipated, and she felt easy with him again. She drew a breath and deep inside her a new happiness dared to raise its tentative, quivering head.

"So, what are you gonna do with yourself today?" he asked, pausing to look back at her as he reached the front door, jingling his car keys in his hand. "You need me to drop you any place? Maybe take you to pick up a rental car?"

"No, that's okay," said Joy. "I told you I wasn't going to need you for this."

"Need me for what?" The jingling sound had stopped. He'd grown ominously still. "Joy, what have you got planned?"

"I'm planning to rent a boat," she said calmly. "I told you. I'm going to King's Island."

Chapter 9

"You're *what?*" He'd heard her perfectly well, he just needed some time to prepare, to keep from yelling at her.

"It's what I came over to your place to tell you about last night, remember? Before everything happened. I'm going to rent a boat. Not a big one, just a little speedboat. One I can drive by myself. Then, I'm going to pretend to have engine trouble, so I'll drift right onto the island, and when they come to stop me, I'll ask to use the phone. How could anyone object to that? Look at me. Seriously, who would suspect—"

"Joy. Have you lost your mind?" Although his skin was prickling and his heart thumping in full battle mode, he said it gently, having learned by this time that going head-to-head with this woman was a losing proposition. "You can't—" No. Wrong word. With her, the word *can't* was like a red flag waved in front of a bull. And speaking of which, *bull-headed* was another word that sprang instantly to mind in regard to Joy Lynn Starr.

He started again, calmly and reasonably. "You don't know what kind of people you're dealing with."

She seemed to be considering that as she gazed steadily at him from across the living room, hands curved around her coffee cup. "Then, why don't you tell me?"

"Joy." He lifted his hands, then let them fall helplessly. "Like I told you, the DelRey family is suspected of—"

"*Suspected,* that's what you said. You told me that so far nobody's been able to prove anything against them. Right? Which means they must be trying very hard to appear legitimate in every way, so as not to give anyone who might be investigating them any ammunition to use against them. So, why on earth would they do harm to an innocent and helpless woman in distress who happens to wash up on their precious island?"

He could only stare at her, hot-eyed and frustrated. The damn woman always had an answer for everything, like it was a tricky book plot she'd already worked the bugs out of.

"There's simply no arguing with you," he said at last. "Is there?"

Her gaze was solemn. "Not when I know I'm right."

He half turned, part of him wanting to go to her and grab her by the shoulders and shake some sense into her, part wanting to get the hell away from her before he did or said something he'd regret. Dammit, she wasn't right, but he couldn't think of any way to convince her of that that didn't involve violating oaths and disobeying direct orders, not to mention compromising a complex multimillion-dollar operation, risking the lives of unknown numbers of his fellow law enforcement brothers, embarrassing his boss and thoroughly annoying several federal agencies, and, in all probability, breaking a few laws.

Finally, as a compromise, he walked across to the table where she was sitting, but across from her, and took hold of the back of a chair, which he gripped hard and leaned on as he said quietly, "Joy. Before you came down here, nobody would even believe your friend was in trouble. Now, she's been reported missing, last seen in the company of a member of a suspected crime kingpin's family. You've accomplished a helluva lot as it is. The wheels are turning. Why can't you leave it in the hands of law enforcement, where it belongs?''

"Because," she replied just as quietly, leaning back in her chair to meet his eyes, "it seems to me that right now 'law enforcement' is more concerned with bringing down this crime family and putting an end to their operations than they are with finding Yancy and bringing her safely home. Not that that's wrong, necessarily, but I think those federal agencies you mentioned would just as soon consider Yancy 'collateral damage,' if it meant getting something provable on the DelReys."

He straightened up with an exasperated sound. "Oh, for God's sake. I think you've been seeing too many Hollywood conspiracy movies."

"Nevertheless," she said, not flinching nor budging a millimeter. "I don't think anybody here really cares very much about what happens to one rather naive young woman from Up North. But I do."

"Dammit, Joy." His voice was rising again. He glared helplessly at her as he drove his fingers through his hair, then asked, "Why is this woman so important to you?"

"She's my friend," she whispered, and to his dismay he saw a sheen come into her eyes and turn the hazel to gold. "More than a friend. She's like a sister, maybe even a daughter to me. She doesn't have anyone else. I'm all she's got, and I'm not going to abandon her. I can't. I won't."

"All right…all right." He caught a quick breath and held up a hand to stop her, knowing if those tears spilled over he'd be a goner for sure. His brain was spinning as fast as it could in search of some kind of solution—a stalling tactic, anything. "Look, just do me one favor, okay? Don't do anything stupid until I've had a chance to talk to some people. Uh, I don't know, maybe we can find a way to work something out." He hoped he sounded convincing. He didn't believe there was a chance in hell of that happening. The only way of "working things out" with this woman, as far as he could see, would be total surrender.

He scowled at his watch. "Right now, I've gotta go to work. Just sit tight, okay? Go for a swim, walk on the beach. I'll stop by after my shift, pick you up, take you to dinner— we can talk about it. How's that?"

She just looked at him and didn't reply.

"Joy?" His heart was really pounding. He swore he'd never known anyone who could rile him up the way this woman could. "Promise me you won't do anything crazy on your own until we've had a chance to talk. Okay?"

Her head was tilted and there was a thoughtful and faraway look on her face, as if she were listening to a recording replaying what he'd just said. "All right," she said, nodding.

"*Promise* me."

"I promise."

She seemed suspiciously quiet, damn her. Almost serene.

He glared at her a long, burning time, trying his darnedest to see what was going on inside her head, before he finally grunted, "Okay, see you later," and turned away and left her there, still cradling her mug of cooling coffee.

But as he slid behind the wheel of his truck he felt as though he'd missed something, and there was a cold uneasiness gnawing at his guts.

He didn't believe she'd actually do it. The idea of a landlubber from Georgia by way of New York City without a spec of seagoing experience renting a boat and motoring out into the Gulf of Mexico alone was just plain crazy. Which he was pretty sure Joy wasn't. Her brother Roy had mentioned "ditzy," but he hadn't said "certifiably insane." No, what bothered Scott was that way she had of working around the little realities of life when they happened to get in the way of her plans. What was it she'd said? Something about being good at solving problems?

Yeah, right. *Her* problems, maybe. Somehow, her solutions seemed to have a way of making *his* problems bigger.

It nagged at him all morning, that uneasiness, enough so that at noon, just before he left the station to get himself something to eat, he tried the number at Roy's beach house.

When he got no answer, he told himself Joy must be taking his advice. Most likely she was out having herself a swim or a nice walk on the beach.

He told himself the same thing when he tried the call again after he got back from Eli's Deli with his usual lunch, Eli's famous Italian meatball sub and a large sweet tea, to eat at his desk while he caught up on long overdue paperwork. When he still wasn't getting an answer an hour later, though, he started to feel more than uneasy. If, he thought, she *had* been out there on the beach all that time in the middle of the day, then she was getting a whole helluva lot more sun than was good for somebody with her fair complexion, put it that way.

He had the local telephone book open on his desk and was flipping through the Yellow Pages looking for Boat Rentals when the phone on his desk beeped at him. He picked it up, punched the lit-up button and said, "Yes, sir, this is Cavanaugh."

"Scotty, I wonder if you'd mind steppin' into my office for a minute."

Smiling a little to himself at the deceptively mild and polite manner of the summons, Scott plunked the telephone down on the open phone book to save his place, then walked down the short hallway to Sheriff Johnny Dolittle's office. He knocked, then opened the door in response to the gruff "Come on in," half expecting to see the same assortment of sour-faced feds lining the walls. But the sheriff was alone behind his desk, busily scrawling notes on a memo pad.

"Shut the door and have a seat," Sheriff Dolittle said without looking up, and he went on writing, tearing off each page as he filled it. After several minutes, he threw down the pen he'd been using. A fleeting grimace crossed his face as he leaned back in his chair. "Got a speech at the Rotary Club tomorrow. Damn job's nothin' but politics nowadays. Nothin' but politics..." He straightened back up with a loud *screech* of his swivel chair and leveled a piercing look at Scott across his cluttered desktop.

"Anyway, I thought you might like to know. Just had a call from the feebs. Scotty, what I couldn't tell you yesterday was that they think their surveillance has finally turned up enough on the DelReys to secure an indictment. Enough, anyway, for them to ask for a warrant to search King's Island. Warrant came through about an hour ago. They're goin' in tonight, after dark so as to minimize chances of escape. We've been invited to send somebody to tag along—" his lips curved downward in a sardonic way "—in a backup capacity only, naturally." He paused to contemplate that, then lifted his eyebrows at Scott. "Thought you might just like to be in on it, given your, uh, prior interest in the matter."

"Tonight." The airless wheeze was the only sound Scott could produce.

The sheriff's gaze sharpened. "That a problem for you?"

"No, sir." *Damn.* Why wasn't there any spit in his mouth?

"Okay, then. Staging's at the Coast Guard terminal. There'll be a briefing there at eighteen-hundred hours. I expect you'll wanna be there for that."

"Yes, sir," Scott said, and was on his feet, half expecting to hear a barked *"Dismissed."*

He was heading for the door when the sheriff said, "Oh, and Cavanaugh…" Scott turned to look back and caught his boss's pained expression as he added, "Don't get in anybody's way. The last thing we want is those damn feebs PO'd at us." Scott nodded, and the last thing he heard before he shut the door behind him was a grumbled, "Politics…"

Back at his desk, Scott didn't sit down, but hauled the open Yellow Pages out from under the telephone that had been holding his place and carried it across the room to where Deputy Duffy was buried deeply in a pile of paperwork.

"Hey, Duff," he said as he plunked the phone book down on his desk, "I wonder if you'd do me a favor."

Duffy looked up from the report he was writing to bare his teeth in a mock smile. "Hey, Cavanaugh. Sure, why not? I live to do you favors. I was getting bored with this, anyway.

Sure has been quiet around here today. So, what's up this time?''

''I've got to go check something out. Could you call every listing in here that rents boats—''

''You mean, like, charters?''

''Charters, rentals, whatever. Ask if they've rented *anything* today to a little tiny lady by the name of Starr. If you come up with anything, buzz me on my cell.''

It was just as he'd feared. The beach house was empty. Joy wasn't there and neither was her pocketbook, but other than that, as far as Scott could see, there wasn't anything to tell him where she'd gone or what she might be up to.

He put it down to the distraction of a growing sense of dread in his heart that he was almost out the door before he remembered she didn't have a car. Heart thumping, he turned back, grabbed up the phone and hit the Redial button. After one ring, a raspy female smoker's voice answered.

''Gulf Coast Taxi Service.''

It didn't necessarily mean anything, he told himself as he disconnected a few moments later, after confirming that a cab had indeed made a pickup at that address at approximately ten o'clock that morning. She could be out shopping. Yeah, that's right. Nothing in the cupboards but instant grits, she'd said. Maybe she was buying groceries.

Yeah, right. He had only a couple of seconds to try to convince himself of that before his cell phone began to vibrate against his hip. He unhooked it, squinted at the caller ID and thumbed it on. ''Hey, Duff, whatcha got for me?''

''Had to go all the way to the *S*'s before I hit paydirt, but I think I found what you want. Sea Breeze Charters. That's down on—''

''I know where it is. Go on.''

''Yeah, well, they had a charter booked this morning by a Ms. J. L. Starr. Went out this afternoon, about two o'clock. Shell hunting. Apparently it was just her, nobody else. Big boat, too. That ain't cheap.''

"Yeah," Scott said grimly. He was thinking Joy either had resources she hadn't told him about, or else she was maxing out her credit cards.

So much for promises.

He thanked Duffy for his help, locked up the beach house and a few minutes later was behind the wheel of his on-duty vehicle, streaking down the coast toward the marina where the office of Sea Breeze Charters was located. He didn't turn on the Crown Victoria's siren but the truth was, he did make use of his flashers a time or two.

He knew Sea Breeze, as he did most all his and Roy's competition, pretty well. They were a good outfit, one of the bigger ones advertised on the Internet, had brochures in all the hotels, motels and restaurants in the area. With several boats of different sizes, the array of signs hanging in the windows of their headquarters said they offered Charters Of All Kinds! Big and Small Groups! Gulf and Bay Fishing! Sportfishing! Dolphin Watching! Shell Hunting! All Day, Half Day, Evening and Overnight Charters!

On second thought, he guessed maybe they weren't really competition of his and Roy's one-boat operation, after all.

As Scott walked up to the Sea Breeze headquarters, a tidy little hut painted white with blue trim situated on the landward end of a long pier, he heard the thrum of powerful diesel engines and saw one of the charter company's bigger boats pulling into its slip. He looked hard, but since he didn't see any sign of Joy either on deck or in the cabin, he pushed open the office door and went in.

"Oh, sure," the cheerfully weathered woman with the gray Dutch-boy bob told him when he asked, leaning her elbows on a display case filled with fishing tackle. "Tom and Randy took her out. In fact, looks like that's them comin' in now. Huh. Haven't been out there that long. Wonder why—"

Scott thanked her and was already on his way back out the door. Down on the pier, he waited until the crewman had gotten the boat secured, then showed his badge and was invited on board. The skipper had levered himself down from the bridge to join them, and he didn't look like a happy man. He introduced himself as Tom and his crewman as Randy, then scowled, spat over the side of the boat and said, "I expect you're wantin' to know about that dizzy broad we just took out to King's Island."

"Yep," said Scott, "that'd be her."

The two men, plainly peeved, told him the whole story while they worked at getting the boat tied down and tucked away.

"She said she wanted to go out to the island," Tom said. "I told her it was private property, off limits to tourists, and she said that was okay, she just wanted to get close enough to take a good look at it. Then, we get out there and she wants to know if Randy can take her in the dingy and get in closer."

"It's just a little outboard," Randy explained. "Use it for puttin' shell hunters off onto the islands, you know?"

"Anyway," Tom continued, "I told her we don't go to King's Island. No trespassing. So she asks if she can rent the damn dingy. Says she'll go by herself, at her own risk. Says she'll pay whatever we ask, sign a waiver, whatever it takes. So, I ask her, I say, what's so all-fired important that she needs to get onto that island so bad? And she tells me— I think she was lyin', if you wanna know the truth—but she tells me she's a journalist, a reporter, and she needs a story that'll make her career for her. She's heard about this 'mystery island'—" he made quotation marks in the air with his fingers "—and she's decided this is just the ticket. So…"

"So you're telling me you let her take your dingy?" Scott said ominously. "Alone? Just like that?"

The skipper and his crewman exchanged looks. Randy shrugged and looked puzzled. "Seemed reasonable enough at the time."

"Truth is," Tom said, frowning and scratching his head, "it was awful damn hard to say no to her, for some reason."

"Yeah," Scott said with a sigh. "I know. Believe me."

"She had it all worked out. She filled out the rental agreement and signed the waiver, just like she said she would, and Randy put her in the boat and showed her how to start it, made sure she knew how everything worked. Seemed to know her way around an outboard, anyway. Then she took off for the island. We watched her until she'd disappeared around to the other side.''

''And you just *left* her there?'' Scott couldn't believe what he was hearing. But then again, this was Joy.

''What kind of a guy you think I am?'' Tom said, angry now. ''We were supposed to wait around and pick her up. She said we should give her three, four hours, and if she wasn't back by that time, we should call the police. So, what were we supposed to do? She's the customer, right? She's paid for the whole damn boat. We said fine, we'll wait, and we were hangin' around out there, Randy was doing some trolling to pass the time and along comes the Coast Guard patrol boat and tells us we have to clear the area. What were we gonna do? We told 'em we had somebody on the island and they said we'd have to leave anyway, that they'd be on the lookout for the dingy and see it got in safely. So, we come on in. Coast Guard escorted us pert' near all the way back to the harbor, too, just to see we didn't double back. Damn humiliating,'' he muttered darkly, dumping a coiled rope into a pile and wiping his hands on his pants.

Since he couldn't think of anything else to do, Scott thanked the two boatmen and turned to leave. Randy called out to him as he was hoisting himself onto the dock. He looked back and saw the crewman holding a woman's handbag, lifting it up to him. ''You might as well take her purse with you. I don't think we're gonna be seein' her again.''

As he walked back along the dock with Joy's purse tucked under his arm, Scott was amazed at how calm he felt, now that the thing he'd been dreading so much had finally happened and there wasn't a damn thing he could do about it.

Yeah, so much for promises.

Maybe, he thought, it wasn't that he was calm, so much as just plain *numb*. He couldn't believe how stunned he was,

finding out that Joy had broken her promise to him. Dammit, she hadn't seemed to him like the kind of person who'd do that. Certainly not the kind to look a man in the eyes and out-and-out lie. He figured he must be numb, because he was pretty sure it would have hurt like hell, otherwise.

He was settling behind the wheel of his patrol car with his radio in his hand, getting ready to call in and wondering how in hell he was going to tell the sheriff about this development and being glad he wasn't the one to have to break it to the feds that in all probability there was going to be one more innocent civilian on King's Island than they'd planned on, when it hit him. Joy Starr *wasn't* the kind to look a man in the eyes and lie. Fact was, he realized, she'd taken great care not to.

Don't do anything crazy on your own. Promise me. That's what he'd said to her. And she *had* promised, but only after carefully playing it over again in her mind. And now he could see how, in her mind, she *hadn't* broken her promise to him. She hadn't done anything crazy, and she hadn't gone on her own. She'd hired a reputable charter company to take her to the island, and figured she had them right there as backup in case anything went wrong. As usual, she'd got it all figured out so it made perfect sense. To her.

Scott didn't know which was scarier, the fact that she'd outsmarted him, or the possibility that he was beginning to understand how her mind worked.

Standing in the well of a DEA Zodiac patrol boat rocking gently on a calm, dark swell, wearing full body armor and listening to the creaks, rustles and whispers of other men similarly outfitted as they waited for the order to hit the beaches, Scott thought he might have a little bit of an understanding of what it must have been like for those young soldiers standing off Normandy on the eve of D-Day. Though, almost as soon as the thought came to him, he was ashamed of it. What he was facing now wasn't really anything like what those kids had had to look forward to. At

least, he didn't have any real expectation of dying anytime soon. The waiting was probably the same, though, and the fear…the tension in the muscles and the sick feeling in the belly, even if his dread of an unknown future wasn't for himself, but for someone else he cared about.

The first strike team had left half an hour ago. The team Scott had been assigned to, made up mostly of crime-scene investigators and forensics analysts, would follow as soon as a safe landing site had been secured. In the meantime there was nothing to do but wait and watch, eyes straining to see through the darkness, ears cocked to catch the sounds of distant gunfire. So far, all seemed peaceful, quiet. The target, King's Island, lay low and dark against the backdrop of the mainland at night, only the usual lights burning in the house and around the grounds. There'd been no sign of unusual activity.

And no sign, either, of Joy or the dingy. Coast Guard patrols, Scott had been assured, had been keeping a close watch on the island since early afternoon, and no one had been observed leaving during that time. So far as anyone was able to determine, Joy must still be on the island. The strike team had been informed of that fact and told to be on the lookout. Beyond that, there wasn't anything anyone could do.

In an attempt to suppress his fear, incipient nausea and a whole slew of unthinkable thoughts, Scott had taken to playing the lyrics to really bad songs over and over in his head. Most of which he hadn't even realized were bad until he'd read a newspaper column on the subject by fellow Floridian Dave Barry a while back. He'd worked his way through ''MacArthur Park'' and a couple of his ex-wife's favorite Neil Diamond songs and was trying to remember what came after the bubble sounds in ''Muskrat Love,'' when the team leader, one of the FBI guys, Scott thought, who'd been up in the bow listening to reports coming in on his radio suddenly threw up his hand to signal for everybody's attention.

The restless stirrings died instantly, as if they'd been choked off. The only sound now was the almost cheerful

sounding splash and gurgle of water against the side of the boat.

The team leader muttered into his radio while everyone waited in dead silence, then he nodded and spoke quietly but briskly to the dark shapes gathered around him. "Okay, looks like we're good to go. We'll go in at landing point A. Everybody check your— *What the hell?*"

With every pair of eyes in the boat focused on the speaker, when the first flash came it was a second or so before anyone realized what was happening. Men started, flinched and began to turn, swearing, some loudly, some in whispers, mostly doing what Scott's grandma would have called "takin' the Lord's name in vain." By that time the sound had reached them, not one boom but a whole series of them, like an artillery barrage. The island looked like the scene of a volcanic eruption. Geysers of flame and billowing smoke rose into the sky, which had become a roiling mass of orange, yellow, red and black.

Then, there were no more explosions. In the sudden quiet, men turned temporarily to stone by shock began to move again with grim and silent purpose. Scott felt the Zodiac vibrate beneath his feet and heard the growl of diesel engines.

As the powerful boat sped full-throttle toward the burning island, Scott's mind stopped screaming the name *Joy!* over and over and finally formed a coherent thought: *I was supposed to look out for her. I was supposed to protect her. I'm sorry, Roy. I'm sorry....*

Chapter 10

"They had the whole place booby-trapped. Trip wires set up all the way around the island, not more than ten feet off the beach. Just far enough to let us get off-loaded, then *wham-o*. Set off a chain reaction."

The speaker was the FBI's special agent in charge, whom Scott had last seen wearing a suit and tie and perched on the corner of Sheriff Johnny Dolittle's desk. He looked a little different now, in a black T-shirt, helmet and body armor, with his face blackened and big white letters spelling out FBI across his back. One thing hadn't changed: He still didn't look happy.

The fire was nearly out. It hadn't taken long. The flames had burned quick and hot and by the time the fire department boats arrived on the scene there hadn't been much left to do but cool down the ashes. The huge mansion, which, like the resort, Spanish Keys, had been built to resemble a Moorish palace, was a total loss. Floodlights had been set up at several locations on the beach, and from there black-clad federal agents were spreading cautiously across the island, making certain there were no additional surprises.

"Casualties?" someone asked, and Scott felt pain in his jaw as he waited for the reply.

"Not so far." The FBI man's eyes flicked to Scott, who thought he might have seen a spark of sympathy there, or compassion. "Couple of our guys, the ones that tripped the wires and set off the first explosion got singed pretty bad. They've been airlifted to the hospital, but it looks like they'll be okay. We'll have to wait for daylight to make a thorough search, but right now we're thinking whoever was in residence might have got away clean. Could have gotten away in the confusion and smoke...could have left a week ago. No way of knowing, now."

Standing a little apart on the edges of the circle of light, arms folded on his chest and expression stoic, Scott listened to the FBI man's words and the thought ticked across his mind like the crawl at the bottom of a TV news channel screen: *Okay, there's a chance she's alive. Maybe they found her and took her with them.*

He wondered when it would hit him. He wondered when he'd start to feel again. Maybe, if he was lucky, he never would.

An agent was talking into his shoulder radio. He said something to the special agent in charge, who stopped talking in mid-sentence to listen. Then he looked over at Scott, made a "come here" gesture and at the same time started walking toward him. Scott met him halfway.

"Thought you'd want to know, uh, Deputy—"

"Cavanaugh," Scott supplied. He still couldn't feel anything, not even his own heartbeat.

"Kevin Harvey," said the special agent in charge. "Looks like we may have located the boat your, uh, friend was using."

Wham went Scott's heart, slam-bang up against his ribs. When he could breathe again, he muttered, "Yeah...okay. Where?"

"It's around on the mainland side. There's a boathouse and dock over there, right below the house. It's empty. Whatever boats are normally kept there are gone, but an outboard dingy was found floating under the dock. No sign of your friend, yet. They're still looking. The boathouse is pretty badly damaged and there's a lot of debris in the water—"

"Take me over there," Scott said. "Now."

Agent Harvey looked like he might want to argue with that for about half a second. Then he snapped his mouth shut and gave a nod to one of the dark-clad, helmeted guys standing nearby. This agent—DEA, according to the letters on his back—led Scott to one of the Zodiac landing boats that had been pulled up on the beach. Scott helped him drag it into knee-deep water, then climbed aboard. The DEA agent started up the motor and pointed the bulky craft toward the surf. It rose gracefully over the gentle breakers, like a ballet-dancing hippo, and headed into deeper, quieter water before turning sharply toward the south.

It was the longest boat ride he'd ever taken. He'd never have believed an island barely a mile long and a quarter-mile wide could seem so big. They had to go the long way around, since the northern end where the house had been was still hemmed in by fire department and law enforcement boats. And once they got to the mainland side they had to go slowly, because there was so much debris in the water. Throughout the trip, Scott crouched in the bottom of the Zodiac, staring into a darkness filled with dancing, wavering light and slippery shadows and praying for the numbness to come back.

Dammit, he didn't want to feel, didn't want to think. But where a short while ago his mind had been a blessedly blank screen, now it was alive with images that came and went so fast that he felt overwhelmed and confused. They were like those montages of old movie clips they always play at entertainment awards shows—tantalizing glimpses of scenes and faces that you wish you could see more of but that are gone before you can grasp exactly what it was you saw. And he couldn't seem to turn it off or control it, no matter how hard he tried. Forget bad song lyrics, they were useless now, buried by an avalanche of those bits and pieces of his life. Faces of people he'd known, some well— Beth and Ryan, his parents, sisters, neighbors and friends—some barely at all, remembered from tragedies he'd dealt with on the job. Joy's face—and he didn't even know which category to put her into. Scenes from his marriage, both good and bad, from his childhood, and Ryan's, conversations with his dad, arguments with Beth. Memories, vivid and gut-wrenching, of Joy, making love to her lush, voluptuous, mature woman's body, and then having her fall asleep in his arms as instantly and trustingly as a baby.

He wondered if this was what people meant when they said at the moment when death seemed imminent, that their lives passed before their eyes. Except, why was it *his* life passing before his eyes when it was *Joy's* that was in question? Was it possible the two had become one and the same? Or at least, interchangeable? And if so, when in the hell had that happened?

The closer they got to the end of the island where the house had been, the more the water was filled with floating debris. His DEA escort cut the Zodiac's engines and picked up a paddle, and without waiting to be told, Scott did the same. Up ahead he could see the outline of the dock jutting out over the water, and under and around it, and on the shore nearby, flashlights flaring and winking and wobbling like a convention of inebriated fireflies. They glided closer to the activity, Scott in the bow pushing charred pieces of wood and tree branches out of the way, while the DEA man propelled the Zodiac silently through the oily, undulating water. As they slid in under the dock, bumping up against a second Zodiac that was already tied to one of the pilings, a dark shape up on the bank hunkered down and a flashlight's beam stabbed through the night.

"Any sign of survivors?" the DEA man with Scott called

in a hoarse whisper, and the man on the bank replied the same way, "Nothing yet."

A surge of unexplained anger rose up in Scott like gorge, and he didn't even try to stop it. "What the hell are you guys whispering for?" he said loudly. "Anybody think about hollerin' out? Maybe calling her name?" There was a moment of dead silence. Scott was already standing up in the Zodiac, one hand braced against a piling, the other cupped around his mouth like a megaphone.

"Joy!" he bellowed. And again, raspy with urgency and hope, "Joy! Can you hear me?" And he looked up into the dark sky, vibrating with tension and praying for a miracle.

Incredibly, it came, not from on high but in the form of a small, tremulous voice from somewhere not far away. *"Scott?"*

"Joy?" It took all the strength he had to keep from wrapping his arms around the piling and breaking into hysterical laughter. Holding his breath, he heard distant sounds that might have been laughter, too, or sobs. "Where in the hell are you?"

He was already using the pilings as leverage, pushing the Zodiac deeper under the pier, when he heard, "Back here…in the boathouse. Or I guess that would be…*under* it."

He still didn't know whether to laugh or cry. "Are you okay? Can you get out of there?"

"I don't think so…."

Jeez. "Are you hurt?" The DEA man shoved a high-powered flashlight into his hand, and he turned its beam into the chaotic darkness at the back of the pier where the boathouse had been. He saw a confusing wilderness of fallen beams and roofing materials, but no sign of Joy.

After what seemed an eternity, he heard, "No, just…a little stuck." She sounded not hurt or scared, but *peeved.*

"Okay, that's all right, stay put. We're coming to get you." And he put his hand over his eyes and finally did give in to laughter, silent and sweet and gently relieving. She'd sounded so much like Joy, the Joy he was coming to know and, God help him, love.

It took half an hour and the combined efforts of the FBI, DEA, ATF and a local fire department crew to free Joy from the wreckage of the DelRey's elaborate boathouse. But in the end it was Scott's hand she took to guide her across the last few yards of exposed cinder-block foundation and onto the safety of the pier. She was shivering and shaking in spite of the warm, humid night. One of the fire department guys gave him a blanket to put around her, and then he wrapped his arms around her, too, and stood there on that pier in the blue-white glare of floodlights and held her.

"I knew you'd come," she said, and her voice was cracked and bumpy with her shivers. "I *knew* you'd come."

"Joy..." *His* voice hurt his throat. "My God, what were you thinking? I can't even—" And then, before she could answer that one, he pulled back so he could look down at her face, ghostly and smudged in the artificial light. "I thought you were dead. Why didn't you call out? When you heard people moving around out here? You must have known they were looking for you."

"Well, yes, I did." He heard a loud sniff, and she swiped a hand across her face. "I just didn't know *why* they were looking for me. I mean, it was dark and I couldn't tell who they were." Her voice had that disgruntled tone again. "The last bunch of people out here looking for me were wearing frogman suits and looked like terrorists."

"Come again?"

"Oh, yeah—" she sniffed again and pulled the blanket tighter around herself "—and they almost caught me, too. There were four of them. Thank goodness I heard them coming and hid in the boathouse. They found the dingy and were starting to look for me, but then one of them said something to the other three, and they all went running down to the end of the dock. I guess they had their equipment with them, because even though it was getting fairly dark by then, I could see them putting stuff on. Then they all jumped into the water and…left. I thought maybe the agents were them coming back after the blast. I'm sorry. How was I supposed to know?''

There was a pause, and she made another swipe at her face with her hand. He could see her looking up at him, her expression impossible to read in the shadowless light.

Then she whispered, ''Did you really think I was dead?''

''Yeah. It did cross my mind.'' And just like that he was angry with her, as angry as he'd been at anybody in a long time. Or maybe it was himself he was mad at, because he'd never meant to let himself care that much about anybody ever again.

But either way, he didn't want to get into it right now, with himself *or* her, so he did what he usually did when his personal feelings threatened to get out of hand. He retreated behind his emotional cop armor.

Exhaling, he said gruffly, ''Anyway, you're not. Sounds like you've got one helluva story to tell, though, and believe me, there are gonna be a lot of people interested in hearing it, so maybe you'd better save it for them. There're gonna be a lot of questions, and I know you're gonna have a lot of answers. Right up your alley.''

Taking her arm in a gentle but firm grip, he began to steer her back toward the wood steps that led down to the waiting boats. She looked over at him but didn't say anything, maybe sensing his mood from his voice. Which made him feel lousier than ever.

Apparently no longer in need of it, she took the blanket from around herself as they walked and folded it over her arm. He was unable to keep himself from looking over at her, maybe to reassure himself that she was really there and all in one piece. And so he got a good look, for the first time, at what she was wearing. Tan slacks and a blouse with a nineteen-thirties look about them, rumpled and sooty, now, the pants with a tear in one knee. A black button-up-type sweater over her shoulders—one shoulder, now, skewed halfway around and hanging by a single button fastened at the throat. And firmly on her head, covering most of her hair, a dark green beret.

"What the hell's this?" He let go of her arm and brushed the beret with his knuckle. "Don't tell me—"

"It's not what you're thinking," she said, glancing at him and quickly away, as if he'd embarrassed her. Smudges of soot on her face made her look like a guilty street urchin.

"No? If not John Wayne, then who?"

"Promise you won't laugh?"

"Trust me."

"I, um…it seemed like something Nancy Drew might wear."

So, of course he laughed. What else could he do? That was Joy, he thought. Always had an explanation for everything.

She'd known right away something was wrong. She'd been told about the security. Scott had warned her, and so had Tom and Randy, those two nice men who'd taken her back to the island, when they'd put her in the dingy. "Watch out for those security guys," Randy had told her. "I think they'd just as soon shoot as look at you. Ask questions later."

So, where were they? As she'd approached the island, her heart had been pounding. She'd expected to hear alarms and sirens, bringing heavily armed security guards on the run to warn her with drawn weapons and bull horns to stay clear. Instead, she saw signs on the sand dunes that said, Private— No Trespassing, but no signs of life.

Abandoning her idea of drifting onto the beach and "allowing" herself to be taken into custody, she'd motored on around to the lee side of the island. Still not a soul to be seen, though she'd wondered whether hostile eyes might be watching her from the shelter of the groves of palmetto and pine that fronted the water there. She'd kept going, growing more and more uneasy by the minute, until she'd come to a boathouse and pier. Surely here, she'd thought, someone would come to prevent her from landing, or at least to question her business. But there had been nothing. No one. It just hadn't seemed right.

That's what she told them, the solemn-faced men from the FBI and the DEA and the ATF that had gathered in the stark and brightly lit Coast Guard terminal office to hear her story. And Scott, too, of course, standing in the back near the door, leaning against the wall with his arms folded on his chest, watching her with a dark and somber frown.

Actually, she told them all that so they would think her reservations had been based on reason and the evidence of her senses. But in fact, she'd only put the evidence together later, during the hours she'd crouched, terrified, in the rafters underneath the boathouse, thinking of all the reasons she should never have set foot on that damn pier. At the time, there'd only been that *feeling,* nothing so clear and specific as what had happened to her in her apartment, this time, just a scalp-prickling, skin-tingling, heart-thumping prescience of danger. And as before, she chose now not to include any mention of it in her accounting to law enforcement personnel. She was pretty sure that like nice Sargent what's-his-name back in New York, the men gathered around her in that room wouldn't understand about her "feelings."

Would Scott? She'd told him about the *feeling* in New York, and he hadn't ridiculed her then, but that didn't mean he hadn't *thought* she was being ridiculous deep down in his heart. She realized that except for a brief flash of something now and then, she *never* knew what Scott was thinking or how he really felt about things, her, especially, deep down inside. Right now, for instance. Was he disappointed in her? Mad at her? Embarrassed or concerned for her? How would she ever know? When she'd first met him, she remembered, he'd reminded her of a giant teddy bear. It occurred to her now that his calm, easygoing, reasonable manner was like a teddy bear's warm furry exterior—nice and cozy to cuddle up to, but it kept you from seeing what was inside.

Joy rarely felt self-conscious, but she'd never felt so exposed, so alone or so foolish as she did sitting there in a straight, hard chair, wrapped in a blanket on a hot Florida night because her clothes were wet and the air-conditioning was going full blast, drinking vending machine coffee and wishing for a beer instead. Oh, how she wished she could be someplace dark and private and alone—well, okay, alone except for Scott. Yes, definitely, Scott would be there. Preferably holding her, kissing her...making love to her.

It's just sex....

Except, it hadn't been. Just sex. Last night. She knew that now. She'd known it then but had been too afraid to admit it. And now, most likely, it was too late. He was mad at her, definitely. Of course he was. *And* ashamed and embarrassed. Concerned a little, too, naturally, because he was a police officer and a caring person and he'd promised Roy he'd look after her.

"So, what happened then? Did you go up onto the pier?"

"What? Oh, well, yes, of course I did. I'd come that far...."

You've come this far, she'd told herself. *You can't go back now without at least trying to see whether Yancy's here or not.* So, she'd tied up the dingy and climbed the steps to the pier. She'd walked up the pier, trying to look as if she had every right to be there, in case someone was watching, but no one came to challenge her. She'd tried the boathouse door, but it was locked, so she'd gone all around the land sides, looking in the windows. It had looked quite nice and comfortable inside, she'd thought, with what appeared to be a recreation area with couches, and even a small kitchen. She'd seen a telephone on the wall, and a television set, and she'd wondered if maybe that was where the security guards slept. Except...where were they?

Then she'd heard something. Men's voices. Furtive rustlings. Not wanting to be found snooping and peeking in windows, she'd scampered as fast as she could around to the pier, hoping to make it back to the dingy before she was discovered so that her original story would have some chance of holding up. Instead, she'd barely had time to duck inside the open-to-the-water boat storage part of the boathouse before four men had come into view. They'd been dressed in black from head to toe. Later, she'd realized they were wearing wetsuits. Perched on a narrow catwalk, she'd watched, then waited while the men moved slowly through the woods close to the shore, passed behind the boathouse and continued on around the northern tip of the island. It had taken them forever—hours, it seemed. They'd been laying some sort of wire, pausing every so often to do something she couldn't see, then continuing on, unrolling the wire, reeling it out, then stopping again. She hadn't known what they were doing, but it had seemed secretive...sinister.

She didn't tell the men from the FBI, the DEA and the ATF about the strange sense of darkness that had come over her then. The sense of, for want of a better word, *evil.* Or that that was when she'd known for sure that she'd stumbled into something way over her head and had begun to be truly afraid.

She did tell them, though, how she'd been afraid to try to make it back to the dingy after that, for fear the men would see her leaving and know she'd seen them doing...whatever it was they were doing. Letting them know she'd seen them, she felt, would be very bad. She'd remembered instructing Tom and Randy to call the police if she hadn't returned in four hours, and had decided to sit tight and wait for help to arrive.

Except...it hadn't. Hours passed, the sun went down, and it began to get dark, and she'd been just about to take a chance on the dingy again, thinking she might be able to slip away in the dusk, when suddenly, there were the men in black again. Running, this time, not in urgency, but with purpose. They'd run past the boathouse and onto the pier, and that was when one of them had spotted the dingy tied up at the bottom of the steps. There'd been several frantic minutes while the men had looked for her, while she'd crouched in the shadows and prayed, knowing if anyone had a flashlight and thought to shine it into the boathouse, she'd almost certainly be found. Then one of the men had signaled to the others, there'd been a brief discussion, and they'd all run down to the far end of the pier, put on their gear and disappeared over the side.

Thoroughly scared by then, Joy had again considered getting back into the dingy—anything to get off that island. Except now those mysterious men were out *there* somewhere in that vast, dark sea. And she'd be alone in a tiny dingy, with nobody to rendezvous with, since surely by now the charter boat, and Tom and Randy, would have given up and gone back to port. Once again, she'd decided she had no choice but to wait for rescue.

She didn't tell the men from the FBI, the DEA and the ATF that it was Scott she'd waited for. That she'd been sure *he'd* come for her. She'd *known* he would.

She did tell them that when it got good and dark, she'd been thinking seriously about breaking a window in the living area part of the boathouse and using the telephone to call for help. She'd decided not to, though, because so far, all she'd been guilty of was trespassing, and she hadn't wanted to add breaking and entering to her rap sheet. Which, as it turned out, probably saved her life.

It began as a series of tremendous explosions, starting some distance away and coming closer—*boom-boom-boom-boom*—one after another. She'd flattened herself on the catwalk that ran along the top of the cinder-block wall that enclosed the boat garage and covered her head with her arms and prayed while the world blew apart and the boathouse disintegrated around her. And after that...

"Okay, that's it. That's enough for tonight."

It was Scott's voice, in a tone she'd never heard him use before—quiet, as always, but edgy and sharp with authority. Her head came up and she watched him come toward her, making his way through the casual assembly of federal agents, some standing, some perched on chairs or leaning against walls or desktops. They shifted to give him room, and his hand found her elbow under the shapeless blanket.

"Come on," he said, his voice low and grating. "I'm taking you home now."

The agent who'd been sitting on the corner of the desk nearest her, the one who'd been asking the questions and who seemed to be in charge, gave a short nod and rose to his feet. "Okay, Cavanaugh, she's all yours for now. We're gonna need to ask her some more questions later on, of course, but right now, just take her home and see she gets some rest."

"And some food. I'm 'bout to starve to death," Joy muttered under her breath as Scott guided her through the door and out into the warm, humid night.

"Serves you right," he said, sounding as if he were gritting his teeth.

He hustled her quickly along a sidewalk to the brightly lit parking lot, which glistened with moisture at that hour—the dark of the morning. The lights were haloed with a fine thin fog that had settled onto the parked cars, making them look as if they were encrusted with jewels. It was quiet, but not still. A ghost of a breeze made the boats in the harbor rustle and creak, and from far out in the darkness came the deep purring of a night-fishing boat heading into port.

Feeling suddenly lonely and a little foresaken, Joy tried to look at the man looming beside her, veering away from him slightly so she could see past the bulk of his chest and shoulder, but he hauled her right back close to him like a misbehaving child, so forcefully that her breath caught and her heartbeat stumbled. She opened her mouth to protest, then closed it and swallowed whatever it was she might have been about to say.

What *could* she say? She didn't even know how she *felt*. Her feelings, as near as she could tell, were a confused mixture of guilt—*I shouldn't have done what I did, he has every right to be angry!* and longing—*But I don't want him to be angry with me. Please, Scott, don't be angry with me!* and righteous indignation—*I'm a grown woman. I did what I thought was right. He has no right to treat me like a child!*

Yes, she felt all that, but what she was most right then was tired. Hungry. Exhausted. Drained. And maybe what she wanted most of all, for just that moment, *was* to be treated like a child. To be held close and comforted, fed and protected. And loved, in *spite* of what she'd done.

Chapter 11

Scott didn't say anything to her, even when they got to his truck, although he did open the door and help her into the passenger seat, being careful to gather up the trailing ends of her blanket and tuck them around her feet before he closed the door. Joy rode beside him in wounded silence, desperately wishing she could go to sleep but too miserable and hungry and uncomfortable even to doze.

It wasn't until they got back to town and she realized Scott hadn't taken the turnoff for the beach that she summoned the courage to break the impasse. After shifting around and clearing her throat, she ventured, "Where are we going?"

He had to clear his throat, too, it seemed, before replying, "I'm taking you home. To my place."

"Why? I thought—"

"I need to feed you. Nothing's open and you told me there wasn't anything to eat at Roy's place but instant grits."

She gazed at his profile, which sort of reminded her of the "Night on Bald Mountain" segment of Disney's *Fantasia*. She thought about telling him she might have exaggerated a *wee* bit about the food situation at the beach house—she'd been subsisting fairly well for the last several days on Roy's selection of canned goods—but since having someone feed and take care of her was exactly what she'd been longing for, she caught a quick, shallow breath and murmured, "Okay."

Then she discovered as she was getting out of the pickup that she'd developed an annoying case of the shakes. Not that she'd have said anything to Scott about it, of course, and he went ahead of her to unlock his front door while she toiled gamely up the steps with the blanket still draped around her, mostly across her shoulders like a refugee in an oversize shawl. Then he turned and saw her, and the next thing she knew he was scooping her up, not gallantly or romantically, but in an offhand way, as if she were a toy or a garden tool somebody had forgotten to put away.

He deposited her just inside the door and went on to the kitchen, turning on lights on the way. Joy dropped the blanket on the couch and followed him, remembering the last time she'd been there and had done exactly the same thing. Remembering everything that had come after that, culminating with his lifting her onto the cool tile counter and kissing her senseless. Tired as she was, sensory memories were zinging around in her head and everywhere under her skin, reprising everything from the chilly caress of the tile on her bottom and the hot and vibrant press of hard muscle between her thighs, to his mouth expertly making lip and tongue sandwiches with hers.

Shaky for more than one reason now, she stepped into the bright kitchen and just like last time, found him in front of the open refrigerator, taking things out and setting them on the counter.

And just like the last time, he plainly wasn't happy with her, throwing her a dispassionate glance as he quietly said, "You'd best get out of those wet clothes."

Choosing to ignore that, she tried to court him with her smile. "I don't suppose you'd have any beer in there?"

But she could see he wasn't going to forgive her so easily. He continued to look at her, but his eyes were veiled and he didn't return the smile.

"No. Go take a shower. I'll fix you something to eat."

Okay, she thought, *be* that way. But it was a dismal attempt at bravado, and instead of annoyed what she really felt was chilled and rejected and lonely. She pulled off her beret and frowned at it.

"I don't have any clothes to put on...."

She could hear him let out a careful breath as, with an air of patience sorely tried, he placed an egg carton and a wedge of cheese on the counter, then took her by the arm and walked her into what was obviously Ryan's room. He opened a dresser and took out a folded T-shirt and a pair of shorts.

"Here," he said, "will these do?"

"The shirt's fine," Joy said, looking down at herself as she held it in front of her. Like all kids, Ryan obviously liked his oversize. The shorts were another matter. She measured them briefly against her waist and handed them back, shaking her head. "I may be as short as a fourteen-year-old boy," she said with a wry smile, "but somebody forgot to tell my hips."

He turned abruptly, before her conscious mind could interpret the expression that had flashed across his sun-darkened face. But something, an instinct, some sense tuned only to *him* picked it up anyway and broadcast it to every nerve cell in her body. She stood where she was, humming, sizzling with sensual awareness, while Scott ducked out of the room with a muttered comment she couldn't understand. A moment later he was back, thrusting a pair of shorts at her. Flannel boxers, she noted as she took them: Black Watch plaid.

"See if those fit you any better," he said, and his voice was a growl. He hesitated, frowning and running a hand through his hair, then muttered, "Towels are in the cupboard to the left of the sink. If there's anything you need... shampoo...just help yourself." And he left her.

Understanding came in a little spurt of warmth. *He's not used to this, having a woman here.* With the thought came an unexpected and undecipherable wave of tenderness. Or possibly, just exhaustion; Scott seemed to have gone and taken her physical strength and support with him. She felt light-headed and clammy and a had strange urge to cry that as far as she could tell didn't have anything to do with emotions.

Maybe everything will make sense when I'm not so tired, she told herself. *Maybe I'll be able to figure all this out tomorrow.* And then she wobbled into the bathroom and concentrated on forcing her unwilling fingers to manipulate doors and faucets and buttons and zippers.

If she wasn't so tired, she'd have liked Scott's bathroom. It was reasonably clean and had the usual facilities—sink, toilet and shower. It also had a big old-fashioned tub, the kind with claw-shaped feet. Joy hadn't seen one in years, and she'd have loved to fill this one with water up to her chin and have a good long soak, but since she was afraid she'd fall asleep and drown if she did, she gave it a longing look and turned on the shower.

Joy came into the kitchen looking tousled and flushed and sleepy, like a small child. Except there wasn't anything remotely childlike about the fact that she was wearing a T-shirt that Scott could clearly see had no bra underneath it and he was pretty sure there were no panties under those boxer shorts he'd lent her, either. Scowling darkly, he pushed a cup of soup in her direction and the thoughts from his mind, the former with considerably more success than the latter.

"Here," he ordered. "You can start with this while I'm making the omelette." Then, as he watched her wander off toward the table like a lost stray puppy, his exasperation with her evaporated, and all he could think about was how terrible it had been when he'd thought she might be dead.

He went over and pulled out a chair for her, then guided her into it and hitched it close to the table, and while he was doing that her scent drifted up and invaded his senses—not roses, this time, just warm, clean woman—and filled his mind with memories and his body with heat and he recalled with vivid clarity what it had felt like to be drunk.

"Drink," he said harshly, moving the mug of soup close to her and folding her hands around it. He went back to the stove and began to beat the hell out of some innocent and undeserving eggs in order to clear disturbing images from his head.

When he carried the omelette to the table, steaming on its blue plastic plate, he thought at first she hadn't moved a muscle since he'd left her. But most of the soup was gone and she looked up when he set the plate in front of her and gave him a sleepy smile. Then she sat and looked at the omelette, and since he thought it seemed likely she might go on doing so indefinitely, he gave a sigh, sat down across from her and picked up the fork. He cut off a piece of omelette that was oozing melted cheese, stabbed it with the fork, blew on it to cool it, then held it to her lips and said, "Okay, open up…" And to his surprise, she did.

He watched the bite of omelette disappear between her soft pink lips and her lashes flutter and her eyes widen and her throat ripple as she chewed and swallowed and he felt saliva pool in the back of his own mouth.

"Good girl," he murmured, and concentrated on cutting off another bite.

"You should eat some of this," she said after the third one, sending an unfocused golden gaze up at him from under her lashes. "You must be just as tired and hungry as I am. After all, you've been—"

"Don't worry about me," he said, growling at her again, and he was sorry when he saw her flush. He didn't want to be touched by her concern for his welfare, but he was.

"Scott, I'm so sorry I caused you…everyone so much trouble. I really am." She frowned, shaking her head at the bite he was offering as she leaned toward him. "I'd never have gone out there to the island if I'd known—"

"I told you," he said, working so hard at keeping himself under control and his voice calm and quiet that he felt as if his jaw had been wired together. "I told you to stay away from the island. I told you the DelReys were being investigated by the feebs. I told you—"

"Yes, but you didn't tell me they were going to—"

"I didn't tell you because I *couldn't*. I didn't know myself they were going in until yesterday afternoon, after you'd already gone off on your own harebrained mission, when I'd expressly told you not to, and even if I had known, I couldn't have told you about it. *Dammit,* Joy."

He dropped the forkful of eggs he was holding on to the plate and leaned back, rubbing a hand over his face in sheer exasperation. With himself as much as her. He hadn't meant to, hadn't wanted to get into this now, tonight, when they were both so tired and probably still a bit in shock. But even though his eyes were burning in their sockets, once they'd started he couldn't seem to stop the words, the questions that had been piling up in him all day and all that long, terrible night.

"What is it with you? Why do you care so much about this...this *girl* that you'd go and do something so god-awful stupid and dangerous? And don't go giving me that 'She's my friend' crap. The Bible and 'Greater love hath no man' to the contrary, most people don't go around laying down their lives for their friends, except maybe in spur-of-the-moment circumstances like jumping into a raging river or running into a burning building. But you—you've been on a campaign to find this girl and bring her back home even if it kills you. And you're like a pit bull, you just aren't gonna give up, are you? No matter how little likelihood there is you'll succeed. Tell me why, dammit. I really want to know."

Through all that, she sat and watched him, owlish with exhaustion. When he'd finished and was waiting like a sentencing judge for her reply and not really expecting one, she first hesitated, then finally spoke, slurring her words a little.

"I'm just so tired. I mean, of losing people. People I love."

"Losing people?" He scowled at her, on the verge of losing himself. "Like—"

She spoke slowly, as if she were adding them up as she went along. "First, there was Daddy. Then…my husbands. Not that they died, but I did lose them, and divorce is almost worse because you lose so much along with him—your home, your friends, his family, your lifestyle. And you might not think so, but I did love them, even Zack, before he hit me."

She pushed clumsily away from the table and rose, mumbling "s'cuse me" as she stumbled from the room.

Scott caught up with her in the living room, where she was looking as if she'd lost her way in a strange city. She didn't protest when he picked her up and carried her into his bedroom, or when he pulled back the blankets and laid her down between his relatively clean sheets. Her eyes were closed, and she gave an uneven sigh and curled on her side with one hand under her cheek, facing toward him.

He stood and watched her for a moment, aching with feelings he didn't want to feel, heavy with thoughts he couldn't allow himself to think. Believing she was asleep, he put out his hand and lifted a lock of damp hair away from her cheek. He tucked it behind her ear and it slipped through his fingers like silk.

He was leaning down to kiss her, just to brush her temple with his lips, when he heard her whisper, "And my babies…my precious little babies." He saw that her lashes were wet and that a tear had begun to trickle across the bridge of her nose.

The heavy weight inside him burst and spread, stinging through every part of him, and he straightened, careful not to breathe or make a sound and left her as quickly as he could. Out in the living room he sank onto the couch, let his breath out in a gust and rubbed a hand shakily across his eyes and back over his hair. His only thought was: *Ditzy? My God…my God.*

* * *

The telephone woke him. He was disoriented at first, finding himself on his own couch, covered by a blanket that smelled faintly of smoke and the sea. Then he remembered. Joy was in his bed, wearing nothing but a pair of his boxers and one of Ryan's old T-shirts. At least he'd had the good sense not to share it with her.

It was broad daylight. He'd overslept—unheard of, for him, and he was swearing as he fought clear of the blanket and the couch and picked up the phone just as the answering machine was kicking in.

"Cavanaugh," he said, but it came out an unintelligible gargle, so he hawked and coughed and cleared his throat and repeated it just to make sure, squinting past the phone at the omelette mess from earlier this morning that was still decorating his stove, sink and countertops.

A vaguely familiar voice said, "Yeah, this is Kevin Harvey."

And Scott thought, *Who?* before he remembered, *Oh yeah, FBI Special Agent in Charge Harvey.*

"Sorry to get you up," the FBI man said, sounding as if he hadn't been to bed yet, "but I thought you'd want to know. I'm out here at the King's Island site. Uh, looks like we've got fatalities. Two, so far."

Scott swore and scrubbed a hand over his eyes. A pulse had begun to thump heavily in his belly. "Any idea who?"

"At this point, impossible to tell. From the condition of the bodies it's gonna take dental records or DNA for a positive ID. There's something else I think you might want to take a look at, though."

"Yeah?" said Scott. He felt sick to his stomach. Something in the FBI agent's voice…

There was a pause, and then Agent Harvey said, "You've got the Lavigne girl's friend there with you, right?"

"Yeah. Still sleeping, though."

"Okay, well, I'd rather not get into this over the phone,

anyway. How soon can you get out here?'' Scott was trying to get his caffeine-deprived brain around the logistics when the FBI agent added, ''Or listen, why don't I meet you at Coast Guard headquarters. Say, in an hour?''

''I'll be there,'' Scott said grimly.

He was hanging up the phone when he heard a yawning voice say, ''Who was that?''

He jerked around, full of heart-thumping, hollow-in-the-belly dread, in time to watch Joy come into his kitchen as if that was something she did every day of her life. And looking a whole lot better than any forty-something-year-old woman who'd survived an explosion and been trapped in a blown-up boathouse most of the night had any right to look.

As a way of avoiding her eyes and giving his hands something to do that didn't involve touching her, he picked up the coffeepot and turned to the sink. ''Work,'' he said as he turned on the water, and since it sounded like something a frog might offer in the way of conversation, he cleared his throat and added, ''Afraid I'm gonna have to leave for a while. You be okay here until I get back?''

''Sure.''

She came to stand beside him, and his skin sizzled and his insides jumped at her nearness. Or maybe it was guilt, because he was keeping the news of those two fatalities from her. But he sure as hell wasn't going to tell her anything until he was sure. Later was soon enough to break her heart.

''Or,'' she went on, ''I can get myself back to Roy's. You don't have to take me. I can always—''

''—call a cab. Yeah, I know. Forget it. I shouldn't be gone that long. If you don't mind hanging out here…'' He didn't know why, exactly, but he wanted her *here* when he broke the bad news. Here, in his house, among his stuff, where he could comfort and take care of her.

''I don't mind,'' she said softly, and then, reaching for the water-filled pot he was holding in his hands, added, ''Here, I can do that for you, if you want to take a shower.''

He surrendered the pot to her, simply because being that close to her and not putting his arms around her was turning his muscles to jelly. "Thanks, but I don't really have time." He turned to the cupboard, got out the can of coffee and put it on the counter, then opened the drawer where he kept the filters. "And right now, coffee's got a higher priority than being clean."

"I can imagine." Her voice was low, her face turned away from him. She counted spoonfuls of coffee into the basket, returned the can to the cupboard, poured water into the coffeemaker's reservoir, flipped the "on" switch, then stood back and looked up at him through her lashes. "You shouldn't have given me your bed. I could have slept on the couch. I meant to." Her brow furrowed, and her gaze slid away from him. "I distinctly remember heading in that direction...."

"You were asleep on your feet. I picked you up. What was I gonna do? You think I could have slept in the bed, knowing you were on the damn couch?"

"I could have slept in Ryan's room."

"No, you couldn't. No telling when those sheets of his were last washed."

She didn't say anything for a minute, just looked at him with those soft brown eyes of hers reminding him of something warm and rich and sweet, like maple syrup.

"You could have shared the bed with me. It's not like you haven't before."

Then it was his turn for silence and looking at her, while his eyes burned and memories of the last time they'd shared a bed careened through his mind. And from the flush on her cheeks, through hers, too.

"All the more reason why I didn't this time," he said with gravel in his voice. "After everything you'd been through... as tired as you were." He jerked his head toward the table, still littered with the remains of the meal she hadn't eaten. "You damn near passed out in your plate."

Her eyes flicked toward the table, then back to his. "You fixed me an omelette, I remember. Thank you."

"You're welcome."

"You could have just…held me."

He raised his voice as the coffeemaker launched itself into its noisy finale. "Yeah, and how much sleep do you think I'd have got? Hell, I was better off on the couch."

He got out mugs and asked Joy how she took her coffee. She told him cream and sugar, which for some reason seemed just right to him, so he poured some milk into a glass and some sugar into a cereal bowl and got a spoon out of the drawer and left her to fix hers the way she liked it while he poured a cup straight for himself. He took the first sip leaning against the counter and gave a nod of approval. She'd made it strong. He could feel the caffeine hit his veins and take off running.

"Good coffee," he said.

She sipped hers, murmured, "Thanks," with lashes veiling her eyes, then set her cup on the counter and began to gather up things from last night's meal and put them in the sink.

He watched her, wondering why she seemed awkward with him now when she'd always seemed so comfortable in his company before. Comfortable, he realized, in her own skin. Which was one of the things he found most attractive about her.

"You don't have to do that," he said, and she looked at him in surprise.

"Of course I do. Do you really think I'd sit here all day while you go off to work and *not* clean up the dishes? Especially after you cooked for me?"

"I made you an omelette. Big deal."

"And soup." She shook water from her hands and turned from the sink, folding her arms across her waist as she looked at him—through her lashes, naturally. "You were very kind to me last night, Scott, considering… I just want you to know—"

"You think I did what I did out of *kindness?*" He didn't

know whether he was about to laugh or get mad, but considering the night he'd had, getting mad seemed like the one to bet on.

Her gaze didn't waver. "I know how angry you were with me. Please don't try to tell me you weren't."

"I wouldn't dream of it." But oddly enough mad was fading fast, although so was laughter, while tenderness, a definite dark horse, was moving up on the outside. "I was pretty ticked off at you for a while."

"You had—*have*—every right to be." Her lips twitched with a lurking smile. "I'm just surprised it wasn't worse. You've been so patient. I'm sure you were overdue for a classic Taurean temper fit."

He almost choked on his coffee. Tenderness dropped back, out of the running. "A *what?*"

Her eyes widened. "You are a Taurus, aren't you? Oh, please don't tell me you're not. Come on, when's your birthday?"

"May the eleventh," he muttered, glowering at her across the rim of his coffee cup.

She beamed back at him. "You see? You really are *such* a Taurus. I couldn't possibly have been wrong about that." Her smile wavered, then vanished, and she was fidgety and uncomfortable again, her eyes looking for a place to rest. "Anyway, I know how angry you were, and trying to understand. I…remember you asked me why it was so important to me, finding Yancy. I think I said some things— I didn't mean to sound maudlin, or dramatic—"

"You weren't. You told me it was about losing people," he said roughly, carrying his cup to the sink while she jerked awkwardly to one side, out of his way. "Which I can understand. You said you were tired of it. First, your dad, then the husbands—not that they'd died, but in the divorces. You said most people don't know how painful divorce is. Unless they've been through it." *And the babies. You told me about them, too. Why did you do that?*

She was trying to smile. "I guess I don't have to tell you about that."

"Actually," he said evenly, watching his hands while he rinsed out his cup and placed it in the drainer, "like I told you, my divorce was fairly painless." And he turned away from her so she wouldn't see his face, because he knew if she did, she was bound to know he'd lied. Damn her, she'd probably know anyway. She seemed to know everything there was to know about him. *Taurus—hah!*

"Well, gotta go," he said with forced brightness. "See you later, okay? Shouldn't be more than two, three hours."

She nodded, and he walked away and left her there, holding her coffee cup and gazing across it at nothing.

Driving down to the Coast Guard terminal, the lie he'd told her played over and over in his mind, like part of a really bad song that had gotten stuck there. *My divorce was fairly painless…painless…painless.*

Painless? That was what he'd told himself and everybody else, all these years. Maybe he'd even believed it. Then along had come Joy, with her warmth and her smile and her golden eyes that could see right through him, telling him divorce was *hell,* divorce was *loss,* divorce was *frightening.* Not to mention wrenching and painful and unbelievably sad. And he'd known she was right.

It helps that mine wasn't personal. Yeah, he'd told her that, and himself, too. But who was he kidding? It *was* personal. Damn right it was. Okay, Beth didn't want to be married to a cop, but a cop was *who he was.* It was all he'd ever wanted to be from the time he was a little kid. He'd wanted to help people, protect them from bad guys, catch the bad guys and lock them up so they couldn't hurt people anymore. He'd been proud to be able to do that, to actually become what he'd dreamed of being. He'd felt good about himself for what he was doing and for who he was.

And Beth hadn't wanted him. Simple as that. Hadn't wanted to be married to him, anyway, which amounted to the same thing. And that had hurt. It had hurt a *lot.*

Now, he wondered if that was why he hadn't been able to let go of her, or force her to let go of him. Why he put up with her calling him all the time, asking him to do things for her and fix things, making demands. Was it because unconsciously he was hoping to change her mind? Figuring if he did everything she asked him to, she'd have to see she'd made a mistake? That he was somebody worthwhile, after all? Even if he *was* a cop.

Was that what he'd been doing? The thought made him feel a little sick, mainly because he was afraid it might be true. And if it was, what on God's green earth was he hoping to accomplish, really? Did he want Beth back? He thought about it, thought about Joy, and decided the answer was a resounding *no*. He definitely did not want back in his marriage, but maybe…maybe what he did want was a little bit of *Beth, eat your heart out.*

That thought, childish as it was, actually made him smile. *Yeah, I'm a great guy, Beth, and you let me go. So eat your heart out.* It was vanity, ego and probably just human nature. He thought he could forgive himself for that.

Half an hour later, though, he wasn't smiling, and forgiveness of any kind was a long way from his mind. He was squatting, balanced on one knee, beside a sheet on the floor of the storage room at the Coast Guard station that was serving as a temporary makeshift crime lab, watching Agent Kevin Harvey carefully poke with a pair of tweezers among the scorched and barely recognizable items spread out there.

The FBI man turned over a plastic card, badly warped and partially burned, but still recognizable as a driver's license issued by the State of New York to a Ms. Mary Yancy Lavigne. He glanced up at Scott and said, "I don't think there's much doubt the handbag's hers."

Not willing to trust his voice, Scott shook his head. After a moment he stood up, brushed off his hands and said with what he hoped was professional detachment, "Anything more on the victims?"

Harvey rose to stand beside him. "One's definitely female.

It'll be a while before we know anything else for sure.'' He threw Scott a sideways look. ''It'd be a help if we had a DNA sample from your missing New York lady. Any chance her friend might have something? I gather they were pretty close.''

''Roommates,'' Scott said. *She was like a sister…a daughter, even.* Oh God… *Joy.* How was he going to tell her? ''I'll ask her,'' he said. He felt hollow and cold inside. ''At the very least she'll be able to get your people into the apartment.'' *I'm so tired of losing people I love.*

Harvey's eyes were keen and sharp, but not without sympathy. ''You want to be the one to tell her? I can have somebody do that, if you want me to. Since we're gonna need to talk to her some more anyway…''

''No.'' Scott took a deep breath. ''Thanks, but I'll take care of it. She's… I've got her at my place, so I'd just as soon…since I'll be going back there…'' He realized how lame he sounded and shut up.

The FBI man said, ''Well, I'll leave you to it, then.'' He held out his hand. ''Thanks, we appreciate your help. Call me when she's up to talking with us.''

''Will do.'' He shook Agent Harvey's hand.

As he left the building and made his way across the parking lot to his truck, he was wondering if this was what a condemned man felt like when he walked out of his cell for the last time and started out on that long and final journey to meet his executioner.

Chapter 12

After Scott had gone, Joy finished cleaning up the omelette mess and washed the dishes. She made the bed she'd slept in—Scott's bed—and straightened up the living room. And then, because she so desperately needed to keep busy, she went in search of a vacuum cleaner, thinking she might as well give the whole place a quick once-over while she was at it.

Not that she expected that would take up a lot of time, because not only was the place not all that dirty, it was also not very big. Just the living room and kitchen, two bedrooms and one medium-size bathroom, plus a service porch in the back that held a washer and dryer. And, yes, there was a vacuum cleaner there, in addition to an assortment of mops and brooms. Beyond the service porch was a small fenced backyard, barren except for a metal shed, a rather anemic-looking lawn that had been recently mowed—Joy wondered if that was Ryan's job—and a dilapidated swing set in a far corner that obviously hadn't been used in quite a while. The whole place had the shabby and impersonal look of a rental, and Joy found it unbelievably depressing. Especially when she thought about the charming brick house with the big wide front porch, the hanging ferns and pots overflowing with flowers and the petite blond woman standing alone at the top of the steps, waiting for her son to come home.

But, that's how divorce is, she thought. *Everybody loses something. And he lied when he said it was painless, because it never is. Never.*

She carried the vacuum cleaner into the living room but instead of plugging it in right away, decided it would be smart to make use of the washer and dryer while she had the chance. Retrieving her damp, dirty and smoke-smelly clothes from the bathroom, she put the sweater and beret in the dryer with a scented fabric softener sheet and set it to tumble at a cool temperature. Then she set the washer for the lowest water level, gentle cycle and cool water, and put in the blouse, underwear—a lingerie bag had been too much to hope for— and socks. She was about to dump the slacks in, too, when she thought, *Oops,* and jammed a hand into the pockets, one by one. It wouldn't be the first time she'd let something important go through the machine. And of course, there was nothing worse than having a tissue go to pieces all over your clothes.

A moment—or an hour or a lifetime—later she was still standing in front of the washing machine, holding something in her hand. And with the roaring in her ears and the cold in her bones and a sense that the world was spinning around and around, she felt as if *she* were inside the washer and somebody had turned it on.

I forgot to tell him. How could I have forgotten something so important?

Not that it looked all that important—just a small plastic rectangle with a picture of a teddy bear on the front...

Scott's cell phone buzzed him on the way home, but he ignored it. It would be Beth's regular morning call, and this particular morning he was in no mood to be patient with her.

He did make one stop at the station to report in to Sheriff Johnny Dolittle and to arrange to take a personal day, part of him wishing there'd been something urgent and pressing come up on the job requiring his immediate attention. But of course there wasn't, and even if there had been, it wasn't his way to shirk a difficult assignment.

True, the evidence still wasn't conclusive that Yancy Lavigne had in fact died in the fire and explosion on King's Island, but it was strong enough that he couldn't put off telling Joy about it any longer. Plus the feds were going to need to talk to her again, and soon, not to mention they'd need her cooperation in getting a sample of Yancy's DNA. He had to tell her now. It wasn't ever going to get any easier.

For the first time in a lot of years he found himself wishing he had a bottle of scotch or something similarly mind-numbing stashed at home in his cupboards.

He mounted his front steps like a condemned man climbing onto the guillotine, grim but determined, heart hammering against his ribs. He let himself in the door, calling her name softly. The first thing he saw was the vacuum cleaner standing upright in the middle of the living room. He bypassed it, feeling tender but exasperated—the last thing he wanted was for Joy to clean his house!—and went on through to the kitchen.

She was sitting at the table facing the door, her back as straight as a Victorian spinster's, her hands folded in her lap as if she'd been waiting for him. Her hair was loose on her shoulders and she was still wearing Ryan's T-shirt and no bra. But he could hear the dryer whumping away out on the service porch and he figured she'd washed her own things and was waiting for them to dry.

Which could explain the fact that she was sitting there like that, he supposed, with that waiting air about her. What it didn't explain was the flush on her cheeks and the shine in her eyes and the little half smile on her lips, as if she had a glorious secret she couldn't wait to share.

His heart dropped into his shoes. God, how eager and

happy she looked, and how he hated what he was going to have to do to her. He wished he could snap a photograph of her the way she was right now, because he knew it was going to be a long time before she looked that happy again.

She said a breathless "Hi," just as he was saying, "Joy—" and he crossed to the table as if the floor had been paved with bubbles of blown glass. He pulled out a chair, sat in it and leaned toward her.

She drew her hands from her lap and put them on the tabletop, then leaned toward him and said, "Scott, I have something to tell you," at the same exact time that he was saying, "Joy, I have something to tell you."

Then she laughed, and it made him ache inside, the way it did to hear beautiful music at a funeral.

"You go first," she said, sitting back in her chair with an air of expectation, as if she just knew he'd brought her something wonderful.

Steeling himself, he cleared his throat and plunged into it. "It seems there were…fatalities in that fire last night. Two of them."

Her brow furrowed instantly and her eyes darkened with compassion for the unknown someones. "Oh, no, that's terrible. I'm so sorry. Do they know who it was?"

"They're pretty sure, yeah," he said gently, and reached for her hand. "Joy, one of the victims was female. They found a woman's pocketbook near the body. It had Yancy's ID in it. God, I'm sorry."

She was shaking her head, quick, frantic little movements. "No—no, it's not Yancy." She withdrew her hand from his.

"Joy…" he said, and he reached for her again, sorry the table was in the way of taking her into his arms. Bad planning on his part. He should have expected denial. "It's not confirmed, yet, but I'm afraid it looks pretty likely that it will be—"

But she evaded him, still shaking her head. "*No.* I'm telling you, it's not Yancy. She's alive. I *know* she is. They've taken her somewhere. She left this behind. Look—"

And it took him that long to realize she was trying to push something toward him across the tabletop.

Frowning, he adjusted his gaze downward, still not getting it that she was trying to show him something, frustrated that she was refusing to hear what he was telling her and unfairly angry with her for making this so hard. Dammit, he supposed denial was normal, but he hadn't thought she'd be so stubborn about it. On the other hand, this was Joy.

He stared at the object pinned by her fingertips to the tabletop, then back at her. Her eyes were shining with excitement again and the flush was back in her cheeks.

She nodded and was obviously waiting for him to say something. So he growled, "What's this?" Then he picked it up and answered his own question. "It's a phone card."

She nodded, so roused and wired that her whole being seemed to shimmer like the surface of water just before it boils. "It's *Yancy's* card. The one I gave her. I marked it— see? There's this little *Y* right here in the corner?" She pointed it out to him, then sat back, triumphant, biting her lip in an unsuccessful attempt to hold back a smile.

He stared at her, frowning intently, hollow with dread, wondering how in the hell he was going to get through to Joy that finding the card didn't mean much of anything. Except maybe to suggest that her friend had been on the island, which they already knew now. Giving up the effort for the moment, he rubbed his burning eyes.

"Where did you find this?" he asked.

"It was on the landing outside the boathouse. Not just lying there like somebody had dropped it. Sticking up between two of the boards. Somebody had to wedge it there. I found it when I was snooping around, looking in the windows. Why would it be there, Scott? Unless someone put it there, hoping it would be found. And who else would have done that besides Yancy?"

"Yes…okay," he said slowly, narrowing his eyes as he studied her. "I see what you're saying. But the thing is, you have no way of knowing *when* she left it. Maybe she put the card there as she was leaving the island, but who's to say she didn't leave it there when she happened to be down at the boathouse?'' He paused and then added gently, ''Joy, she left her purse. Tell me honestly, would a woman do that? Go away and leave her purse behind?''

Her eyes gazed unwavering into his, no longer shimmering but dark and determined. ''Maybe she would,'' she said quietly, ''if she wanted someone to know she'd been there.''

''Joy…'' He covered his eyes with his hand because he couldn't bear to see the hope in hers. ''You don't know how much I wish you were right. I know you want to believe—''

''I don't *believe*,'' she said in a rasping voice, like something tearing. ''I *know*.''

He lifted tired eyes to look at her. Her face had gone pale and still and he was ready to concede to her the possibility of a miracle if that was what she wanted, at least until the DNA results were in. But she rushed on breathlessly, as if she feared he might not let her finish.

''I didn't want to tell you this. I thought if I showed you concrete evidence, something you could see…touch… I wouldn't have to. But…okay.'' She struggled to draw in a breath, then plunged. ''I told you about the *feeling* I had back home in New York? The feeling that Yancy was *there*. Well, I had it again. Out there on that island, when I found the card and picked it up. Just for an instant, I felt her *there*, as if she was with me. And then those men came along, and I shoved the card in my pocket and ran and hid, and with everything that happened after that I guess I…forgot. Then a little while ago I wanted to wash my slacks, and I was checking the pockets and I found the card and… I felt it again. I *felt* her, Scott. I don't know how else to describe it. But I know I couldn't feel that if she wasn't…here on this earth anymore. And I wouldn't make something like that up. I swear I wouldn't lie—''

''Joy—''

''I *couldn't*. I—''

''*Joy. I believe you.*''

She stared at him, her lips still forming the words she'd been about to say, though no sound came. He stared back at her, heart pounding, and was surprised and a little defiant to discover he meant what he'd said. Call him a ditz, too, but dammit, he believed her. Or maybe he simply believed *in* her, but the point was he no longer gave a damn whether she was right or not. If she was so certain Yancy Lavigne was alive, by God, he was ready to accept that on faith and proceed accordingly, until incontrovertible evidence or, more important, Joy's own *feelings* proved otherwise.

"I believe you," he repeated, gently this time, and he shrugged as his lips curved into a rueful smile.

He was utterly stunned when she gave a stricken cry, covered her face with both hands and burst into tears.

This is it. The thought was suddenly there inside her head, the revelation so clear and bright and overwhelming it was almost Biblical. *He's for real. This is real. Oh God…*

He was around the table in a heartbeat, long before she was ready, pushing back her chair, reaching for her, dragging her into his arms. She didn't try to evade him, knowing it wouldn't have been possible, anyway, even if she hadn't wanted it so badly. Yes, *wanted* it—wanted *him,* even though he scared her. And then his arms were there, and his chest, and his heartbeat thumping against her cheek, and he was so big and solid and strong, like a fortress around her, and yes, a teddy bear and she knew she'd always be safe there if she only had the good sense to stay. If only…

"I can't figure you out," she heard him say in a ragged voice. "Do you know, the only time you ever cry is when I say something nice to you? Why is that?"

Because you scare me to death, that's why. "I don't know," she said. She drew away from him with a sniff, and every nerve and sinew screamed in protest. His face was a study in bewildered compassion. Looking at it made her eyes fill again, so she tried to pretend the tears were laughter. "I guess I just can't deal with 'nice.' I don't have the right defenses."

She felt his stillness, his strength. His hands were gentle on her arms, but they were enough to hold her there so she couldn't escape his scrutiny, couldn't retreat into the shelter of his embrace nor turn and run away.

"Why," he asked softly, "do you think you need to defend against me?"

She didn't answer. The silence stretched and stretched, and she couldn't think of anything to say that wouldn't sink her hopelessly into quicksand.

"Joy?"

Finally, almost angrily, she snapped, "Don't confuse me." It wasn't what she had wanted to say. *You terrify me. You excite me...thrill me. You make me feel hot and sexy and young and alive. You make me feel like a girl again. You make me believe in the possibility of all sorts of things I'd stopped believing in long ago. And that's what terrifies me, because what if I'm wrong...again? What if it goes bad...again? What if I lose...again? I couldn't bear it. I couldn't.*

That's what she wanted to say, but she couldn't, because to do so would make this...whatever it was between them something she couldn't back away from, or ignore or joke about, or dismiss as "just sex."

"We can't run away from this," he said, as if he'd heard her thoughts.

Except, he'd said "we." *We can't run away from this.* And somehow that only made it worse.

"Why couldn't I have met you during summer vacation?" she said furiously, swiping at her nose with the back of her hand. "Have a nice little fling and go home with a smile on my face and some really hot memories. This isn't a good time for this, dammit!" She glared at him and found him watching her with narrowed eyes.

"A good time for what? A fling? Sex? I thought we'd agreed just the opposite."

She looked back at him a long time, and the world around her became a vibrant stillness. It was like something she remembered from a long ago time. She'd been ten years old, or so and she'd been standing on the edge of a dock of some kind. Down in the water had been Daddy, holding out his arms and calling to her to "Jump! Jump, baby girl, it's okay, I'm gonna catch you...."

Shaking her head slowly, warily, she'd said, "No...not for that."

"What, then?"

Jump, baby girl, jump.

She closed her eyes. "For falling in love."

It had seemed an eternity to the ten-year-old Joy, that she had fallen and fallen through terrifying space before the water and Daddy's arms had enfolded her, both at exactly the same moment. It seemed the same eternity now before forty-two-year-old Joy heard a gusty sigh and the words, "Yeah, I know what you mean," and felt Scott's arms come around her, both at exactly the same time.

She whispered, "You do?" and felt a mystifying urge to cry.

"Yeah." His voice was raspy in her ear, like the purr of a tiger.

She felt his hand come between her cheek and his shirt front and a finger gently compel her chin upward, and she saw, through a wavering blur, his beautiful mouth smiling down at her.

"So, what are we going to do about this? I hear you've sworn off men."

She sniffed and pulled away from him—not far, but so she could focus on her hand resting on his shirt right over his thumping heartbeat, and her fingers rubbing back and forth on the soft fabric in an exploring, questioning way, and she was remembering that she'd never actually *seen* his chest. Kissed and licked and nuzzled and tasted it, yes, but it had been dark the night they'd made love.

"Well, obviously not *completely*," she said with a prim little cough. Though "prim" wasn't easy to pull off when her heart was thundering and her eyes were wet, heat was pooling on her skin like dew on summer roses and her entire body felt honeyed and heavy and ripe for the picking.

She heard the beginnings of a chuckle and felt his arms moving to bring her close again, and even though it was what she wanted more than anything in the world because she wanted to be completely honest with him, she quickly added, "It's not men I've given up on, actually, so much as marriage."

"Really?" And now it was his turn to pull away, while inside her head she was squalling in protest and resisting the urge to hang on to him with tooth and claw. But his eyes held a soft gleam and his lips the beginnings of a wry smile as he murmured, "Well, it's okay, then. So have I."

She sniffed, beginning to hope but at the same time feeling ambiguous in a way she couldn't understand. "You have? Really?"

He nodded. "Definitely. Once was plenty for me." His smile died before it was fully born, and without it he looked grim but somehow vulnerable at the same time.

Overwhelming tenderness and her own vulnerability became too much to cope with and she began to tremble. *Maybe…it will be okay, then. Maybe this can work. Maybe…* "So it's probably okay, then," she said, her voice frail. "As long as we're perfectly clear—both of us—on the situation."

"Which I think we are, definitely. No talk of marriage or any of that 'from this day forth' stuff. Nothing legal, nothing binding."

"Right. No strings, just…love. For as long as it lasts. And when it ends—" *Which it always does, and why do I feel so sad already?* She took a deep breath and repeated it, firmly. "When it *ends,* we say goodbye and walk away, no harsh words, no blame and no regrets. Agreed?"

"Agreed."

But then he just looked at her, eyes narrowed and head a little bit to one side, as if he were waiting to see what a possibly dangerous animal was going to do next. And she looked back at him the same way, except her heart was beating so hard she thought he could probably see it.

Finally, he said in a croaking voice, "Shall we shake on it, or what?"

Somewhere in the maelstrom of emotions inside her, laughter formed, though she managed to keep her face solemn as she held out her hand and watched it disappear, swallowed up in his. And she was remembering, suddenly, the last time that had happened, the first time she'd set eyes on Scott Cavanaugh, the first time he'd touched her. She remembered the *zing* that had shot through her then. *Why didn't I see it? That first day—why didn't I know?* Well, so much, she thought, for ESP.

"Does this mean we can have sex now?" Scott said in a bumpy voice.

And she replied, "No, but maybe we can make love."

"Hmm. I'm a guy so I don't know. Is that supposed to be better?"

Now his breath, his whisper, his soft laughter…all mingled with hers.

"I think so. Kiss me and let's see."

And then his mouth stopped her breath *and* her laughter and she gave a gasp of purest joy, her heart and her whole being *lifting*, like a baby on a swing. *Oh God, I'm going to make love with Scott Cavanaugh. Not just sex—love. Yes, I love him!*

She lifted her arms around his neck and he picked her up and settled her against him, chest to chest and belly to belly, with her legs coming around his hips as if they were meant to do that. And all the time he was kissing her as if he'd never have enough of her.

She couldn't ever have enough of him, either, she was sure of it. She twined herself around him as if she were trying to climb inside his skin, and she couldn't seem to make herself stop. His hands slipped inside the legs of her borrowed boxers and cupped and kneaded her bottom, and when he touched her nakedness her pulse shot off the charts and sent her blood rocketing through her veins until it found the part of her body that was in the most intimate proximity to his, where it slammed and thundered against the barriers of flesh and skin and clothing like a wild thing.

She was like a wild thing. She'd never wanted anyone or anything so much or so mindlessly as she did this man. *Never.* What was happening to her? She was out of control. But she was a forty-two-year-old woman. She shouldn't be like this. Should she?

I don't care! I'm forty-two years old and I've never felt like this before. Dammit, I've got lost time to make up for.

He pulled his mouth away from hers and she whimpered in protest. "Have to deadbolt the door," he gasped against her mouth. "Ryan has a key. Wouldn't want him walking in on us."

"Nope...definitely wouldn't want that." Laughing, breathless, she clung to his neck and distracted him with kisses as he carried her down the short hallway and across the living room.

"There," he said, and she heard the dead bolt click into place.

Then he was pressing her bottom against the locked door so that the open, vulnerable, throbbing part of her was wedged even tighter against him, as tight as it was possible to be with clothes on, and his new kiss was so deep it made her dizzy. Dizzy with wanting him, wanting the clothes *gone,* wanting him wedged as tightly as he could be inside her.

"Make love to me *now,*" she said. The fierce, growly voice startled her. She hadn't thought she could produce such a sound.

"Yes, Miss Joy, ma'am." *His* growl was tender rather than fierce. "Right here? Or there's the floor...couch... kitchen table...or would you prefer the bed?"

"All of the above, please. But—" She pressed a finger to his lips to interrupt him as his hands dug into her buttocks and he bent with renewed urgency to kiss her again.

Momentarily conceding, he kissed the tip of her finger and smiled. "I do have a condom— I think…somewhere…if that's what you're asking."

Shamefully, she hadn't given it a thought. She gave her head a rapid shake, then breathlessly amended, "Well, that, too. But I want to *see* you. It was dark before. I've wanted…" Longing stopped her voice and breath.

He made a sound deep in his chest that made her shiver. "I've wanted to see you, too, believe me."

His eyes, the look in them, glittering with desire, made her weak, and it was all she could do to whisper, "Well, that's easy, why didn't you say so?" and trembling, she lifted her arms over her head, taking fifty percent of her current ensemble with them. The T-shirt slipped from fingers that had turned to liquid, something warm and syrupy. She felt his hands on her sides—so big, so warm, measuring the span of her waist, torso and back, while his eyes gazed at her breasts as if he were a starving man at a banquet.

He muttered something low and guttural that she couldn't understand, then leaned to kiss her mouth, then her throat. She thrust her fingers into his hair and cradled his head close, moaning softly, then slid her hands to his shoulders and gripped them, arching back against the support of his hands and forearms as he lifted her higher. She felt his breath, expelled in whispered words she couldn't hear, then his mouth…his lovely, gifted mouth. When it gently closed over the tip of one tight and nerve-roused breast, she felt a shaft of something so bright and sharp it was almost pain, as if he'd pierced her there.

It was pleasure too intense to bear for more than an instant, but it didn't last for only an instant, it went on…and on…forcing from her throat a cascade of high, desperate whimpers. Tears sprang to her eyes.

One of his hands thrust strongly downward, forcing the elastic band of her boxer shorts over the curve of her buttocks as far as it would go, given her position, then pushed roughly, impatiently inside. And having gained access to her most intimate and vulnerable places, his occupation was as gentle as the invasion had been ruthless. His hand glided like silk over the nerve-rich backs of her thighs until her whole body sang and shivered, then tenderly cupped the swollen petals between, so that they pulsed and fluttered against his fingers and she twisted and moaned, wanting—*needing*—to feel them inside.

"That's not fair!" Her voice was high and thin and airless. "I said...I want—"

"What? Anything you want..."

"I said I want to see you—"

His chuckle was a delicious pooling warmth against her throat. "All in good time..."

"—and I want you inside me—*now*."

"I want that, too, believe me. Wait a minute, sweetheart..."

Sweetheart. With that word playing in her head, lovely as a single soaring note from a violin, she didn't even realize they were moving until she felt the giving firmness of a mattress against her back.

"Wait..." She felt an aching emptiness where he'd been.

Too dizzy with desire even to protest, she opened her eyes and watched him undress, drinking in the sight as each new part of him emerged from its cover, and wallowing in the pleasure of it like a lush on a binge. His chest was as broad and well-formed as she'd imagined it must be, paler than his neck and arms and dark-shadowed with hair in the right places. His torso tapered nicely, with only a hint of love handles to come, to a flat belly, slim hips and hard buttocks and corded thighs. His body wasn't lithe and slim like a very young man's, nor solid sculpted muscle like a bodybuilder's—simply that of a big, tall man, nicely proportioned and in very good shape for his age. *A grown-up,* Joy thought, and smiled.

"What?" he asked, watching her, and she felt a flutter of tenderness when she realized the wary look in his eyes was self-consciousness.

"Nothing. I just like the way you look," she murmured.

"Mmm… I like the way you look, too. Definitely." He leaned down to kiss her where she lay sprawled on his bed amidst the folded-back sheets, pulling the boxer shorts off and tossing them on the floor, then bracing his hands on the mattress on both sides of her.

But she placed a hand on his chest to stop him there and instead rose to meet him halfway, kissed him hungrily, then kept pushing him back until she was sitting upright on the edge of the bed and he was standing in front of her, hands resting tentatively, uncertainly on her shoulders.

"You said…anything I want," she murmured, gazing up at him through her lashes while her hands glided slowly up the outsides of his thighs.

He laughed uneasily, and his voice had become a croak. "Why do I think I'm going to regret saying that?"

"Not a chance." Smiling, blissfully happy, she leaned forward and kissed the silky, incredibly fine skin at the very top of his thigh. She touched it with her tongue, and was thrilled beyond measure when he groaned.

Incredible was his only thought, as she began, then, to "have her way with him," licking and kissing her way across his belly and down into the hair-matted regions below. Then, just when his knees were beginning to buckle, upward again, following the hills and valleys of torso and rib cage and chest while her hands explored and measured his buttocks and back and her body glided over and around him like an Egyptian dancer's silken shawl. Scott wasn't sure how he endured the exquisite torture, but he did, standing rigidly at attention, every inch of him, shivering a little and trying hard not to moan, until his breath felt trapped in his chest and his heart was ready to explode.

"Joy…" His voice was appalling—feeble like that of a dying man. She was standing now, every inch of her body caressing, it seemed, every inch of his, somehow all at the same time, while he could only stand helplessly, hands on her undulating hips, wondering how much more of this he was going to be able to stand. "Joy," he said, his voice barely audible, "don't you think we should lie down?"

She shook her head, nuzzling her lips against his chest, and murmured, "I like it this way. I get to see you...touch you all over. It's kind of like...dancing."

His laugh was weak and desperate. "When do I get to lead?"

"Now." Amidst husky laughter, her arms lifted around his neck and her breasts pillowed against his chest. His heart surged into his throat as she came weightlessly into the cradle of his arms, wrapping her legs once more around him, *this* time with nothing whatsoever between them. "Now," she said again, husky and fierce, her eyes gazing down at him, dark with passion. "I want to have you inside me. Please..."

And maybe it *was* a little like dancing. The world revolved slowly as he lifted her higher, every muscle and nerve in his body quivering with tension and suspense and self-control, then carefully lowered her, penetrated her, and she shifted and writhed and settled herself around him and he felt her body pulse and throb inside with laughter and lust and...yes, with *joy*.

Breathlessly laughing, she looked down into his eyes and murmured, "I guess there are some advantages to being small."

"Not *too* small," he said, laughing, too. "Feels like a perfect fit to me."

"Mmm." The laughter died, and she swallowed. "So what now?"

Her skin had grown moist and warm and tight. He could feel her trembling.

"So...we dance," he said softly. "I lead."

"I love you," she whispered as she kissed him.

And suddenly he was the strongest, mightiest man in the world, filled with power and passion and the strength to move mountains. His muscles felt like iron, the woman in his arms no more a weight to carry than the parts of his own body.

She *was* part of his body, she was one with him and he with her, and once again he didn't need to think about what his body was doing, or hers, they simply *were,* together and moving in perfect harmony as naturally and easily as breathing.

Then she cried out, a sound that tore at his soul, a sound both desperate and glad like that of a returning wanderer at long last seeing the first glimpse of home. She threw her head back and sobbed aloud, her fingers digging into his shoulders, and he buried his face against her neck and held her as tightly as he dared, held them both, bracing against his own cataclysm. Held himself and her both for as long as he could and when he couldn't any longer, tumbled them both laughing and breathless into the waiting bed.

"Oh, mercy," said Joy, when the tumult had died down enough for coherent speech, "I'm glad you don't have close neighbors."

He was trying to think of a response, lying facing her with his mind full of awe and his hand cradling her face, his thumb dazedly stroking the swollen mounds of her lips, feeling drained and warm and heavy with a kind of happiness he'd never imagined he would feel again. But he couldn't think because there was a noise, an annoying, persistent ringing in his ears.

It was several seconds more before he realized it was the telephone.

Chapter 13

"Let it ring," Scott murmured, when Joy flattened herself back against the sheets to allow him access to the phone on the nightstand. "It's probably just Beth, wondering why I haven't been answering my cell phone."

"Why haven't you?" She raised herself on one elbow to gaze down at him.

He looked at her, lightly brushing her throat and the upper part of her chest with the backs of his fingers. His eyes were indigo shadows, his brows knitted and solemn. "I had other things on my mind," he said softly. "I guess I didn't feel like dealing with her today."

"What if it was about Ryan?" she asked, and he didn't answer right away.

The phone had stopped ringing and from a distance came a high-pitched *beep* and then Scott's voice, gruff and unnatural-sounding: *"Hi, this is Scott, I can't come to the phone right now, so leave a message."*

Then, breathy and childlike, a Marilyn Monroe voice: "Scotty? Where *are* you? I've been leaving messages on your voice mail all morning. Okay…anyway. *Please* call me back. I really have to talk to you. It's important. 'Bye.''

He lay back and covered his face with his forearm, swearing under his breath.

Joy looked down at him, at her hand on his chest, liking the way it felt, stroking him like that—the rough-silk textures of hair and skin.

''Does she really call you every day?''

He uncovered his eyes and a wry smile. ''Yeah. At least.''

Joy watched her hand glide down over his stomach. Something clenched inside her. She fought it, then said tightly, ''I know it's none of my business, but why? I thought she was the one who divorced *you.*''

Scott thought, *Good question.* And he thought, too, how strange and amazing it was that in such a very short time it *had* become her business. He knew he owed her an answer, and probably himself while he was at it, but the truth was he'd never had a reason to come up with one until now. He'd never looked at himself and his relationship with Beth closely, possibly because he'd known he wasn't going to like what he saw.

Rather than answer her, he touched her wandering hand with his and said softly, ''Do you have any idea how good that feels?''

She smiled in a vulnerable, bruised-looking way, and said, ''Well, yes. It feels good to me, too.''

He sat up and pulled her across his lap and kissed her deeply, his chest clutching with a fearsome tenderness he didn't know what to do with. Lacking any other outlet for it, he cradled her as close as he dared and gave his hand permission to wander as hers had done—down over the soft, sweet roundness of belly and hip and bottom. The muscles of her torso spasmed and she curled inward, coiling herself around him and pressing pillow-soft breasts against him as she kissed him back.

It was some time later that she drew back and breathlessly asked, ''Don't you have to go to work?''

He shook his head, intertwining his smile with her moist, parted lips. "Uh-uh, I took the day off."

And he could feel *her* smile now, playing hide-and-seek with his.

"Not that I mind, but…how come?"

There it was again, that terrifying tenderness, like a knife in his heart, and his smile twisted into a grimace as though it was actual, physical pain he felt. He pulled Joy against him with a fierce protectiveness that bewildered even him, though he'd been protecting people most of his life.

"I thought—" he grabbed at a breath and began again "—I was going to have to tell you Yancy was probably dead. And I wanted…" His voice ground to a halt.

You wanted to be here for me, Joy thought, shivering and trembling inside with the unbearable wonder of that. "But she's not dead," she said, nestled against his heartbeat.

"But I didn't know that. All I knew was what you'd told me about losing people and that I was going to break your heart."

Hearing the anguish in his voice, she held him as tightly as she could and whispered, "You could never break my heart."

He couldn't speak. Emotions filled him, great rocks and boulders of emotion, until he thought he would burst. The pain of it was unbearable and at the same time exquisitely, overwhelmingly, gloriously sweet.

"Joy," he said when he could finally trust himself again, "tell me about them—your husbands—the marriages."

"My husbands?" She jerked slightly and looked up at him as if the question had surprised her.

Then for a time she was quiet, and he thought, *Please, Joy, trust me…. Don't shut me out. You don't have to protect yourself against me.*

She stirred restively in his arms and said, "I thought I had. There's not much more to add, Scott, really." She moved to sit up and he let her go, and cool air rushed to fill the place where she'd been so warm against him, making his skin shiver. She lifted her arms to gather her hair away from her face and neck and, with her back to him, went on in a matter-of-fact tone, "Zack couldn't live with his own failures and took it out on me. I probably put up with his cruelty a lot longer than I should have, but...well, you know. Marriage was supposed to be forever, right?" She looked at him over one bare shoulder, a classic pose worthy of an Old Master. "For better or worse?"

Her smile was wry. Then it vanished, and she looked away. "It took him hitting me to convince me it was okay to give up on that idea. And as for Freddie..." She sighed deeply, as if the memories depressed her. "Quite frankly, he was only the best example of the type of man I normally attract. Spoiled and shallow. But charming, of course, and handsome, convinced every reasonably attractive woman within range is fair game. And never *ever* acknowledging responsibility for anything he does or who he hurts. That was Freddie."

"He cheated on you?"

Joy threw him a look. "I think he probably cheated on me on our honeymoon, although I can't prove it. But I actually believed he loved me, deep down, and would eventually settle down. Maybe because I did so want it to work, especially since I'd already been through one divorce. I was sure a second one would just about kill my momma and send me straight to hell besides. Plus, I thought the world of his daddy and granddad. They were good people. Sweet as can be. I think it must have been Freddie's mother that spoiled him so rotten. Anyway, like I said—they saw to it I got treated well in the divorce. I think they'd have disowned Freddie if they'd had anybody else to leave the family business to."

He stared at her naked back, fighting the urge to put out his hand and touch the soft, pale skin, the vulnerable bumps of her spine. Softly, he said, "Tell me about the babies."

She flinched and her spine contracted, not as if she'd been struck but as if something—a fly, or a feathered wing—had brushed her lightly. She shifted half around and looked at him in genuine confusion. "You mean, the miscarriages? I told you—"

He shook his head. "You told me you'd had miscarriages, but the other night when you were talking about loss, that's not what you said. You said babies. My precious babies."

She tried to make her voice light. "Did I? Good heavens." And at the same time she was pulling and tugging the chenille bedspread around her hips and gathering it up in front of her exposed breasts. Suddenly her nakedness made her too vulnerable.

He understood that and part of him ached for her. But in his determination to gain her trust he put out his hand and grasped the bedspread and pulled it away from her—not roughly, but slowly…inexorably. She let it go with an exhalation of defeat, then closed her eyes while he began to brush her breasts with the backs of his fingers.

"Joy, look at me," he ordered, his whisper harsh and ragged as he gently brushed her skin as if it were the finest, lightest down, telling her with no more words than those that she and all her secrets and heartaches were safe with him.

She looked at him for a long time while her nipples puckered and grew hard and a dusky flush crept over her skin, then sadly smiled. "You know, it's funny," she said softly, "about that word…'miscarriage.' People say it like it's some kind of illness, one that's common, not too serious and easily cured, like appendicitis, maybe. And maybe it used to be like that years ago when so many babies died and babies born too early almost always did. I know when I had my first one Zack and I had been married only a month, and Momma and lots of other people, too, told me, 'Oh, it's nothing to worry about, it's not unusual to miscarry the first time,' and they were sure next time everything would turn out just fine. Plus—they didn't say it, but I knew they were thinking it— we were both so young and hadn't a pot to pee in, so it was just as well.

"But we were young and stupid, and I got pregnant again right away. This time I made it to five months. I'd begun wearing maternity clothes. I'd felt the baby move. I thought it felt like having a butterfly living inside me. We talked about names, tried to guess whether it was a boy or a girl. You know…it was *real*. Losing it was painful. Physically, of course, I mean it was *labor*. The whole thing. Except afterward there was just this terrible emptiness. Sadness. I never even saw him. They told me it had been a boy. After a day or so in the hospital, I just went home and picked up…as if nothing had happened. I mean, it was just a miscarriage, right? Miscarriages are so common, even normal, so I shouldn't make a big deal out of it. So I tried hard not to. I kept the sadness inside.

"After that one, I wasn't so eager to try again, but eventually I guess the maternal urges got the best of me and there I was, pregnant again. This time I was nervous and scared about every little twinge. I 'bout drove myself and everybody else crazy. And in the end it didn't make any difference."

She looked up and away, toward a far corner of the room. "I think it must be genetic. My sister Jessie had Sammi June early, too, and now she's an NICU nurse—that's in the Neonatal Intensive Care Unit. Anyway, I lost my little girl at twenty-two weeks. It was just too early…."

"Back then," Scott said, his voice thick. "Nowadays…"

"No." Joy shook her head, jarring loose some tears that had gathered behind her lashes. "No." She brushed the tears away and straightened her back, lifting her head high. "I got to hold her, just for a few precious moments. I wouldn't trade that for anything in this world, but I also know I won't go through such a thing again. I won't *ever* hurt like that again."

Without another word, Scott pulled her across his lap and silently held her. Her body felt quiet, relaxed in his arms. She neither trembled nor cried, but he knew if he looked at her face he'd see the jewel-like shine of tears among her lashes.

He was holding her like that, rocking her slightly, his mind empty of everything but the woman lying against his heart and the love he felt for her when the phone rang.

They both jerked convulsively. Joy struggled to sit up while Scott swore and muttered, "Not now, dammit."

"Maybe you should answer it," she said, sliding out of his arms and lap. "It must be something pretty important or she wouldn't keep calling you."

"I'll call her back eventually. Whatever it is, it can wait another minute. Let the machine get it. I'm gonna take a shower first."

He stood up, then leaned down to kiss her, the darkness and defiance fading from his face. The tenderness that came to replace it made her chest go warm and tight.

"And after that...if you want to put some clothes on...how 'bout if I take you out to lunch? I don't know about you, but I'm starving half to death."

"Sounds good." She smiled into his eyes at close range, feeling her smile stretch with his. He kissed her once more, then walked naked into the bathroom while she gazed at his magnificent backside in admiration and a kind of stunned happiness. *I can't believe this is happening. This doesn't happen...to me.*

The phone had stopped ringing. Smiling and giddy, she picked up the Black Watch-plaid boxers from the floor and went into the living room to retrieve the T-shirt she'd abandoned so wantonly there. As she crossed the hallway and passed the kitchen she heard the *beep* signaling the conclusion of the outgoing message. There was a pause, and then, instead of Marilyn Monroe's breathy whisper, a deep, male voice with a pronounced Florida drawl said, "Yeah, Scott, Johnny Dolittle, here..."

Joy started toward the kitchen, then stopped. *It's Scott's phone, not mine,* she reminded herself. *It's his business.* And she went on into the living room to look for her T-shirt.

But the voice was loud and firm, and it was impossible not to hear.

"...wanted to let you know the feebs have located our mutual targets and will be moving on them this evening. Call me if you want to be in on the takedown.'' *Click.* The answering machine beeped and went silent.

Joy walked into the kitchen, pulling the T-shirt absent-mindedly over her head. As she approached the phone and answering machine, which was on the countertop farthest from the stove and sink and closest to the table surrounded by the usual clutter of junk mail, advertising flyers, notepads and phonebooks, her heart was pounding. She felt wired and jittery, and her skin tingled as if she'd been hooked up to a low-voltage electrical current. *Johnny Dolittle? The feds? Mutual target? Takedown?* What was that about? It must have something to do with Yancy, she was sure of it. She had no idea who Johnny Dolittle was, but the *feds?* What else could it be?

Never known for her patience at the best of times, it was all Joy could do not to charge into the bathroom and haul Scott bodily out of the shower. Instead, she forced herself to breathe deeply and count slowly to ten. ''Clothes,'' she said aloud to herself. ''I should get dressed.''

She went to the service porch and got her clothes out of the dryer and put them on standing right there, except for the sweater and beret which she carried into the kitchen, folded neatly and placed in a pile on the table. She was perched on a chair with her legs pulled up and her arms wrapped around them, rocking gently to the suspenseful pounding of her own heart when Scott came into the room at last.

He was wearing khaki slacks and a white T-shirt and his dark hair glistened, spiky and wet from the shower. He looked good enough to eat with a spoon but Joy's vital signs were already as far off the charts as they could possibly get, and she just held on to herself even more tightly and watched him with dry mouth and burning eyes as he came toward her.

''What's up?'' he said warily as he leaned to kiss her. *Something* was up, he'd known the minute he'd walked into the kitchen. He could smell adrenaline like an engine running hot.

''You need to listen to your message,'' she said. Her voice

was tight and air-starved and he knew it was only partly thanks to the cramped-up way she was sitting. "It wasn't Beth."

"Oh? Who was it?"

"Somebody named Johnny Dolittle."

She was watching him with narrowed eyes, to see if he'd lie to her about it, maybe, but they were long past the point where he'd have tried to keep anything from her.

"That's the sheriff," he said. "My boss. What'd he want?" She shrugged, still watching him, and he felt a sinking in his gut as he walked past her and punched the "play" button on the answering machine.

Tense and frowning, he waited through Beth's message again. His stomach clenched when he heard Sheriff Dolittle's familiar rumble. He played the message through, then punched Erase. He didn't want to look at Joy, who'd unfolded herself from the chair and come to stand beside him.

"It's about the DelReys, isn't it? They've found them. The feds. Haven't they?"

"Joy." He looked down at her, struggling to keep his voice calm and his expression cop-stern, fighting against an undefined sense of danger and dread. "I need to return this call. Would you mind waiting in the bedroom?"

She was shaking her head rapidly and he understood that it wasn't so much in defiance of his request, but more a general denial, a rejection of circumstances and coming events they both knew were unavoidable. And probably beyond their control.

"Yancy's with them. I'm sure of it. And they think she's dead, Scott. They're going to go in and take them down and they don't even know she's there." She was speaking rapidly and in a low, trembling voice, and even with the ambiguous pronouns, he knew exactly what she was saying.

And his heart ached for her because there wasn't a damn thing he could do about it. There was a hard, burning lump of pain right in the middle of his chest.

"Joy—" he took her gently by the arms and faced her

"—listen to me, love. This is police business. I'm sorry, but I have to ask you to go in the other room while I make this call. Okay? Please?"

"Police business." The anguish in her eyes was almost more than he could bear. "It's the police's business to 'take down' the DelReys, not to save Yancy. They're going to go in with guns and battering rams and body armor and tear gas, and they don't even know Yancy's there. They think—"

"We don't know—"

"*I know.* Where else would she be, if not with them? She's with them and she's alive. Somehow she must have convinced them she's not a threat, so they haven't killed her. But she tried to let someone—me—know she's there, so she's not really *with* them. But nobody knows that except us. Scott, you have to stop them!"

"You must know I can't do that," he said harshly. "For starters, I don't have the authority. Nor do I have the necessary evidence to convince those in authority that Yancy might—*might*—be with the DelReys. I'm not even sure it would make much difference if I did. Joy, the federal government isn't going to let drug and arms dealers and possible financers of terrorists off the hook because they happen to have a hostage. And by the way, if the DelReys mean to use Yancy as a hostage, they're going to have to let somebody know she's there, right?"

She gazed up at him in silent despair.

He leaned down to kiss her, his chest aching. "Look, I'm gonna do what I can. I'll tell whoever's in charge of the operation that we've found evidence that points to Yancy having survived the fire and that she could still be traveling with the DelReys. Beyond that, there's not much I can do. It's out of my hands, and it's definitely out of yours." He kept his hands gentle on her arms, though it wasn't an easy thing when what he wanted was to hold on tightly enough to keep from drowning in her eyes. "We'll just have to trust that the takedown goes smoothly and without anybody getting hurt. Which, nine times out of ten, by the way, is what happens. Okay?'' He waited, silently pleading for her to understand, then said huskily, ''I have to call the shop. Let me do this, Joy. Please.''

She nodded, her eyes darting from side to side, and her lips moving though she didn't make a sound. Then she turned and walked out of the kitchen. A moment later he heard his bedroom door close.

He took a deep breath, waited a long five-count, then picked up the phone and pushed the one-button code for the sheriff's office. He waited again, counting heartbeats, until he heard the familiar growl.

''Dolittle.''

''Yes, sir, it's Scott Cavanaugh. Got your message.''

''Yeah… Scott. Kinda figured you'd want to be in on this. That feeb SAIC—what's his name, Harvey?—made a point of mentioning it, too.''

''Yes, sir, I definitely would,'' Scott said, marveling at how calm his voice sounded when his heartbeat could most likely be heard over the telephone.

''Okay, then. Here's how it's gonna go. Feeb's surveillance picked up the targets this morning, out at Sun-Tek. That's that big manufacturing outfit… I think they make those automatic patio cover thingamabobs that go up and down on rails. Anyway, they're out on Route—''

''I know it,'' Scott said. ''Don't they have their own airstrip?''

''They do. That plant is in the tri-county jurisdiction, so our SWAT's gonna be goin' along on this deal. And it's gonna have to happen fast, because according to the chatter the feebs are picking up, our friends are plannin' on leaving the jurisdiction, not to mention the country, sometime early this evening. The feebs don't want to move in before the plane gets here. I guess they're hoping to snag whoever's on it at the same time, but you're gonna need to get in here so you can get briefed and set up. I know you're takin' a personal day—''

''That's okay, sir, no problem.''

"Everything okay, son?"

"Yes, sir, everything's been straightened out. I'll be there in twenty minutes."

"All right, then. See you shortly." The line went dead.

Scott was just about to hang up. He had actually moved the receiver about a foot away from his ear when something instinctual, a sixth sense—one of Joy's *feelings*, maybe, made him stop and bring the instrument back. He listened, holding his breath, and heard a soft but unmistakable *click*.

His whole body went ice-cold. He had no idea how long he stood there, gripping the receiver and not breathing, not moving, not wanting to believe he'd actually heard what he'd heard. No more than a second or two, probably; it only seemed like eternity. He came back to life like a rusty windup toy, jerkily thrusting the receiver onto its cradle and crossing the kitchen and hallway in long clumsy strides. He gripped the doorknob, silently turned it and pushed open his bedroom door.

The room was empty. The bed was still a tumbled reminder of earlier, happier associations. A lifetime ago. The bathroom door was closed. Beyond it he could hear water running.

Could he have been mistaken? He stood beside the bed, bathed in icy sweat and vibrating with unspent adrenaline, staring down at the phone. I should give her the benefit of the doubt, he thought. *I should trust her. If I love her, I should trust her...shouldn't I?*

Baloney. He loved her, all right, there was no longer any doubt of that in his mind. And he did trust her. Sure he did. He trusted her to behave just like Joy.

He let out a gusty breath through his nose and reached for the phone. He held it against his cheek and was sure it felt warm. Though he knew it was probably impossible, he even thought it smelled like roses. Grimly, he looked toward the closed bathroom door. *Aw, dammit. Dammit, Joy.*

What the hell was he going to do with her? If she'd heard the whole conversation, she'd know when and where the takedown was to take place. And he'd seen that look on her face before—not long ago, in fact, just before she'd hired herself a dingy and set out to invade a mobster's private island. He *knew* her. If she thought Yancy's life was in danger—and she did—nothing in this world was going to keep her from trying to do something about it. What was *he* going to do? He had to leave, and he couldn't very well handcuff her to the bed...

The hell I can't.

The thought had barely popped into his mind before he was moving to his closet, opening the door, reaching for his clean uniform in its dry cleaner's bag. He shucked off his pants and dressed quickly, one ear cocked to the sounds coming from the bathroom, then took his heavy-duty belt from its hook and buckled it around his hips. He hefted it once to settle it firmly, then strode across the room and knocked with one knuckle on the bathroom door.

"Joy," he called in a soft, rasping voice, "you decent? I have to go now. Just wanted to say goodbye."

The door opened and there she was, her face flushed and unbelievably lovely, a hairbrush in her hand and her hair loose on her shoulders, a shimmering, shifting cascade of honey-colored silk, looking innocent as a five-year-old in footy pajamas. His belly clenched and electricity hummed behind his breastbone.

Her eyes traveled over him from head to toe. Then she smiled and murmured, "Wow."

"What?" He'd begun to sweat.

"I've never seen you in your uniform before."

"Oh." He was unbelievably nervous. He'd faced down knife-wielding gang-bangers, drunk-and-disorderlies armed with everything from guns to bowling balls, even a coked-up fisherman with a spear gun and he'd never been this nervous.

He let out a breath, took her in his arms and closing his eyes, bent over to lay his cheek on the top of her head. Inhaling the sweet rose scent of her hair, he murmured, "It's going to be all right, Joy. I promise you I'm gonna do everything I can to see that it is. You know that, don't you?"

"Yes," she whispered. "I know you will."

He straightened, his hands sliding from her shoulders and down her arms to close gently around her wrists. "I hope you also know that I love you," he said thickly, "and that you'll understand why I have to do this."

And then, swiftly, smoothly, with the ease borne of much training, experience and practice, he slipped the handcuffs from his belt and snapped one end onto Joy's delicate wrist.

Chapter 14

Joy glanced downward, uncomprehending, at the stainless steel bracelet that encircled her wrist. She looked back up at Scott, and a smile twitched uncertainly at the corners of her mouth. "Scott? Wh-what are you doing?" Something inside her clung to the notion that it was a joke, a game.

His face was averted, his attention focused on making adjustments to the size of the cuffs. "Making sure you don't do anything stupid," he said, "since promises don't seem to work...." Adjustments completed, he raised his head and looked at her.

Her breath caught. She'd expected his eyes to be glittering like sapphires. Angry. Hard...as hard as his jaw and the set of his mouth. Instead, the softness in them made her stomach clench. She opened her mouth, but no words came.

"You heard, didn't you?" he said quietly. "You were listening in on the bedroom phone."

She stared at him, wanting desperately to lie, her throat and jaw cramping with the effort to force out some words of denial.

His lips softened into a smile. "It's okay. You couldn't lie to me even if you tried. Anymore than you could keep yourself from picking up that phone. Or from taking off out there to try and rescue your friend. That's why I'm not giving you that choice."

"Wait—where—what are you going to do?"

"I'm going to handcuff you to the bedpost." His smile broadened momentarily, then darkened into a frown. "I just hope you're not desperate enough to gnaw through it with your teeth. Wouldn't put it past you. Come on, quit stalling. Let's go."

"No, wait—" She pulled back, a silly and futile defiance. She couldn't believe he was going to do it. *But he was.*

Inspiration struck. "What if I have to go to the bathroom?"

He paused, frowning, while he considered that. Then he said, "You're right." He led her, like a puppy on a leash, to the toilet, put down the lid and said, "Okay, sit."

Too stupified to object, she did as she was told.

"Now, lean over. No, this way, toward the sink. Stretch out your arm. Good. Okay...that'll do it."

There was a *snick,* and then a *clink,* and Joy found herself staring once again in disbelief at the other end of the handcuffs, now firmly fastened to the drainpipe underneath the old-fashioned wall-mounted sink.

"That works," Scott said, sounding smug.

He straightened, dusting his hands, then leaned down to drop a kiss on the top of her head. "Okay, I'm off. I'll be back as soon as I can. Meanwhile, *try* and stay out of trouble, hmm?"

"As if I had any choice," Joy managed to say, breathless with impotent fury but unable to come up with a single syllable to offer in her own defense. Oh, she was angry, you bet she was. But at the same time a voice of reason in the back of her mind was reminding her that she'd earned this. "Scott, wait. Don't do this. Please. I promise—"

The bathroom door closed softly, and he was gone.

She listened, hunched over and miserable, to the sound of fading footsteps. She felt the house shake slightly when the front door slammed shut. She heard the truck start up with its customary roar, and then…silence. Whimpering with frustration, heart hammering, she slid off the toilet seat and onto the floor.

Time passed. Joy had no idea how much time, or how it passed, but somehow or other, it did. The telephone rang twice, but she couldn't hear whether anyone had left a message on the machine. For a while she entertained the fantasy that she could find a way to free herself. She tried tugging on the pipes to see if she could pull them loose. She tried soaping her hand to see if the cuffs could be slipped over it, but apparently Scott was good at his job. Short of removing her thumb, there was no way out of the cuffs. Her brain raced randomly and futilely around the problem until her head ached with the tension.

Then she got the idea of writing the next chapter of her book in her head, more as an exercise in mental discipline than anything else. She knew she'd never remember any of it later. She was actually well on her way to working out the details of the second murder when something sent a blast of adrenaline through her system and knocked every word she'd assembled in her mind into an incomprehensible jumble.

The house had shuddered. Minutely, but unmistakably. Someone had opened and shut the front door!

Her heart leaped into full thundering gallop. He'd come back! Surely, the raid couldn't have happened yet. He must have changed his mind about leaving her here like this. He was going to set her free! She held her breath, straining her ears for the sound of footsteps.

She heard a voice, but it wasn't Scott's. It sounded far away and uncertain. And young.

"Dad?"

Ryan.

Her second thought was, *Oh God, no.* She put her free hand over her eyes while her heart went *trip-trip-trip* and she tried to think which would be worse—to stay silent and pray he'd go away, resigning herself to remaining a prisoner, or to suck it up and call for help from a fourteen-year-old boy who, by all indications, resented her very existence.

Footsteps, light and hesitant, came into the bedroom. "Dad? Hey, you in here?" The footsteps came closer, and there was a knock on the bathroom door. "Dad? That you?"

She took a shallow breath. "No, Ryan. It's me, Joy."

"Oh—" the voice cracked and suddenly deepened "—sorry." There were shifting, scuffling sounds and mutters of embarrassed apology.

"No! Wait, it's okay, don't go. Please. You can come in. I mean, I can't come out. I'm sort of…stuck."

The doorknob turned slowly. The door opened a cautious inch, and the top of Ryan's head appeared. Then one eye.

"I'm down here," Joy said breathlessly. "On the floor."

The door opened farther and Ryan stood there, a backpack slung over one shoulder, his body hunched and coiled like a wild animal poised to bolt for the underbrush at the slightest threat of danger.

"What're you doing down *there?*" The new, deeper voice cracked and soared higher on the last word, and he cleared his throat as if it had embarrassed him. Joy wordlessly lifted her chained wrist as high as she could. He focused on it, blinked, and said, "Oh." He frowned and sidled warily closer, his eyes moving from the end of the handcuff attached to the drainpipe to Joy's face. "Are those my dad's hand-cuffs?"

"Yep."

The frown changed to complete noncomprehension. "What? Why did he—" He jerked around suddenly, turning his back to her, and put a hand up as if to shield his eyes from a dreadful sight. "Wait, don't tell me. I don't want to know."

"*Ryan!*" In spite of everything, Joy was laughing, half embarrassed, half amazed. "What in the world are you think-

ing? I can't believe you even know about...what you were
thinking.''

He gave her a look along one shoulder, wary again. "I've
seen stuff. On *Law and Order, CSI*...lots of places. I'm not
a kid, you know." He came back and perched on the edge
of the bathtub, letting his backpack slide to the floor.

"So," he said, sounding interested now, "what was it,
some kind of joke? Where's Dad? Is he gonna be back anytime soon?"

She closed her eyes briefly and sighed. "Ryan, it's kind
of a long story. And I'll tell you all about it, but right now
I'm more interested in getting out of these things. I don't
suppose you'd know if your dad has a spare key anywhere
around here..."

He shook his head, looking troubled. "I don't know if he
does or not. I wouldn't know where to look, even if he did."

"Okay." It had been too much to hope for. She took another breath and went for door number two. "What about
tools? Does your dad have any tools he keeps around here?
You know, for doing repairs, plumbing, stuff like that?"

Ryan's face lit up. "Yeah. Oh, yeah. I know he's got tools.
He's always fixing stuff for my mom. He keeps everything
in the shed out back, because it has a padlock on it—"

"Oh, no!" Joy's heart, which had grown buoyant with
hope, sank like a stone once again.

"It's okay, I have a key." Ryan was scrabbling around in
his backpack, so his voice sounded muffled. "So I can get
the lawn mower out. Sometimes Dad's not here when I need
it. Here—see?" He held up an assortment of keys, dangling
from the end of a Harry Potter key chain.

"Oh, thank God. Okay, what we're gonna need is a monkey wrench. Do you know what I mean? The kind with the
adjustable—"

He snorted. "I know what a monkey wrench is."

"Sorry." She smiled at him. "Of course you do, I wasn't
thinking. Heavens, you probably know more than I do about
how to take apart a bathroom sink."

Ryan had the grace to look doubtful about that. "Well, I've never actually *done* it." He squatted down to peer at the pipe, then looked sideways at Joy and shrugged. "How hard could it be? It's not exactly rocket science."

"Right," said Joy, beaming at him. "I know you can do it. Why don't you go and get whatever you think you'll need? Maybe some of that stuff you spray on to help it come apart—"

"WD-40?"

"Yes, that's it! I knew you'd know. Okay go, quick."

Looking earnest and intrepid, Ryan left. Joy listened to his youthful footsteps clomp through the house and onto the service porch, and heard the screen door bang, and then settled back with a sigh and a smile and a thumping heart to savor the beautiful irony that it should be Ryan, of all people, who'd come to her rescue. *Who'da thought it?*

He was back in less time than she'd expected, lugging a large metal toolbox. The lid was partly open, and even before he set it down on the linoleum floor, Joy could see a can of WD-40 sticking out of the top.

He lowered himself to one knee in front of the sink and shot her a troubled look. "I don't know if I should do this. I mean, I was just thinking…" His blue eyes regarded her steadily, and they reminded her so much of his father's— without the grown-up's confidence and wisdom and patience, of course, but with all the intelligence and honesty and courage and the promise of more strength and character to come. "Dad must have done this for a reason, right? I know my dad. He wouldn't just leave you here for the heck of it. What if I let you go, and it turns out I was wrong?"

Joy returned his look for a long, silent moment, and she was thinking that it would be a very big mistake for anyone to underestimate this boy, and that if her own son had lived, she would have wanted, hoped, prayed that he would grow up to be a young man just like this one. She swallowed an unanticipated lump in her throat, cleared it and nodded.

"You're right," she said quietly. "Your dad didn't do this

for the heck of it. He did it to protect me. Because he's afraid I *might* do something dangerous that *might* get me hurt. I'm sure that's something you're not exactly unfamiliar with.'' She offered him a wry smile and was ridiculously touched when she got one in return.

''Yeah…'' For a moment, his voice was almost as deep as his father's, and he coughed as if it had startled him. ''So, what is this dangerous thing he thinks you're going to do?''

So Joy told him everything. She told him about Yancy, her life and hopes and the dream vacation she hadn't returned from. She told him how dear her friend was to her, and about the phone card and the *feeling,* about trying to convince the police that something bad had happened, and about coming to Florida to look for Yancy herself, expecting to get help from her brother, Roy.

''And instead, there was my dad,'' said Ryan. For some reason his eyes looked vulnerable.

''Yes,'' said Joy softly. ''There was your dad.''

She told him about going to the Spanish Keys Resort and finding the photograph of Yancy with the suspected mobster's son and about blackmailing Ryan's dad into taking her out on the boat to scope out the DelReys' private island. She did *not* tell him about going to look at the dead body that wasn't Yancy's or what happened after that.

She told him about her certainty that Yancy had been on King's Island and about her decision to go there without involving Scott because of his professional conflicts. And the consequences of that decision. Ryan's eyes got big when she told him about the frogmen and the explosion and being rescued by his father along with a whole bunch of federal agents.

She told him about the two dead bodies found in the burned-out mansion and that the feds were certain one of the bodies was Yancy's, and about finding the phone card and the recurrence of the *feeling* that made her just as certain it wasn't. She did *not* tell him what had happened between his dad and her…good heavens, could that have been just this morning?

When she told him about the phone call from Sheriff Dolittle and how she'd listened in and overheard the details of the operation against the DelReys planned for that evening, Ryan covered his eyes with his hand and said, "Oh man."

Joy said, "Tell me about it."

"So," said Ryan, frowning. "Dad caught you listening and that's why he handcuffed you? Why, does he think you're gonna go get mixed up in their big raid? You can't be *that* stupid."

"Thank you," Joy said, beaming at him. "No, of course I wouldn't do a thing like that. But you see, here's the thing. I believe Yancy's with the DelReys and that they're going to take her with them when they try to leave the country. I don't know why. Maybe they plan to use her as a hostage for as long as they need her, and then they'll kill her. But anyway, since the feds believe she's already dead, they're not going to be doing any negotiating. They don't know the DelReys have a hostage, do you see? And I'm afraid, if they just go in shooting—" she threw Ryan a dark look "—I watch TV, too, you know. I'm afraid Yancy is going to wind up getting killed."

Ryan nodded somberly, thinking hard. He shot her a look. "So, what *were* you going to do? What *can* you do?"

"I intend to go there," she said with more confidence than she felt. "To the plant where the DelReys are. It's a manufacturing plant, a perfectly legitimate business, right? Why *shouldn't* I go there? I mean, maybe I want to buy a mechanical awning. Why not? And, once I'm there, I'm going to try to find out once and for all whether or not Yancy's there, and then I'm going to tell the police so they can conduct themselves accordingly." She concluded in a flush of righteousness. Ryan, however, was shaking his head. *"What?"*

"Your plan's bogus, that's what. I mean, for starters, how're you gonna even get there? You don't have a car."

That one was easy. "I'll take a cab."

"Okay, that's cool, and *then* what? From what you told me, the feds have this place under surveillance. That means they're gonna be watching it like hawks. You think they're just gonna let some taxi drive right in there?"

"Hmm," said Joy, gnawing on her lip. "Well, I guess I'll just have to sneak in some way."

Ryan looked skeptical. "Okay, let's say you do. Let's say you even find your friend. What makes you think these DelRey guys are gonna let you leave? What if they wind up holding *you* hostage? And then how are you gonna let the feds know?" He shook his head emphatically. "Dad's right. This *is* stupid. And dangerous. You could get killed."

"Maybe," Joy said, quietly pleading. "But if I don't do it, Yancy almost certainly will. So, what should I do? Sit here safe and sound and let my best friend get killed? How could I live with myself if I did that? If there's even a chance I can save her, I have to try. Don't you see?" She held his eyes for a long, tense time, then sagged back against the toilet bowl and covered her eyes with her hand. She rubbed them hard, then lifted them again to confront the boy crouched before her, holding a wrench—and Yancy's life—in his hand.

"Ryan, I'm not a child. I'm a grown woman. I don't need a dad to make decisions for me. I'm way past that. This decision should be mine to make. Your dad—granted, for all the right reasons—took that choice away from me. That said, I do realize I'm asking you to make a decision that's just as grown-up and just as tough. First of all, I'm asking you to disobey your father. I shouldn't do that. And I wouldn't, unless I truly believed a young woman's life was at stake. What I'm really asking you to do, Ryan, is to let *me* make the choice as to whose life to risk."

There was another endless pause. Then Ryan reached for the toolbox and dragged it closer. "What the hell," he said, throwing her a grin as he hefted a monkey wrench as long as his forearm and almost as thick, "I'm grounded anyway."

Joy went limp, too overwhelmed with relief and gratitude to even say thank you. Overwhelmed, too, with belated guilt.

As if he'd heard her, Ryan added with a shrug, "Anyway, I'm not really disobeying Dad. He never told me I couldn't let you loose. What am I, a mind reader?" He gave her another grin before he lifted the wrench to measure the span of the pipe fitting.

Joy watched his bony, rough-knuckled boy's hands as he adjusted the wrench, fitted it over the pipe, tightened it and gave it a testing tug, then a harder one that made the muscles in his arms and neck stand out. When he paused to reach for the can of WD-40, she said, "By the way, speaking of grounded, why are you here?"

He sat back on his heels. "Oh, yeah." He shot her a look that for some reason seemed slightly shifty, or at least, evasive. Then he gave one of his all-purpose shrugs and attacked the pipe joints with WD-40. "My mom's been calling. Guess Dad never got her messages. Anyways, she, um, had to go somewhere, so she told me I should come here after baseball practice."

"Well," Joy said lightly, wondering what he wasn't telling her, "I'm very glad you did."

"So," he said, his expression earnest as he attacked the pipes with the wrench again, "are you and my dad getting married?"

If she'd had anything in her mouth, she would have choked. She almost did anyway. "What? No, why would you—"

"Why not? You like him, don't you? He must like you a lot, or he wouldn't have done…this." He sat back again, redfaced and sweating, and looked at her. "I know he likes you. I saw the way he looked at you, that day on the boat."

"Which," Joy said, still breathless with astonishment, "you weren't exactly thrilled about, as I recall."

"Yeah, well…" He shifted around to get at the pipe from a different angle, and she couldn't see his face. His ears, however, were bright red. "I've been thinking about that. I was probably being pretty childish, actually. Selfish, you know? Anyways, I think Dad should probably have somebody." He threw his body against the wrench. There was a cracking, grating, screeching sound, and a triumphant grunt. *"There."*

Joy scrambled up onto her knees, heart pounding. "Did you get it?"

He sprayed more WD-40 and threw himself on the wrench again. "It's...coming."

"Oh God, what can I do? Can I help?"

"Just keep out of the way. Okay...that's got it, I think. Oh, *yuck,*" he added as the trap fell to the floor with a *clunk,* splashing soapy gunk across the linoleum. And just like that, Joy was free.

She gave a whoop of delight and threw her arms around Ryan's neck, narrowly missing hitting him in the head with the dangling end of the handcuffs. "Oh, Ryan. Oh my God, how can I ever thank you?"

"For starters," he said dryly, sounding a lot older than fourteen, "you could try not to get yourself killed. Dad would never forgive me."

Laughing, Joy hugged him one more time and let him go. "I'll do my best." She got stiffly to her feet while Ryan was putting the tools back in their box, stepping over the dismantled plumbing to look at herself in the mirror. Murmuring "Merciful heaven," she lifted her hands to comb her fingers through her hair and clonked herself in the ear with the dangling handcuff.

"What're you going to do with that?" Ryan's face, still pink with exertion, came into view beside hers.

She regarded the cuffs with a frown. "I don't know. I hadn't thought about that. I don't suppose there's anything in that toolbox that would cut through—"

"Uh-uh, no way," said Ryan, backing away, hands held up in front of him. "Even if there was, I'm not ruining a pair of Dad's cuffs. Those things are expensive."

"Oh, well... I'll think of something." The sleeves of her

blouse wouldn't cover the cuffs, but her sweater would. Of course, she'd also look like a lunatic, wearing a sweater in Florida in May. Maybe if she folded it over her arm...

Her stomach growled, reminding her that she'd missed lunch. "I'm starving," she said, smiling at Ryan. "Want a sandwich?"

"Sure." A loose-jointed and ungainly fourteen-year-old once more, he scooped up his backpack and followed her out of the bathroom.

In the bedroom, she turned to him with a smile. "Ryan, am I mistaken, or is your voice changing?"

"Yeah." His smile flickered like a faulty lightbulb. "I guess it is...maybe."

She gave a low whistle. "Wow, that's kind of a big deal."

He shrugged, then gave up trying to be cool. "Yeah," he said breathlessly, grinning in a way that lit up his whole face and made Joy's heart turn over. Then the smile tilted wryly, and suddenly he looked so much like his father she felt her chest clench. "Guess it's about time."

"Well, you know, you sound just like your dad," Joy said, smiling at him, and when she saw his face turn pink with pleasure, she knew her life, and loving Scott Cavanaugh, had just become a lot more complicated.

In the kitchen, she dug through her purse until she found the piece of paper on which she'd written the number of the cab company she'd used before, and called them to arrange for a pickup. Then, handcuffs clanking, she took cold cuts, mayonnaise, mustard, a loaf of bread and a tomato out of the refrigerator and assembled four enormous sandwiches, while Ryan, without being asked, got out plates, paper towels, glasses and milk. They ate—wolfed—the first of the sandwiches standing at the counter.

After they'd washed them down with milk and were wiping mouths and taking deep breaths in preparation for tackling the second, Ryan burped politely and said, "So...*are* you gonna marry my Dad?" But he wasn't looking at her, and his eyes had that shifty, evasive look again.

Joy drank milk, wiped her mouth and pushed the plate and her second sandwich away. The squeezing sensation in her stomach had taken away any desire for food. Ignoring it, she said lightly, ''Ok-ay, Ryan…what's goin' on here?''

''What?'' He widened his eyes, trying, not very hard, to look righteous and wounded.

''For starters, I've only known your father a few days. And for most of that time, you haven't been all that happy about the fact. Now, all of a sudden, you think we should get *married?* So come on, what gives?''

He picked up his sandwich and examined it minutely. Then he slid his eyes to hers, and she saw it again—that look that reminded her so much of Scott. A very young version, but unmistakable nonetheless. Character…integrity…courage. He shrugged and focused on the sandwich again.

''Okay. Here's the deal. My mom wants to move to St. Petersburg, and I don't want to. All my friends are here. Plus, I wouldn't get to spend as much time with Dad…help on the boat…stuff like that. But if Dad got married, I could stay here and live with him. And… I think you'd make an okay stepmom.'' He gave another shrug and bit into the sandwich.

Joy burst out laughing. What else could she do, with such a sweet aching inside and tears gathering, and no words at all to say? She was desperately trying to find some when she heard a horn honk on the street outside.

''Oops, that's my cab.'' She grabbed for her purse, heart hammering. ''Well, wish me luck.'' She dodged around the end of the counter, pausing to snatch up the sweater from the kitchen table and arrange it in a casual drape over the handcuff.

She was halfway across the living room when she realized Ryan was right behind her, his backpack slung over one arm. She halted and turned. ''And…just where do you think you're going?''

He gazed back at her, unblinking. ''I don't think you should go alone. I'm going with you.''

Joy's heart turned to mush. She didn't know where in the

world she found the strength to keep her face and voice stern, but somehow she did. "Uh-uh. No way." She placed her unshackled hand flat on his chest, and feeling his heart tap-tapping against her fingers, wanted more than anything in the world to hug the stuffing out of him. "Risking my own neck is one thing. No way in this world am I letting you do something that could get you hurt."

"But you said…all that stuff about it being your own decision. How come you get to make yours, and I don't?"

"Because I'm a grown-up and you're not," Joy said firmly. She smiled and leaned over to kiss his cheek. "Honey, I wish I could let you come with me, believe me. You'd make a terrific partner. But you know I can't. Your dad would never forgive me if I let anything happen to you." *And neither would I!*

Out on the street, the horn honked again, less politely. "Gotta go," she said huskily, and again, as she turned away from Ryan's unhappy face, "Wish me luck."

"Wait."

Something bumped her arm. Looking back, she saw that Ryan was rummaging frantically through his backpack. "At least take this." His voice was deep, a grown man's growl, as he thrust his cell phone into her hand. "It's got Dad's cell number programmed into it. It's number one. If you get in trouble, maybe you could, you know, call him."

He lifted one shoulder, and she saw his throat—his budding Adam's apple—bob convulsively with his swallow.

"Thanks," she whispered. As she ran down the steps to the waiting cab, she was thinking, *Oh God, now I have two men to love. What in the world am I gonna do?*

Chapter 15

"Whoa," the cabdriver said, putting on the brakes and steering his car onto the grassy shoulder, "looks like this is as far as we gonna go."

Joy hitched herself forward to peer over the seat, taking care to keep her handcuffed arm wrapped in the sweater and tucked down out of sight. "What is it? Why are we stopping?"

The driver, a chunky Latino with a brushy walrus moustache whose name, according to the ID above his rearview mirror, was Luis, tipped his head toward the road ahead where a clot of official vehicles of various colors had formed, shimmering in the early evening heat. "Cops got a roadblock up there. Looks like somethin' big goin' on. Looks like they not lettin' nobody in there." He shrugged, shot a look over his shoulder and hung a sharp U-turn, jouncing across the pavement, up onto the opposite shoulder and back onto the pavement.

"Wait!" Joy was frowning and thinking hard. Dammit, Ryan had been right. Federal agents and local police had the whole area blocked off. She had told him she'd have to think of something. Obviously, the time for that was now. "Isn't there another way? What about the other side? Or in back?"

Luis shook his head. "There's an airstrip back there. I think they gotta fence, too, a big one—chain-link, you know? Other side?" He waved his arm in a vague but sweeping gesture. "Nothin' over there but swamp. Those palmettos, you know? Maybe snakes, 'gators, too. No way through over there." His eyes found hers in the rearview mirror. "Why you wanna go in that place so bad? Maybe you come back tomorrow, no? Cops be gone by then."

Ignoring him, Joy chewed on the inside of her cheek while she thought about it. How much time did she have? The phone conversation she'd overheard had said only "this evening", after a plane had arrived. Who knew when that might be? Was the plane even now circling the airstrip, preparing to land? She took a deep breath.

"How close can you get me to that swamp?"

Luis abandoned the mirror to look at her over his shoulder, the expression on his face stating clearly his opinion that she was *loco* in the *cabeza*. Meeting only Joy's unblinking stare, he gave a fatalistic shrug. "I don' know, I guess we go see."

Fifteen minutes later, the cab pulled to a stop once more. "Okay," Luis said flatly, "this is close as I can go."

Joy ducked her head and peered through the windows on both sides of the cab. They were on a service road that ran alongside a canal, the grassy dirt bank rising on one side of the road, a thicket of pine and palmetto scrub on the other. The road had dead-ended at a chain-link fence, which intersected the steep canal bank at roughly a right angle. Obviously meant to deter motor vehicles rather than foot traffic, the fence didn't abut tightly against the sloping bank but left a V-shaped gap plenty big enough for a determined child— or one small woman—to slip through.

In the unlikely event one would want to.

Beyond the fence, the palmetto thicket had been allowed to swarm right up to the top of the canal bank, forming a natural barrier around the plant's manicured grounds. Like a moat, Joy thought, around a castle. The castle in this case being the low-slung, utterly innocent-looking sprawl of beige buildings that was Sun-Tek Industries, Inc., maker of mechanical awnings and patio covers. If she was right, there was a princess in the castle awaiting rescue. *Whatever made me think I was cut out to be a knight?*

"Thanks, this will be fine," she said, trying hard to keep her voice steady. She reached over the back of the seat to give the cabdriver a handful of money, including, she hoped, enough of a tip to overcome his fears and scruples about leaving her here alone. Because plainly he had some.

"You sure you don' wan' me to wait for you?" Looking like a doleful walrus, Luis leaned his head and one elbow out of the window to watch her as she got out of the car.

Joy resisted the urge to kiss his cheek and instead gave him what she hoped was a confident smile. "No, thanks. But...you don't happen to have any mosquito repellent, do you?"

Luis shook his head, gave her a despairing wave, rolled up his window and drove away.

Joy watched the cab disappear in a cloud of dust, then unwrapped the sweater from her arm and draped it over her head like an Arab's *kaffiyeh*. It would be hot, but she hoped it would provide some protection against mosquitoes. Then she looked down at her feet, at the leather stack-heeled boots she'd been forced to wear on her last two escapades, since her only pair of running shoes were somewhere at the bottom of the fishing boat harbor. Not the best footwear for a long walk in the heat, but they'd probably be impervious to snakes. 'Gators, on the other hand...she really didn't like the idea of meeting an alligator.

Then inspiration struck. She rummaged through her purse, hoping and praying that what she was looking for was still there, since she'd never had occasion to use it before. *Yes.* There it was. Clutching the purse-size container of pepper spray no single New York woman would ever be without,

Joy climbed the bank, squeezed through the gap at the end of the fence and set off into the swamp.

Inside an FBI surveillance van parked behind a warehouse roughly half a mile from the entrance to Sun-Tek Industries, Scott resisted the urge to check his watch one more time. The waiting was always the worst. This was pretty much par for the course on ops he'd been involved in—ninety-eight percent boredom and maybe two percent pure, unadulterated adrenaline.

"What the *hell?*"

Everyone in the van turned to see who had spoken. The agent sitting in front of the bank of monitor screens was leaning forward, frowning at one of them. He pointed. "Jeez, who in the hell is that?"

Agent Kevin Harvey moved in behind him. So did Scott. Every pair of eyes in the van was fixed in horror on the small figure moving across one of the screens. Someone was swearing. Scott's heart dropped into his shoes.

"Where the hell did *she* come from?" Harvey murmured disbelievingly.

"She just came out of the woods," the agent monitoring the screens replied the same way. "That swamp right there. Where the hell is she going?"

Nobody had an answer to that, and Scott wasn't about to open his mouth. Not until he absolutely had to. Everyone watched in fascinated silence as the small figure trudged off the edge of one screen and a moment later appeared, from a slightly different angle, on another.

"What the hell's on her head? Zoom in, zoom in, dammit."

The figure sprang into out-of-focus close-up. The image sharpened.

"Uh, looks like some kind of clothing—a jacket, maybe. No, it's a sweater. Wait, she's taking it off."

"What the hell is that on her arm? Is that— It looks like...*handcuffs.*"

Scott closed his eyes and braced himself.

"Cavanaugh?" Scott could feel the FBI man's breath. *"Tell me that's not who I think it is."*

He grimaced and opened one eye. "I'm afraid it does appear to be."

"I thought you said you'd taken care of the situation."

"Well," Scott said, exasperated, "I did try." He paused. "Those are my cuffs she's wearing."

Agent Harvey swore. "Who the hell does she think she is, *Houdini?*" He bent to peer at yet another screen, this one showing the circular drive and landscaped flower beds of the front entrance to the plant's office complex. The figure, now clearly recognizable as the woman Scott had last seen chained to his bathroom plumbing, had stopped on the wide shallow steps. She now had the sweater draped over her arm, hiding the dangling cuffs from view, and was taking something out of her purse. "What the hell's she doing *now?*"

"Look's like she's making a call on her cell phone," the agent at the console said.

At that same moment, Scott felt his phone vibrate. He looked down at it, startled. *No,* he thought, *it can't be.* He unhooked the phone and looked at the readout. Ryan's number. *Ryan. Damn!* Things fell into place. With a sense of growing dread, he hit the "on" button and slowly lifted the phone to his ear, feeling almost every eye in the van turn to him as he cautiously said, "Hello?"

"Uh-oh," the agent monitoring the screens said. "She's just been busted."

Scott scowled at the screen, where he could see a security guard twice her size closing in on Joy. "Hello?" he said again. "Joy, is that you?"

"Yes, hello. Triple-A?" It was definitely Joy's voice.

A combination of relief and terror weakened his knees. He opened his mouth to reply, then closed it as she went on without waiting for one.

"Yes, hi. Uh…my car broke down and I was wondering how soon I could get a tow truck?"

This time Scott knew better than to fill the pause. Motioning for silence, he covered the bottom half of the phone with his palm.

"Well, I'm at the Sun-Tek plant right now. I thought maybe you could have a truck meet me here. I'm not sure I can explain where my car is, but I can take somebody there. Would that be all right?" Another pause, then: "Okay, thanks. Oh, how long do you think it'll be?" Pause. "That long? Uh-huh… I see. Okay, well, thank you. 'Bye."

Then, instead of silence, Scott heard muffled scufflings, followed by a man's voice, gruff and officious.

"Sorry, lady, office is closed. I'm gonna have to ask you to leave the premises."

Agent Harvey's eyebrows were lifted in silent query. Scott frowned at him and shook his head, listening.

The smaller figure on the screen was gesturing. Then came Joy's voice again, muffled and distant this time, but clearly distressed. "Oh, oh, no, please don't tell me that. I was *so* hoping… You don't suppose I could just come in and use the bathroom, do you? My car broke down, and I've called Triple-A, but it's going to take *forever* for them to get here, and I'm *so* hot and thirsty…not to mention the mosquitoes have just about eaten me alive. Please? I'll only be a minute, just long enough to…*you* know…freshen up a little bit?"

"Well…" said the security guard.

Scott almost laughed. He didn't have to watch the monitor to know what that "look" of Joy's was doing to the man. He'd seen her work that particular magic before.

"Okay…" There was a gusty sigh. "I guess it'd be all right. I'm gonna have to take you, though. Come around to the employees' entrance. You can go in through there."

"Oh, thank you *so* much. You are a lifesaver…." The voices faded into rustles and whirs of static as the two figures walked side by side off the edge of the screen.

"Okay, you want to tell me what the hell's going on?" Agent Harvey demanded, all but vibrating with impatience.

Scott held out his cell phone, and as mad at Joy as he was,

he couldn't keep a grin from spreading across his face. "She's left the connection open," he said, his chest swelling with admiration and pride. "She might as well be wearing a wire."

Joy walked beside the security guard down a brightly lit hallway, her boots sounding loud on the vinyl tile floor as she struggled to keep up with his longer stride. As rapid as her footsteps were, her heart beat faster. She felt strange, jerky, as though her body wasn't quite under her control, and she thought of her junior year in high school, walking onto the stage on opening night of the school play. They'd done *Our Town* and she'd played Emily. She'd felt just like this, she remembered—as confident and prepared as she knew how to be, but nevertheless terrified she wasn't going to remember her lines.

It was eerily quiet. This was the huge plant's office wing, and they passed office after office, open doors revealing empty desks where screen savers marched silently across darkened computer screens. Down at the far end of the hallway, a glass door opened onto a patio—an employees' eating area, perhaps—enclosed by a low block wall. Beyond it Joy could see the airstrip, a dark slash across the green grass like a lead pencil mark on a giant pool table. The last door on the left side of the hallway before the exit stood open and she could hear the murmur of voices coming from inside.

For an eternity her heart seemed to stop. Those voices... one was a woman's, she was sure of it. But was it Yancy's? It seemed familiar, but that might be wishful thinking. If only she could see with her own eyes.

"There you go," the security guard said. He'd halted before a women's rest room. He pulled a key out of one of those snap-back thingies attached to his belt and unlocked the door, throwing a nervous look toward the open door near the end of the hallway as he gruffly added, "Be quick about it."

But, Joy thought, if I go in there now, I'm done. He'll wait for me to finish, then escort me back the way we came, and I'll never get to see who's in that room. *I have to see who's in that room!*

Why she was so certain she didn't know, but that certainty gave her both courage and inspiration. "Oh, wait. Is that the employees' lounge?" she cried, and she slipped past the guard before he had any idea she was going to and went hurrying down the hallway toward the open door, talking loudly as she went. Loudly enough, she devoutly hoped, that if it *was* Yancy in that room, she'd hear Joy's voice and be prepared. Prepared enough, she hoped even more devoutly, not to give her away.

"They'd probably have vending machines, wouldn't they? Could I just get myself something to drink, as long as I'm in here anyway? You know, I've been wanderin' around out there in that awful heat, and I am about to *die* of thirst...." *Bad choice of words, Joy.*

She could hear the guard's footsteps, feel the heat of his body, the rush of air that meant he was almost upon her. In another second he'd grab her arm. *Oh, but two steps more and I'll be able to see!*

A shadow moved across the doorway. Joy all but hurled herself into the opening and found herself sandwiched between two enormous men, the one behind her in his security guard's uniform, complete with weapon, the one in front wearing a tropical-weight suit that had a noticeable bulge under the jacket. It was pure instinct that made her continue on, plough full tilt into that massive chest, when all good sense should have told her to stop in her tracks. Caught unaware, the man in the suit actually took a step back, although her weight couldn't have affected him more than a fly's.

"Oh, goodness," she cried gaily, steadying herself with her palms against his shirt front, "I'm sorry about that! You sure did startle me. I didn't know anybody was in here. I was just lookin' for the vending machines. You don't happen to—oops, I see where they are. If you'll just excuse me..."

And she slipped under his outstretched arm and into the room.

It was, as she had supposed, an employees' lounge or break room. On the left were cabinets and a sink, microwave oven and coffeemaker, several round tables and chairs. Several men were sitting at one of the tables. Most looked to one degree or another to be Latino. All of them looked tough. An assortment of vending machines stood along the wall opposite the door and to the right of these, several comfortable chairs were arranged around a coffee table covered with sections of a newspaper and some well-thumbed magazines, facing a TV set on a cabinet against the wall. At the far end, a couch sat in front of a large window that looked out on the patio and airstrip. A woman was sitting on one end of the couch. A man was perched on the arm of the couch beside her, one arm draped possessively across the cushions behind her shoulders. All this Joy absorbed in the first couple of seconds, along with the fact that the woman sitting on the couch was Yancy.

A strange calm settled over her—a feeling of tremendous relief and happiness and vindication, too. She thought she knew how the Victorian explorer Stanley must have felt, finding Dr. Livingstone alive against all odds in the jungles of darkest Africa. She thought she understood the exact feelings, the enormous calm behind that classic greeting: *"Dr. Livingston, I presume?"* She felt just that way now.

Instinct told her to keep talking, so she did, babbling on about how hot and tired she was and what a terrible day she was having, with her car conking out and all, and at the same time she was rummaging madly in her pocketbook, finding her wallet and pulling out dollar bills to feed into the vending machine. And at the same time she was doing *that,* she looked toward the couple on the couch and gave them a big smile, along with a head shake that could have meant just about anything to a casual observer. Afraid to risk making direct eye contact with Yancy, Joy could only hope she'd gotten the message, which was, essentially, two words: *Shut up*.

Meanwhile, not only Yancy but *everyone* seemed to have turned to stone. Everyone except her. It was as if she moved through a garden of statues, except that the tension in the room was like a living, breathing thing. She could feel its hot breath on the back of her neck, hear its high-pitched keening in her ears, *smell* it, like ozone during a thunderstorm. Any second, now, she expected lightning to strike her dead.

She prayed no one would notice her hand shaking as she tried to thread a dollar bill into the vending machine's slot. Behind her she could hear the mutter of voices, but the thunder of her own pulse was so loud, she couldn't make out words. She could hear uneasy stirrings and feel hard, suspicious eyes watching her as she tucked her wallet back into her purse, leaving it open and praying nobody would notice that, either.

She pushed a button at random. A can fell into the tray with a rumble that sounded like a rock slide. She fished it out, popped it open and took a long drink, then turned to face the room, holding the can pressed against her cheek.

"Oh, my goodness, that does feel good. Thank you so much. I'm really sorry to barge in on your break like this." And she was encompassing the room with her smile, appearing to take notice of her surroundings for the first time. "Y'all sure do have a nice place here. You're lucky. Where I work, we pretty much have to go out and sit on the back stoop."

She passed around her smile again, this time focusing on the faces of the people in the room—counting them, taking stock: two men sitting at the table, one middle-aged and heavy, with a hard, slightly pockmarked face, the other somewhat older, leaner, grayer and considerably more handsome, with a nose like a hawk's beak and a thin, cruel mouth. Both, like the big man who had tried to intercept her at the door, wore light-colored suits and tropical print shirts. She couldn't tell whether they were armed. *The DelReys,* Joy thought. *Brothers? Father and son? In any case, they looked dangerous, armed or not.* Then the big man standing beside the security guard—*he* definitely had a gun underneath that jacket. *A bodyguard?* All three wore looks of consternation and Joy thought with a little thrill of excitement and hope, *They don't know what to do with me. I'm a glitch in their plans.*

The man sitting on the arm of the couch she had seen before, in a photograph in a glass case at the Spanish Keys Resort. Diego DelRey, known as Junior. He looked young, not out of his twenties, and bored, sleek and lithe as a cat and movie-star handsome, wearing slacks and a polo shirt. No weapon in sight. He looked, Joy thought, like the man of Yancy's dreams.

So, a total of five men…and Yancy. Yes, Yancy, wearing a pale green halter-top sundress she'd bought especially for her trip from a designer she really couldn't afford, and her hair, grown out some from its usual spiky, pixie style and wilting in the heat and humidity, looking more waifish than fashionable. Her huge green eyes looked frightened and Joy's heart swelled inside her chest with maternal rage and resolve.

"Well, I don't want to be in your way," she said brightly. "I hope it's okay if I just use your rest room, before I go?" She started toward the door, her heart pounding so hard it hurt, aware that the big man in the suit had moved to intercept her. She thought of Scott and the FBI, out *there,* somewhere, poised to strike—listening, she hoped and prayed, to her every word.

Is this the moment? Should I give the word…now?

Chapter 16

She shifted her purse, lifting it onto her sweater-shrouded arm, bringing it and the cell phone inside closer to her mouth. Her heart danced into her throat as she watched the face of the man standing between her and the door, and gauged the moment....

A low droning sound filled the room. The bodyguard seemed to freeze in place, and the tension in the room kicked up to a new level.

"Plane's here," Junior DelRey said, looking out the window.

"Oh, my goodness, is it gonna land?" Joy cried, moving quickly toward the window, toward the couch, toward Yancy, chattering like a fool again. "Isn't that exciting? Y'all have your own landing strip and everything?" And while everyone's attention was on the twin-engine executive-type jet, watching it touch down on the runway and flash past the window, she looked straight into Yancy's eyes and made a small jerking motion with her head.

Yancy sat up as if she'd been poked, and for one awful

moment Joy was afraid she'd misunderstood. But then, in a tired, bored-sounding voice, Yancy whined, "Diego, honey, I should probably use the rest room before I get on that plane. Goodness knows how long it's going to be before I get another chance."

Junior DelRey smiled indulgently at her. "*Querida,* there will be a rest room on the plane."

Yancy made a face. "Oh, I know, but I hate those little tiny things, and sometimes the air is bumpy."

"Let her go. There is enough time." The hawk-nosed man had spoken. He jerked his head toward Joy. "Her, too." Another jerk, this one aimed at the uniformed security guard. "Go with them. But be quick."

Joy beamed at Yancy in a chummy way as she joined her. "Y'all are going on a trip? How excitin'. Is it for business, or just for fun?" Chattering again, she edged past the stone-faced guards and through the doorway. Yancy fell into step beside her and they walked together rapidly down the hallway toward the ladies' rest room, the guard trudging heavily behind them. Joy thought, *How fast and hard can my heart beat before it kills me?*

The security guard pulled out his key and unlocked the rest room. "You heard what the man said," he growled as he backed away to let them through the door, and there was no longer any hint of friendliness in either voice or expression. "Be quick about it."

Yancy nodded. Joy chirped, "Thank you so much!" Then they were together inside the rest room, and the door was clicking shut behind them. It had barely done so before Yancy gave a sob and turned blindly into Joy's arms. Joy hissed a frantic *"Shh!"* and reached behind her to ease the thumb-lock into place. The guard had his key, of course, but at least it might slow him down. Grabbing Yancy's arm, she pulled her into the disabled-persons stall, closed the door and locked it.

"What—"

Joy held a silencing finger to her lips. She grabbed the cell phone out of her purse, impatiently pulling the sweater off her handcuffed arm when it got in her way, and Yancy got out one tiny horrified squeak before she stifled it with both hands clamped over her mouth.

"Scott," said Joy, trying hard to sound calm, "if you're listening, I have Yancy. We're in the rest room. The DelReys are down the hall in the employees' lunchroom, first door on the right inside the patio exit. There are five. At least two are armed. Can you hear me? Scott? Oh God...please. Are you there?"

And then she heard the most beautiful sound. Scott's voice, controlled, maybe a little out of breath, a bit ragged.

"I hear you. We're coming in."

She had begun to laugh, silently and with tears running down her cheeks, when she heard him again.

"Joy? Do me one little favor? *Stay put!* Do you think you could do that? For once in your life? Keep your head down, *dammit!*"

Laughing, crying, Joy dropped the cell phone back into her purse and turned to take her best friend into her arms.

"I knew you'd come," Yancy said, sobbing. "I *called* for you to come. And you did. You did...."

Unable to speak, Joy just nodded. Then she pulled Yancy down into the corner as far from the door as she could get, and they held on to each other and kept their heads down, while all hell broke loose outside.

"So, what happens next?" Scott nodded toward the two women sitting together on the concrete steps of a floodlit loading dock, talking animatedly the way women do after an emotional event, with a lot of gesturing and hugging mixed in.

Following his gaze, Agent Harvey said, "To Yancy, I assume you mean." Scott nodded. The FBI man hesitated, then glanced over at him, not smiling. "I can guarantee we're going to have a few questions to ask her."

"Sure," Scott said, and then was silent. This was the eye

of the storm, he thought. There'd be a lot of havoc still
to come.

The storm was already beginning, in fact, swirling around
them where they stood near Sun-Tek's loading bays. Vehicles
of all shapes and kinds representative of various law enforcement agencies, federal and local, were parked helter-skelter
in the parking lot, with more arriving all the time. The raid
had been a complete success—the best kind of success, with
a minimum of destruction and bloodshed. Diego DelRey, Se-
nior, family patriarch and by most accounts head of its business operations as well, had been taken into custody, along
with his younger brother, Mario, reputed chief of security,
and playboy son, Diego Junior. A DelRey bodyguard and a
plant security guard had sustained gunshot wounds, not life-
threatening, and had been transported to a hospital. Now,
though night had fallen, armies of crime scene technicians
and forensics experts, including bookkeepers and computer
scientists, were preparing to fan out over the huge plant and
pick it clean of any and all possible evidence that might link
the DelReys with organized crime or international terrorism.

"And after that?" Scott asked, thinking of Joy and all
she'd been through, all she'd risked to find her friend and
bring her home. He felt his heart flutter with burgeoning
pride, but squelched it quickly. He wasn't ready to give up
being angry with her yet, not by a long shot. He'd lost a few
good years off his life tonight, no doubt about it. If she ever
put him through something like this again... He shook himself and tuned in to what the FBI man was saying.

"After that? For now, we'll put her in protective custody.
For how long... I guess that'll depend on how much she
knows and is willing to testify to."

Scott nodded. After a moment, he said, "What about
Joy?"

"You mean, your partner?" Agent Harvey looked over at
him and it was the first time Scott had seen him smile. "Take
her home. Feed her, put her to bed, do whatever you need
to do, as long as it keeps her the hell out of my operations."

"Well," Scott said dryly, lifting the cuffs he'd been juggling restlessly from one hand to the other, "I did try."

"A word of advice," Harvey said under his breath as they walked over to where the women were sitting. "Next time cuff her to something that can't be taken apart with a monkey wrench."

"I'll try and keep that in mind," Scott said darkly. He hadn't gotten to the point where he could laugh about all this yet, though he guessed he would eventually. Maybe. First, he was going to have to find Ryan and skin him alive. He hadn't quite decided what he was going to do with Joy....

"Sorry to have to break this up," he said, and two faces swiveled toward him, one probably the most beautiful face he'd ever seen in his life, up close and in person. Her pictures didn't begin to do her justice. Still, it was the *other* face that filled his eyes, and his mind and heart as well. The only face he ever wanted to see, the first upon waking up in the morning and the last before he went to sleep at night. A face with soft brown puppy-dog eyes and a warm and generous smile. A face filled with life and love, compassion and joy. *Yes, Joy.* And he suddenly knew exactly what he wanted to do with her, what he ached to do with her and fully intended to do the minute he got her alone—grab her and pull her close to him and wrap his arms around her and hold on to her and never let go.

The two women rose and faced them, looking dazed, smiling uncertainly. Joy, the shorter of the two by half a head, touched Yancy's arm and said, "Scott, this is my friend, Yancy. Yancy, this is Scott."

Yancy held out her hand. Scott took it and murmured, "Yancy," and she murmured back, "Nice meeting you, Scott."

Agent Harvey cleared his throat and she turned to him with a determined smile. "Is it time to go already?" She turned back to Joy and caught her in a quick, hard hug. Or it would have been quick, except Joy held on to her for a while and by the time Yancy pulled herself free, tears were falling.

"Oh..." she said, laughing and sniffling, "you take care, now."

And Joy said fiercely, "Okay, you, too. I'll see you *soon.*"

They broke apart. Agent Harvey took Yancy's arm and led her away. The look on Joy's face as she watched her friend go made Scott's throat ache. It was the look of a mother watching her child go off into the care of strangers on the first day of school.

He touched her elbow and said, "Let's go home." Her eyes flew to his, shimmery with tears, and his heart lifted with the pain of loving her. It was all he *could* do, he realized. Embrace the pain...rejoice in it. Because he was going to be living with it for the rest of his life.

He's so angry, Joy thought. "Scott, I want you to know—"

"Not now. Wait until we get home." His voice sounded growly and strangled, and she wondered whether he was ever going to *not* be angry with her again.

He took her home in a Sheriff's Department patrol car. He didn't say a word to her the whole way, and she sat hunched in the passenger seat a million miles away from him, feeling as tired and miserable as she'd ever felt in her life. She kept silent, too, until they were turning onto the street where Scott lived.

She swallowed painfully and said, "Scott, I know you're angry with me, but please don't be mad at Ryan. It wasn't—"

"Joy. Don't." He didn't even glance at her. "Don't tell me it wasn't Ryan's fault. He sure as hell bears a share of the blame for this...escapade, and he's damn sure old enough to take the responsibility for it. He made a choice. He let himself be talked into doing something he knew damn good and well was wrong. You really think he ought to get away with that? How many bad choices does it take to ruin a kid's life? I'll tell you how many—*one.* That's all. Just one—" His voice cracked.

Joy swallowed back tears and whispered, "I'm sorry."

Scott didn't want to look at her. *Couldn't* look at her. Instead he stared narrow-eyed through the windshield, preparing himself, girding himself emotionally for the coming confrontation with his son. And it was going to be a bad one, because since he couldn't bear to be angry with Joy, most of his anger over this crazy stunt had gotten transferred to Ryan. Except that now it wasn't anger, if it ever had been, so much as it was *fear*. Just now, the responsibilities of fatherhood seemed terrifying to him, the task of raising a "good kid" into a good man almost too daunting to contemplate. The odds seemed long against him indeed.

He pulled the car into his driveway and cut the motor, then sat holding the steering wheel, his muscles weighed down with his fear. Beside him, Joy unfastened her seat belt and turned her head toward him, not saying anything. And as they sat there in the dark car, enveloped in that shimmering silence, the front door of Scott's house opened, throwing a broad ribbon of light across the yard. They watched as Ryan burst through it, then halted in frozen silhouette, as if in dread.

Joy uttered a muffled sound, like a sob or a laugh, and yanked open her door. And then, as Scott watched, too stunned and uncomprehending to move or utter a sound, she launched herself from the car and was half running, half tripping over the scruffy grass toward the house, and Ryan was running, clattering in the awkward way of teenage boys, down the steps to meet her. They came together—like…what? Long lost friends? Brothers? Like parent and child in a joyous embrace, holding each other and stumbling and turning to keep their balance, laughing…sobbing, talking over each other in breathless phrases.

"Is it really you? You're okay?"

"Oh, Ryan. Yes…yes—"

"Did you do it? Is she—"

"She's fine. Everything's—"

"I can't believe it, you're alive—"

"Yes, yes, I'm fine… I'm fine…."

Alone in the dark patrol car, Scott felt a great tremor go through him, and a sudden *loosening* inside him, as if the entire superstructure of his being had collapsed without warning. He put a hand over his face and sat shaking his head, silently laughing until the tears came, and swearing because like most men, he wasn't any good at crying.

They were coming toward him now, his only son and the woman he loved, walking side by side but not touching. Even in the meager light he could see that Ryan was looking a little embarrassed by his display of emotion, not to mention uncertain. Joy looked…hopeful. Hopeful *and* uncertain. He got out of the car, moving slowly and stiffly, like someone coming home after a long hospital convalescence.

"Dad," Ryan said. Only it wasn't Ryan's voice. It was a stranger's voice. Deep but a little unsteady. A man's voice, not quite broken in. "I'm sorry—"

"Not now, son. We'll talk about this later." His own voice was calm, almost gentle, but what he felt was more a tremendous weariness—numbness, almost. Too much in his life had changed too suddenly—turned upside down, done a complete one-eighty, and he was feeling overwhelmed by a sense of awe and wonder. "Is your mom home?"

"Yeah," said his son's new voice, followed by some throat clearing—obviously Ryan wasn't quite used to it yet, either. "I was gonna go over there, but I wanted to wait…"

"Hop in," Scott said quietly, "I'll take you home."

Ryan hesitated, threw an uncertain look back at Joy, then opened the passenger door of the patrol car and got in. Scott started the motor and backed out of the driveway, then pulled up the wrong way to the curb and rolled down his window. Joy took a few steps toward him, her arms wrapped around herself as if she were cold although the night was sultry and soft with the promise of summer. Her eyes clung to his, dark-shadowed in the stingy light of the yard lamps, and he thought of all the times he'd thought of them as being like a puppy's. Right now, what she looked like was a puppy dog expecting to be kicked.

That realization made his chest clench with pain and a lump of sickness rise into his throat. He thought of the way she'd been, that wonderful self-assurance, that complete lack of self-consciousness he'd found so attractive. What had changed?

He knew what had changed. She'd fallen in love with him. Up to now, the men she'd loved had always let her down, so naturally she was expecting him to do the same. *That's what love does to you,* he thought. *It makes you vulnerable.*

"Go on in," he said, his voice tight with the pain he felt for her. "I'll be back soon, okay?"

She nodded. *I'm never gonna let you down.* He made the vow to her silently. *If it takes the rest of my life, I'll make you believe that. I'll make you believe in me.*

Yes, he thought, as he drove away and left her standing there, his chest, his whole being swelled with a fierce and protective love. Love did make you vulnerable. But the right kind of love could make you strong, too.

Joy watched the big car's taillights flash and wink out around the corner, then she slowly turned and walked across the barren little yard, up the steps and into the house.

She'd never felt so tired. She felt weary clear to the bone. What a day...what a night it had been! She'd been focused for so long on Yancy, getting someone to believe her friend was in trouble, then finding her...rescuing her. Her mission had been accomplished, and she felt strangely let down—directionless.

But that wasn't all. She felt unbearably sad...heartsick. Because somewhere along the line she'd fallen in love. And she'd even begun—dangerously, perhaps, to believe in Forever After again. But ironically, in the process of finding Yancy, she'd destroyed any hope of such a thing for herself.

I don't regret it, she thought. *I don't.* She'd really had no choice. But why did it have to cost so much?

Scott was never going to forgive her. Of that she was certain. Not for going against his orders and risking her own life—she was pretty sure he'd get over that, as he'd gotten over it the other times she'd done it. No, what she'd done this time was something truly unforgivable. She'd come between a father and his son. She'd incited a son to disobey his father. She'd interfered with Scott's efforts to teach his son responsibility, to instill in him strong character, and to make good choices. The *right* choices. In a way, she'd endangered Ryan's life, his future. How could *any* man forgive that?

She wandered into the bedroom, trying not to think of how it had felt to lie with Scott in his bed, to make love with him, to laugh with him, to talk of love, to make deals with him. *As long as we're clear...just love...for as long as it lasts...and when it ends we walk away, no harsh words, no regrets....* Her heart twisted with a pain so sharp she almost cried out.

She went into the bathroom and her heart twinged with a completely different kind of pain when she saw that Ryan had cleaned up all traces of their prison break—put the pipes back together, put away the tools, tidied up the mess. What a sweetheart he was, really. A son anyone would be proud of. *The son I wish I'd had.*

She was so hot and itchy and tired. She couldn't bear to look in the mirror, sure her hair must be a nightmare of dust and debris, as her clothes were. The skin on her face and arms was covered with scratches and mosquito bites. Surely, she thought, Ryan wouldn't begrudge her a bath, no matter how angry he was. She'd feel much more able to face him if she were clean.

She plugged the tub with its old-fashioned stopper on a chain, turned on the faucets and began to undress. A shower would have been quicker, but what she really wanted—just once—was to immerse herself in that huge old tub. Bubbles would have been nice, but as this was a bachelor's bathroom, she had no hope of that. Unless...yes, there was a bottle of shampoo. She poured a generous amount into the water gushing from the tap and watched a mound of bubbles grow. Then she slipped off her bra and underpants, climbed into the tub and leaned back with a tremulous sigh. Oh, she was so tired. She ached all over, inside and out. Especially inside…deep in her heart.

She might have dozed. Suddenly she was sitting up, adrenaline-cold inside and realizing that once again she'd felt the house quiver. *The front door had closed.* Her heart thumped in time to the beat of footsteps crossing the bedroom floor. The door, which she hadn't closed, swung silently inward.

Scott stood in the bathroom doorway looking not at her, but around her in a vague, lost way, as if he'd been searching for something. Joy gazed at him, suspense pounding in her chest and singing in her ears, every nerve in her body trembling…waiting for the inevitable. She held her breath as he moved slowly into the room. The suspense rose to a screaming pitch.

Still not meeting her eyes, he picked up a sponge she'd left on the edge of the tub and gazed at it as though he'd never seen anything like it before. Then as her throat began to swell with sobs, he knelt down on the floor beside the tub, dipped the sponge into the water and slowly, slowly lifted it to the nape of her neck.

A sob burst from her and tears ran down her cheeks as she lifted unbelieving, incredulous eyes to his face. He didn't say a word…didn't smile…still didn't meet her eyes…but gently, gently wiped the tears from her face with the sponge.

Trembling, she opened her mouth to say something…his name. He touched his finger gently, gently to her lips, then leaned over and kissed her.

He kissed her a long, sweet, unimaginably lovely time, before he pulled back to gaze at her with a sigh. "Miss Joy…what am I going to do with you?"

She gave a small, disbelieving, sniffling laugh, touched her nose and said thickly, "Forgive me?"

He shook his head. "Already done."

Hesitantly, hardly daring to say it, she whispered, "Then…love me?"

"Already do." He said that with a shrug, his beautiful mouth softening into a smile of exquisite tenderness.

Her own smile emerged, then, blossoming like something newly born. "Then...make love to me?"

His smile became a grin. "Come out of there and I will."

Trembling and tearful with wonder, she caught her lip between her teeth and murmured, "Why don't you come in here? There's plenty of room."

His heart hammered as he laughed and leaned to kiss her. "I'm too old to make love in a bathtub."

"Says who?" And she gazed up at him through her lashes.

What could he do? He'd seen her work that magic before. The next thing he knew he was shucking off his clothes and climbing into the tub, feeling awkward and excited and a little bit silly and overwhelmed, like a kid again.

Joy moved around to give him room, facing the back of the tub as he eased himself down into the warm, slippery water. Then, graceful and lithe as an eel, she slid astride his body and leaned to kiss him. She sank onto him, slick and tight and pulsing with vitality and sweetness and warmth, everything he'd ever hoped for and had been missing for so much of his life.

The loving was slow and intense...hearts and bodies swollen and interwoven, wrapped and fused together with moisture and heat and love. The climax was silent and overwhelming, and they held on to each other and rode it out together, trembling and dazed, like survivors of a storm.

Sometime later, an eternity later, from the moist and steamy pillow of Scott's chest, Joy stirred and whispered, "What am I going to do with you?"

He was silent for a long time, heart pounding...gathering courage. Then, with agony, he said it. "Marry me."

She went still in his arms. She lifted herself away from him and with regret and a sense of inevitability in his heart, he let her go. She eased back into her end of the tub, not saying anything, just looking at him. At least, he thought, gazing warily back at her, she didn't say no.

She wiped sweat from her nose, then said in a matter-of-fact tone, "Ryan asked me if we were going to."

Scott swallowed his fear and answered just as calmly. "His mother's moving to St. Petersburg. Some friend she met at her sorority reunion wants to open a garden shop and asked if she wanted to partner with her. She...thinks it's time she let go."

"Ryan wants to stay here," Joy said. "He thinks if we got married—"

Scott nodded. "He could stay here with us."

She licked her lips. Her eyes looked dark and scared. "It's not a very good reason to get married."

"No." His voice felt like boulders in his chest. "The only good reason to get married is if you love each other."

Her eyes seemed to shimmer...her lips not to move. "Which we do."

"So much...you can't bear to live apart...can't imagine growing old without each other?"

She felt so afraid. Her heart was beating like a trapped bird inside her chest. "Do you?" She could barely hear her own voice. "Feel that way?

"Yes." And she could see the same fear in his eyes. "Do you?"

"Yes." She took a trembling breath and her eyes darted away from his. "So... I guess it could work. As long as we're perfectly clear, both of us, on the situation."

He nodded somberly and cleared his throat. "As long as both parties understand...that this is forever. No divorce. No letting each other down..."

"So..." Her eyes came back and swallowed him. "We're clear on that. Definitely."

His voice was ragged. He could scarcely breathe, couldn't feel his own body. "Definitely."

"Then," she whispered, and she looked like an orphan who'd found a new home—hopeful...scared...happy...dazed. "I guess it's okay."

"So...we can get married, then?"

"Yes." She came back into his arms with a shaken but blissful sigh. "As long as it's forever."

The telephone was ringing. Joy opened her eyes and saw that it was morning. Beside her, Scott stirred, swore and stretched out an arm to pick up the bedside extension. He growled, "Cavanaugh," then lay back to listen, responding from time to time with monosyllables, while Joy lay on her side and watched him, drinking in the newness and unimaginable sweetness of the miracle of him. Happiness lay on her like sunshine. Yancy was safe. And Scott loved her. Scott…who was good and kind and honest and real, and even if he did come with a little bit of baggage, she could deal with that. Yes… And she smiled, thinking of Ryan, who was so much like the son she'd lost…

Yes, she thought, I maybe think my karma's finally changed.

Scott cradled the phone, lay back on the pillows and reached his arm around her to pull her close. "That was Agent Harvey," he said.

"About Yancy?" Joy craned to look up at him. "Have they finished questioning her? When can I see her?"

"Joy…" He enfolded her in his arms, and her heart began to thump against his chest.

"What's wrong? Scott? When can I see her?"

His sigh lifted her like a boat on a swell. "Sweetheart… I'm sorry. I'm afraid that's not going to be possible."

"Why? What—"

"Yancy's going into the federal witness protection program," he said softly. "Immediately. She's a witness to the murder of the DelRey's housekeeper and her husband. Plus, it seems Junior was really in love with her and planned to marry her. He told her enough about the family business she's never going to be safe as long as any of the DelRey's or their organization are running around loose. She's got no choice, sweetheart. I'm sorry."

"I can't…" Joy swallowed, pain rushing into her chest and throat. "I can't even…say goodbye?"

Scott shook his head, bumping her head with his chin. His voice was rusty with sympathy and compassion. "I'm afraid not. She's already gone. They did it last night, right after she left you. It's done."

She was silent, weeping without shaking, without sobs. Scott held her, saying nothing, simply giving her his love…his strength.

After a while she stirred, and lifted herself on one elbow to look down at him, her heart aching with loss…and at the same time with joy. "It's so ironic, isn't it?" she whispered, smiling through her tears. "I've lost someone…again. But I've found someone at the same time. Someone I never thought I'd ever have. Someone to love…and to love me…forever."

"Yes," Scott said, aching with love for her, holding her as close as he dared. "Definitely."

Drawing her close again, he held her as tightly as he dared, one hand soothing her, stroking her back…her side…. After a while, in the peaceful silence that follows emotional cataclysm, he gave a shaken and wondering sigh and dared to relax…to allow himself to believe. His body grew still…his hand came to rest, fingers splayed over the gentle, nestlike hollow of her belly. Smiling, he closed his eyes.

And it came to him, creeping into his consciousness like fog…like smoke…like dreams. Only it wasn't a dream, it was real, more real than anything he'd ever known. It was a feeling, not felt with any of his five senses. A feeling that someone was there. That it wasn't just Joy and him lying together in his bed. There was another person with them, a little girl, a tiny baby nestled against her mother's breast, one tiny hand unfurled like the petals of a delicate pink flower. He could hear, though not with his ears, the soft sweet sounds she made. He could smell, thought not with his nostrils, the scent of baby powder mingling unmistakably with old roses…

So this is what she meant, he thought in awe. It's not just a feeling. I know.

"What?" Joy asked breathlessly, and he realized he'd gone tense and utterly still.

"Nothing," he murmured, smiling at the ceiling, shivering inside with the most incredible, the most complete happiness he'd ever known. "Just thinking about how much I love you...and what wonderful things there are to come."

*   *   *   *   *

INTIMATE MOMENTS™

From reader favorite
SARA ORWIG

Bring on the Night
(Silhouette Intimate Moments, #1298)

With a ranch in Stallion Pass, Jonah Whitewolf
inherited a mysterious danger—a threatening
enemy with a vendetta against him. When he
runs into his ex-wife, Kate Valentini, in town,
he comes face-to-face with the secret she's kept—
the son he never knew. With the truth revealed,
Jonah must put his life in peril to protect his
ranch and his family from jeopardy. But can he
face the greatest risk of all and give himself up
to love a second time around?

STALLION PASS:
TEXAS KNIGHTS

*Where the only cure for those hot and sultry
Lone Star Days are some sexy-as-all-get-out
Texas Knights!*

Available June 2004 at your favorite retail outlet.

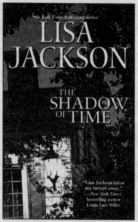

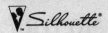

INTIMATE MOMENTS™

A new generation begins
the search for truth in...

A Cry in the Dark

(Silhouette Intimate Moments #1299)

by Jenna Mills

No one is alone....

Danielle Caldwell had left home to make a new life
for her young son. Then Alex's kidnapping rocked her
carefully ordered world. Warned not to call for help,
Dani felt her terror threatening to overwhelm her
senses—until tough FBI agent Liam Brooks arrived on
her doorstep, intent on helping her find Alex. Their
clandestine investigation led to a powerful attraction
and the healing of old wounds—and the discovery
of a conspiracy that could unlock the secrets of
Dani's troubled past.

The first book in the new continuity

FAMILY
SECRETS

THE NEXT GENERATION

Available June 2004 at your favorite retail outlet.

COMING NEXT MONTH

SIMCNM0504